The Dead Angel

by
Carolyn Rowe Hill

Carolyn Rowe Hill

PUBLISH
AMERICA

PublishAmerica
Baltimore

First printing

ISBN: 1-59286-376-0
PUBLISHED BY PUBLISHAMERICA BOOK PUBLISHERS
www.publishamerica.com
Baltimore

Printed in the United States of America

DEDICATION

In honor of my grandmother who loved to write

ACKNOWLEDGEMENTS

I'd like to acknowledge and thank my readers for believing in THE DEAD ANGEL whether they read all or only part of the manuscript. Jennie Hill read Chapter One and couldn't wait for Chapter Two. John Rowe helped find the "missing" quotation marks. Carol Swingle just "loved the story." Sharon Meldrum kept wondering why the book wasn't in print yet. Elaine McDonald liked it so much she shared her copy with her son-in-law. Dr. Ruth Fennick, lent a professional's perspective to the work, and Larry Hubbard said from the beginning that the book would make it.

A special thank you goes to my agent, Richard Lawrence, of the Eaton Literary Agency, for his efforts on my behalf; and to my husband, Bob, for his considerable help with the final editing.

To all of you, your support and encouragement helped make this dream a reality. I am grateful. Thank you.

Carolyn Rowe Hill

CHAPTER ONE

She looked so peaceful with her hands folded under her small, youthful breasts, her long, blonde hair falling softly against the lace pillow beneath her head. She looked like an angel in repose.

Detective Hannah Bell, looking down at the lovely young woman on the bed, felt a pang of sadness that forced her to look away for a moment. A wave of nausea passed through her. In ten years of police work, she never grew accustomed to the sight of a dead body. Seeing what appeared to be senseless death was even more painful. Why and how had this young woman died?

"Any obvious cause of death?" Hannah asked the forensic specialist who arrived at the expansive Victorian mansion sometime ahead of her. He was carefully checking the body for wounds, sniffing here and poking there.

"Not yet, but I doubt it's natural causes, even though looking at her might make you think it. One thing is certain there were drugs involved." The doctor paused, then continued as if talking to himself, not Hannah. "My first guess is suicide, possibly without intention to follow through. Perhaps it was an effort to gain someone's attention."

He studied the girl again.

"She must have had help arranging herself. It's too perfect. She couldn't have laid herself out so well alone. Curious. I hate to disturb her. She looks so beautiful and serene."

Dr. Garrett Adams was very good at his job. Not only had he

been at it for years, but he was an excellent and humane scientist. He also had an uncanny sixth sense. Often his wild guesses turned out to be right.

For a moment, an overwhelming sense of grief for the loss of that young life gripped the pit of his stomach.

"Who found her?" Hannah asked.

The doctor returned to reality. "Her sister."

"Where is she?"

"I don't know. She showed us the way up here, then excused herself. She's pretty upset."

"I can understand that." Hannah turned to leave the room, noting the décor one last time. *Too frilly for me,* she thought.

The room was decorated almost entirely in a single shade of beige, and there was so much lace! The only other colors she noticed were small touches of cranberry and hunter green in the floral touches in the wallpaper fabric, along with the potpourri that filled a cream-colored china bowl sitting atop the jewelry armoire just inside the door. The pungent, pleasing fragrance filled the room.

The wallpaper was beige satin damask with tiny flecks of gold. The pattern was varying arrangements of beige roses tied with thin, cranberry-colored ribbons. It looked very expensive, very new, and very Victorian.

The furnishings were also Victorian and seemed quite sparse for such a large room. An enormous, ornately carved wardrobe took up most of one wall.

I'll bet that cost a pretty penny, Hannah thought.

The huge, high-poster, lace-covered canopy bed was placed against a section of wall that had been designed to create a diagonal corner, allowing the bed to be positioned against it and totally dominate the room.

The ornately carved headboard was six feet high. On either

side of the bed was a matched pair of equally ornate nightstands. A pair of crystal lamps, one each, sat on the nightstands. One table also had a box of tissues in a beige lace tissue holder, while the other held a modern clock/radio that looked strangely out of place in that highly baroque setting.

A combination vanity/writing table and dresser sat between the two large windows on one side of the room. Except for the jewelry armoire near the door, that was all.

The most striking feature of the furniture was the color – all the same shade of beige. The pieces almost blended in with the wallpaper. Each window was covered with a veil of beige lace with more beige lace draped around the frame and flowing to the floor.

I wonder what a shrink would say about all this beige, Hannah mused. *It would make me crazy to spend much time in here. It's pretty enough, but incredibly boring. This room needs more color, more cranberry and green and a lot less beige.*

Then she noticed the six paintings on the walls. Each portrayed a romantic scene of a man and woman in an exotic pose. Hannah guessed they were all by the same artist, because they were the same style, and the colors in all of them had the same varying shades of beige, cranberry, and hunter green.

They may be commissioned pieces, she thought, *painted just for this room.*

Her gaze returned to the young woman on the bed. For the first time, she saw how extraordinarily beautiful she was—beyond lovely. Her eyes were closed, but her skin was like that of a china doll framed by long, shimmering, ash-blonde hair. Her skin looked fragile enough to tear if touched. Her cheeks held a tinge of pink blush, just enough to brighten her pale skin.

Remarkable, Hannah thought.

She also noticed the victim's dressing gown for the first time.

It appeared to be made of beige lace of the same color as her hair, fitted over a beige chiffon undergarment. A cranberry-colored rose with dark-green ribbons streamed neatly down from the modest neckline.

It was amazing. Everything in the room blended into all the other parts, letting nothing stand out. There was no center of interest except for the bed, which was so large one couldn't help noticing it. If the victim had stood against the wall, she would have been almost invisible. She was as beige as the rest of the room.

Like Dr. Adams, Hannah wondered how the girl could have arranged herself so perfectly, right down to the ribbons laid precisely down the front of her gown. The obvious answer was an assistant, and that person must be found.

Hannah left the room and walked down the nearby stairs to find whoever might be able to shed some light on the unfortunate incident. At such times, the question that always came to her was *Why?*

Why would an attractive, apparently healthy, young woman with so much life ahead kill herself, especially when there were no apparent financial difficulties? Of course, that didn't take into account other factors, including mental stability.

When Hannah reached the landing, she saw a young woman standing at the bottom of the stairs, looking up.

"Who are you?" she asked.

Hannah was startled to see someone who was almost, but not quite, a twin of the victim. She was more robust and had wild, flaming crimson hair. She looked harder, too, holding a cigarette near her mouth for a puff, but instead she repeated her question, apparently impatient at Hannah's lack of quick response. The woman's voice was raspy and cool.

"Who are you and what are you doing here?" she asked.

"I'm Detective Bell." Hannah flashed her badge and walked down the remaining stairs. "I'd like to ask you some questions."

When Hannah reached the bottom of the stairs, the woman took the badge from her outstretched hand and studied it while Hannah studied her.

She was the same height as the victim, probably five-feet-seven-inches. Her hazel eyes were surrounded by thick, dark lashes, and her tan skin was much coarser than the victim's.

Is the skin difference genetic or a result of too much sun and too many cigarettes? Hannah wondered, watching the young woman scrutinize her and her ID card. *Was her skin once as lovely as her sister's?*

The woman took a long drag on her cigarette before handing back the ID card.

"I've already spoken with Lieutenant Mayer. Why do I need to speak with you?" she asked in a surly tone.

Hannah looked into her eyes and said firmly, "You'll be talking to a good many people before this matter is closed. Mine is probably the friendliest face you'll encounter."

The young woman turned and led Hannah to a nearby room that appeared to be a combination music room and library. A black baby grand piano stood in one corner, with a mandolin mounted on a corner shelf behind it. The adjacent wall to the right appeared to be a music library.

I'd sure like to look at that music, Hannah thought. *Someone in this house must be a musician. What I wouldn't give for a setup like this. Does anyone play that mandolin, or is it just part of the décor?*

All the other walls had built-in bookshelves, even the space between the large windows directly across from where the two women stood. The center of the room was filled with heavy, overstuffed furniture arranged neatly on a Persian carpet.

"Please have a seat, Detective." The woman pointed to a nearby sofa.

"Thank you."

They sat and faced each other on the long sofa nearest the baby grand. After a few moments, Hannah broke the silence.

"Who are you, and what is your relation to the victim?"

"I'm her sister, Gloria Allen."

"What was your sister's name?"

"Angela Allen."

"Who else lives here with you and your sister?"

"Our mother, Mariah Allen, and the household staff. They have quarters inside the house."

"No other siblings?"

"No."

"What about your father?"

"He died years ago when we were children."

"How did he die?"

"In a car accident."

"I'm sorry."

"That's OK. It was a long time ago."

"How old were you and Angela when your father died?"

"Nine."

"It was a long time ago, but the pain never goes away completely does it?" Hannah asked with genuine sympathy.

"No." Gloria looked out the window.

After a few minutes, Hannah asked, "Can you tell me what happened here this evening?"

Gloria sighed and spoke while still looking out the window. "We were about to sit down to dinner. Since my sister hadn't arrived, I went to get her. That's when I found her. When I realized Angela was dead, I called for my mother. She called Dr. Blum, and he called the police."

"Who is Dr. Blum?"

"Our family physician."

Hannah wrote down the name in her notebook. "I'll need his phone number, please."

Gloria recited it from memory.

"Thank you," Hannah said. "When did you last see your sister alive?"

"This afternoon."

"Where, and what was she doing?"

"She was in her room…."

"Go on. Doing what?"

Gloria seemed reluctant to answer.

"Doing what?"

"Writing at her desk."

Hannah sensed that wasn't true, but she continued with her next question. "What was she writing?"

"I…I don't know." Gloria sounded annoyed.

"It would be best if you told me the truth. It'll come out eventually."

Gloria squirmed but remained silent.

"Because of the questionable circumstances surrounding your sister's death, you don't want to draw negative attention to yourself. You can answer my questions truthfully in the comfort of your own home, or you can come downtown with me and answer them in far less pleasant surroundings."

Gloria looked at her in confusion. "Why should anyone suspect me? She was my sister, for God's sake!"

There was an uncomfortable silence.

"Besides, Angela killed herself," Gloria continued. "That's obvious, isn't it?"

Hannah concealed her surprise at the nature of the assumption. "Is it?"

"Well, isn't that what those people upstairs think?"

"Do they? Is that exactly what they said?"

"Well, no, not exactly."

"What does *not exactly* mean?"

"I thought I heard someone say it. That's all." Gloria waved her hand dismissively.

"What makes you think Angela killed herself?"

"I don't know. What other explanation is there?"

"There are natural causes, and then there's murder."

"Murder?" Gloria was startled by the suggestion. A quick look of fear flashed in her eyes, then it disappeared. "That's impossible. Who would want to kill Angela? She was perfect. No one would want to kill *her.*"

Hannah caught the sarcasm in Gloria's voice. "Why would she want to kill herself?"

"I don't know," Gloria said slowly. "She suffered from depression occasionally. Maybe she died from natural causes. Like you said, that's possible. It never occurred to me, though. She seemed too young for that."

"You're right. Death by natural causes at her age is unlikely, but it happens. Exactly how old was Angela?"

"Twenty-six, the same as me. We were fraternal twins."

"I thought you might be. You look a lot like her, but not exactly." Hannah was surprised. Angela barely looked twenty, while Gloria looked at least twenty-six.

"Gloria, did Angela take any drugs, prescription or otherwise, during her bouts with depression?"

"No."

"What about physical health problems."

"None."

"She was healthy, then?"

"Yes."

"You're sure she didn't take any drugs, not even over-the-counter ones?"

"I just told you, she never took drugs. She didn't believe in them. She wouldn't even take aspirin for a headache." Gloria was clearly irritated. "Nor did she indulge in any other self-destructive behavior."

"As far as you know."

"I knew her better than anyone."

"Then tell me what she was really doing in her bedroom the last time you saw her."

"What do you mean? I already told you."

"That was a lie."

Gloria said slowly, "It's going to seem really strange. I haven't figured it out myself yet, but here it is:

"Angela wanted me to photograph her in the pose in which I later found her. I arranged her hair, dressing gown, and ribbons just the way she asked. I asked what she was up to, but she wouldn't tell me. When I said I wouldn't help unless she told me, she gave in.

"Angela had commissioned a portrait of herself. She wanted to be photographed to show the artist exactly what pose she had in mind. I pressed her about it, asking why she wanted a portrait of herself looking dead. She said she wanted to see what she would look like."

"A photograph would accomplish that," Hannah said.

"That's what I said. She said it wouldn't be like a portrait, and she wanted to hang it above her headboard. I said that was not only vain, it was weird. She said I had no sense of the dramatic.

"After I took the photograph, she dismissed me, saying she was going to take a nap and would see me later. When I left, she was still in the pose we set up for the photo.

"Then, when she didn't join us for cocktails and dinner, I went up to get her and found her lying the way I left her."

"Exactly what time was that?"

"Just before six o'clock."

The room was silent for a moment. Then Gloria added, as if confiding a secret, "My sister was a little eccentric for one so young. She was also very bright and easily bored. She always wanted new, different things to do. I guess she outdid herself this time."

"Who else was in the house at the time you found your sister?"

"Just my mother and me," came the weary reply.

"Where was the household staff? Weren't they serving dinner?"

"No," she said nervously. "It's their day off." Exhausted, Gloria sank farther into the couch.

Hannah wasn't quite finished. "What about your mother? Where is she, and how is she holding up? This is a terrible shock for her, too."

"Yes, it is," Gloria said in a small, tired voice. "I guess."

As if on cue, Mariah Allan entered the room. Like the victim, she was an extraordinarily beautiful woman, although smaller in stature than her daughters. Instead of ash-blonde hair or wild, red hair, her hair was jet black, pulled away from her face and tied neatly at the nape of her neck with a white chiffon scarf, the ends of which fell a short distance down her back.

Her eyes were a light, icy blue, and her skin, like Angela's, resembled flawless porcelain. She wore a blue-and-white lounging gown, where the blue matched her eyes. She was a striking woman, and, when she entered a room, everyone noticed.

Gloria stood from the sofa, spoke briefly, and, it seemed, rather awkwardly, with her mother, then left.

As Hannah watched them interact, she became increasingly aware that something was missing. There was no appearance of shared grief between mother and daughter. Gloria looked distressed but not grief-stricken. Instead, she seemed frightened.

Her mother showed no expression whatsoever that Hannah could see. There was no display of affection, nor warmth or compassion in the hushed voice, and no physical contact. Considering the tragic circumstances, that was very odd.

Hannah thought of her own family under similar circumstances. When her identical twin sister had been kidnapped, the strong bond among the family members kept them from falling apart. There was a lot of touching, hugging, and crying. They helped each other. From the moment it was apparent that Heather was missing, parents, relatives, and friends united in their grief. That had helped tremendously in surviving a difficult time, one that wasn't over, because Heather had never been found.

Family dynamics come in many different forms, she reminded herself. *This might just be their way, affected by the shock they're experiencing.*

Setting her thoughts aside, she approached Mariah. "Hello, Mrs. Allen. I'm Detective Bell." She displayed her badge. "I'm very sorry about your daughter."

"Thank you," Mariah said coolly. "Angela would never kill herself. She was murdered."

"Why would anyone want to kill your daughter?" Hannah was taken aback by the woman's forthrightness. *Another assumption,* she thought. *Suicide by the dead girl's sister and murder by the mother. Very odd.*

"Because she was rich, bright, and beautiful, and some were jealous of her. My Angela could do anything she set her mind to."

"What about natural causes? There's a small chance she might have died of a heart attack, stroke, aneurysm, or other biological failure."

"No. She was murdered."

Hannah didn't know what to say. *Gloria thinks it's suicide, Mariah thinks it's murder. Why? Neither is apparent. To an inexperienced eye, seeing Angela lying so peacefully on her bed would make one assume an unknown natural cause, not suicide or murder.*

"Is there someone you suspect of killing Angela?" Hannah asked.

Without hesitation, and still showing no emotion, Mariah said, "Yes. Her sister."

CHAPTER TWO

The phone rang as Hannah opened her front door. She picked up just before the answering machine came on. "Hello?" she asked breathlessly.

"How did things go at the Allen estate?"

It was her boss, Lieutenant Robert "Rob" Keys, who never identified himself when he called. He just stated what was on his mind.

"All right," she replied.

"I haven't heard from Doc Adams about the cause of death. What do you know?"

"The cause wasn't obvious when I last saw Doc, but he said drugs were definitely involved. It looked like suicide to him, though it might have been unintentional, like a scare tactic.

"It's an odd situation, Rob. Angela Allen was laid out on her bed all neat and tidy. Her hair and dressing gown were perfectly arranged. It turns out her sister, Gloria, helped her set herself up for a portrait Angela wanted to have painted of herself. Angela had Gloria photograph her to give the picture to the artist. We don't know how much more Gloria was involved, but the mother thinks Gloria killed her sister."

"She actually said so?" Rob was astonished. "How very strange. Generally, even when parents believe a child is guilty of such an act, they try to protect them. The wealthy, in particular, don't like paying for their, or their children's misdeeds."

"She spoke so heartlessly it gave me the shivers."

"Why does she think Gloria killed her sister?"

"I don't know, but she made it sound like jealousy. Mrs. Allen said some people were jealous of Angela's wealth, brains, and beauty, all of which Gloria also has to some extent. I didn't get any more from Mrs. Allen than that incredible statement, but I will."

She described her conversation with Gloria and her observations of the interaction between mother and daughter.

"I didn't interview anyone else, including the household staff. They were away, because it's their day off. That might also have been a factor in Angela choosing to kill herself today, or for a murder to take place, or whatever it was.

"I'll go back and speak with the staff and again with Gloria and her mother. I also want to look around. We'll need a search warrant eventually. It'll depend on how cooperative the Allens are and what we learn from the interviews. I'm very interested in learning more about this family's dynamic and its emotional makeup. Something's wrong."

"I'll get the wheels in motion for a warrant so it'll be ready when we need it. Get some rest now. We'll get back to this in the morning. See you at eight."

"Yep."

Hannah hung up and saw she had three calls on her answering machine. The first was her mother, the second was a newspaper reporter, and the third was Laine Daniels, a friend.

She called her mother and chatted about the usual things—the unending search for Heather, dead or alive, an upcoming dinner on Sunday, and Dad's failing emotional and physical health.

She didn't call the reporter. She did call Laine.

Laine and Hannah had been close friends since they started kindergarten. They shared a passion for vocal music and loved to play old records and sing along. As children, they whiled away many hours that way.

Laine and her parents were visiting the Bells at their summer cottage in Northern Michigan the day Heather disappeared at the age of eleven. Laine was largely responsible for helping Hannah stay sane throughout the ensuing time period. She had a marvelous sense of humor, for one so young, and seemed to be able to handle whatever came her way.

"Hi, there, gal pal," Hannah teased when she heard her friend's voice. Laine intensely disliked that expression.

"Hey, Girlfriend. What's up?"

"Turn about's fair play." Hannah laughed at the trite pseudo-intimate term she'd grown to so dislike.

"I heard about that young woman's death. It was on the news. They don't know how she died, but it seems a bit strange how she was found, don't you think? One reporter said someone told him she looked perfect, totally unmarked, like an angel without wings."

Laine liked to play amateur detective, which amused Hannah. She knew Hannah couldn't discuss a case with her, but that didn't stop her from trying.

"Yes, it's strange. We'll figure it out eventually." *The angel comment had to come from Doc,* she thought. *It certainly sounds like him.* Still, she was surprised that Doc would say something publicly so early in the investigation. *He must have been unusually moved by this one.*

To Hannah's surprise, Laine didn't pursue the topic. One small question in a death case usually started her on a grand odyssey of questions and theories. That evening, however, she had other things on her mind.

"We need you for the concert on Saturday. Mary Ellen has laryngitis and can't sing a note. All you'll need is a quick brush-up on tempo and timing."

"You're out of your mind. That's only three days from now. I'm up to my neck in a new murder case, not to mention the other twenty-one cases on my docket. I haven't sung in ages, and you want me to get on stage and make a fool of myself? I don't think so."

"Hannah, we need you. It's close to you, too, at Pletcher High School. It'll take all of five minutes to drive there."

"You don't get anywhere in five minutes in Chicago unless it's to your next-door neighbor's, and even then you might be mugged."

"Stop being difficult, Hannah. We need you."

"I got that part already."

There was a moment's silence.

"Oh, all right. I'll do it." As usual, Hannah caved.

"Thanks. Stop by tomorrow when you can, and we'll go over the numbers. I'll be here. With three little kids, I don't go far. Just try to miss naptime between one and three. That's about the only sleep I'm getting these days."

"OK. I'll try. By the way, Laine, do you still have your mandolin?"

"It's probably in my folks' attic someplace. Why?"

"Just wondered."

"You want to play the mandolin?"

"No, I just wondered if you still had it. I'll see you tomorrow."

"'Bye."

"Hasta la vista." Hannah hung up. *So much for an uplifting conversation with my good friend. Let's see what I have to wear that still fits.*

Pulling out her favorite royal-blue gown from the closet, she tried it on. "It won't be this one," she moaned. "I need to lose a few pounds to get back into this. Let's try the emerald-green one."

She tried it on. "That's better. At least in this, the ten pounds I've gained don't show so much."

Hannah set about finding the remaining pieces of her ensemble for the performance. The music was in her music bag, which she'd take to Laine's.

"I must be out of my mind to do this," she muttered. "I need to develop some backbone. Laine gets me every time. I just can't say no to her, and she knows it."

Hannah remembered her grandmother saying, "No one takes advantage of you unless you let them."

Hannah glanced skyward. "I'm still working on that one, Grandma."

Grandma Mullen had been a huge influence in Hannah's life. She was long gone, but Hannah thought of her often. She was the one who gave Hannah confidence, who made her believe she could do anything she wanted if she was willing to work hard enough for it.

Grandma Mullen, her father's mother, never said things like, "Girls don't do that," which Hannah heard at home. Her mother meant well, but she was the product of a male-oriented home where girls were thought to be less capable at worldly pursuits than men.

Grandma Mullen also had a lot to do with Hannah going into police work. After Heather disappeared, and time passed, Hannah wanted to have an active hand in finding her. As she grew older, police work seemed the best way to go about it. The memory of Grandma Mullen's encouraging words helped her stay focused on her goal.

It was eleven o'clock, and Hannah was beat. She slipped on her favorite nightshirt and climbed into bed. Her last thoughts were, *Why, Angela? How, Angela?*

The ringing phone startled her awake. It was Doc.

"My God, Doc, it's after two in the morning. Not everyone stays up all night like you do."

"Sorry, Han, but I had to call you. I need to talk to someone I can trust. You're it."

Doc was the only person allowed to call Hannah by a nickname. Her name was Hannah, and that was what she wanted to be called, but somehow, coming from him it was different. She didn't mind. She took it as a sign of his affection for her, and she returned the feeling.

Over the years, they developed a profound respect for each other's abilities and integrity. The relationship helped them solve difficult cases that others had given up on.

"What's up, Doc?" Her mind was in a fog, but she sensed the angst in her colleague's voice.

"The Allen thing."

"Oh, yeah. What's going on? What did you find?" Hannah propped herself up on one elbow.

"All I can say is that something is rotten in Denmark. It looks like someone may have been playing a practical joke that went wrong. It's a tragic waste of a young life. At first, I thought it was suicide, but now I'm not so sure."

Hannah sat straight up in bed, suddenly wide awake. "OK. Fill me in."

He paused for a moment. "I have a theory. Actually, it doesn't qualify as one, because it's far too speculative." He paused again.

"Are you still there?" Hannah asked.

"Yes," he said uncertainly, taking a deep breath. "Bear with me, Han. This is going to sound pretty bizarre. Some of what I have to say I can prove. Some of it I can't."

Hannah waited.

"I have a strong gut feeling about some aspects of this case.

It's one of those times I get the feeling there's more to the situation than meets the eye. This isn't a cut-and-dried case of any kind, suicide, homicide, accident, or natural causes."

"Go on."

"I'm not even trying to understand the why of it, I'm just trying to determine what happened."

He paused again, and Hannah thought, *This thing really has him going. He's really stressed out over it.*

"I believe that Angela, for whatever reason, wanted someone to think she was dead, even if only for a short time. Maybe she wanted to make a point or gain attention. Who knows? She took a drug that feigns death, but from which the person awakes in a few hours. I can prove that much.

"Whether her plan included having the police involved is another matter. At best, it was a dangerous game. At worst, she could have ended up suffocating in a body bag. I wonder if she ever considered that. Anyway, whatever she was thinking, we'll never know. She ended up dead, regardless."

Doc didn't seem to know what to say next. He was rambling, which wasn't like him, trying to articulate his tangled thoughts.

"I certainly don't understand how she managed to have herself so perfectly laid out. She had to have help."

Hannah thought he was talking to himself, almost unaware that she was on the phone, so she waited.

"Tomorrow, we should have the report of the fingerprint tests. That'll tell us something."

"Her sister helped," Hannah interjected. "She was the so-called accomplice, although it was probably without her conscious knowledge."

"How so?"

Hannah explained the photographic session in Angela's bedroom the afternoon of her death.

"OK. That makes sense." Doc sounded relieved. "As strange as it is, it works in this scenario."

"No warmth, no breath, shall testify thou livest," Hannah quoted. "The rose in thy lips and cheeks shall fade to wanny ashes, thy eyes' windows fall like death when he shuts up the day of life. Each part, deprived of supple government, shall, stiff and stark and cold, appear like death…. This borrowed likeness of shrunk death. And then awake as from a pleasant sleep."

She smiled. "I forgot some of the words, but it's close."

"What was that?" Doc asked.

"Don't you remember your Shakespeare? It's from *Romeo and Juliet.* I had to learn that passage in a drama class in college. The good friar gives Juliet a vial of liquid so she can feign her death to get out of marrying Paris. Although Juliet's trick lasted longer than Angela's, at least Juliet woke up."

"Not that it did her much good."

His words made Hannah think. "Good grief, do you think Angela was trying to pull a Juliet?"

"You may have something there. It's possible. It wouldn't surprise me if she was into something like that. From the look of that room, she was a hopeless romantic. Did you see the paintings on the walls? They're all of men and women in romantic settings. At least she may have gotten the idea from it. Good thinking."

"Thanks. Yes, I noticed the heavy dose of romanticism in the décor, including the paintings."

They paused for a moment.

"Anyway," Doc continued, "it could be, then, that after Angela dismissed Gloria, and she left the room, Angela took a pill concealed in her hand. There were traces of the drug and its odor on her hands and around her mouth when I sniffed the corpse. She could have popped the pill without disturbing her hair or gown. I can prove she took a death-feigning drug, but I don't know why.

"After that, she fell into her feigned death sleep. She had to be certain someone would find her before she awoke, or the game would be for nothing. From what you've told me, she must have counted on Gloria to do that. If Angela didn't show up for supper, she knew her sister would come looking for her. If, by some unlikely chance, Gloria didn't show, Angela would awaken in bed with no harm done, although she would have had a doozy of a headache."

Doc stopped to catch his breath, which came slowly and with difficulty.

"Then the game would end. Angela would be alive and would have the last laugh on someone. Who knows what she was thinking. That's not very angelic behavior for one who looked like an angel lying on that bed." He took another labored breath. "Then something went wrong. Angela didn't wake up. She died, but it wasn't from the drug." He stopped to breathe again.

Hannah tried to follow Doc's theory, but she was becoming more and more concerned with her friend's breathing. "Are you feeling OK?"

"Oh, yeah. I'm just tired tonight. I guess it shows in my voice."

"More in your breathing."

"I'm fine. Really." He took a deep breath. "Then the question becomes, was this a suicide, an accidental death, a homicide, or death from natural causes? Natural causes is out. It wasn't suicide, because the pill she took wouldn't have killed her unless she overdosed, which she didn't. Accidental death would be possible, again if she overdosed. I'll get to homicide in a moment.

"She took a risk by taking that drug. Someone of her slender stature could have been unconscious much longer than anticipated. She could have awakened in the middle of her own autopsy."

"Ouch."

"However, from what I could determine, she would have awakened in about three hours. I estimate she took the pill around three-thirty, so she would be awake again at six-thirty. That fits with what you said about the session in the bedroom.

"She planned her waking around dinnertime, because she knew Gloria would be the one to come for her. When Gloria couldn't wake her, she'd call her mother and set off a death-scene panic from which Angela would soon awaken."

"She was counting on a lot of things going right."

"Yes. It might have turned out the way she wished if she hadn't died. At least she would have had a dramatic moment or two. In her mind, she might have thought of it as a romantic adventure. We don't know anything about her state of mind. Was she stable, naïve, sick or something else?"

"I hope to learn more about that when I speak with her family and the others who were close to her."

"I would be very interested in her young psyche. This lady has me mesmerized, and she's dead." He spoke softly as if not wanting to admit his fascination.

Hannah waited.

"Was anyone else in the house besides the Allen women that afternoon? Were there any guests or visitors? I was wondering about dinner guests. Angela might have wanted to get all she could out of her faked death by scaring a lot of people simultaneously."

"Gloria said she and her mother were the only ones in the house at the time of Angela's death. It was the staff's day off. No one mentioned guests or visitors. I'll ask.

"The two girls could have planned this charade together just to get their mother's attention. Mrs. Allen struck me as very remote and cold. She's probably almost unreachable."

Hannah's voice trailed off as she tried to remember what she'd told Doc. "Doc?"

"Yeah?"

"Did I tell you, or was it Rob, that Mariah accused Gloria of killing her sister?"

There was an uneasy silence, then Doc said, "No, you didn't tell me that."

"That's another can of worms, isn't it?"

"Yes. I'll have to think about that."

Hannah changed the subject. "What about the death-feigning drug? How would Angela get her hands on it? I can't imagine she walked into her neighborhood pharmacy and asked for it."

"I don't know. That's one of the things we need to figure out. The drug can be found, but it's not easy. She may have had a friend get it for her. That would be accomplice number two." He hesitated, then said, "This is where it gets murky. Just hear me out. "As I said, I found traces of the death-feigning drug in her blood and on her palm. That's how I know she must have held it there for a period of time. That's concrete evidence." He took some deep breaths.

"While Angela was in her feigned death state, someone came into her room. I assume this person knew she was supposed to be napping. That person pricked her bare foot with a needle tainted with a potent poison. It killed her instantly, leaving no trace, because it dissipates quickly from the body.

"The only evidence I have is a tiny puncture wound on the bottom of her foot. It would have gone unnoticed unless someone went looking for it. In these days of overflowing morgues and overworked medical examiners, places like the bottoms of the feet are more unnoticed than usual, unless there are obvious lacerations. It was a clever idea, but it didn't work. The killer wasn't counting on an old fart like me, someone who checks every part of a body and is insatiably curious."

"I don't mean to be impertinent, Doc, but you sound like you need rest. You're really tired. We can finish this tomorrow."

"No. I'm almost done. If I don't tell you now, I won't be able to finish. As far as we know, only Gloria and Mrs. Allen were in the house. It seems reasonable to suppose one of them is the murderer. We have no clear motive, but I'm sure one will turn up. It always does.

"Disposing of the murder weapon was easy. A small, innocuous weapon like a needle would be very difficult to find. Even if it was found, it's possible there would be no trace of the poison left on it. Even a tiny vial, in which the needle was carried, would be hard to find. If we get lucky, though, it might have fingerprints on it."

Doc's breathing sounded labored on the phone.

"Is there more?" Hannah now wanted the conversation to end for her own sake. She felt very weary, and a bit overwhelmed.

"Just a little more. The killer then put slippers on Angela's bare feet to cover the mark he left."

"What makes you think that?"

"The mark the slippers left on her feet indicates they were put on after she died. From the way the room was kept, I doubt Miss Allen kept slippers under her bed. That means the killer had to know where to find them, and that implies familiarity with the victim and the room."

"You should be the detective on this one, Doc." Hannah was amused.

"A forensic specialist is part detective."

She smiled.

"When we brought the body to the morgue, I performed a prelim and started with her feet, as usual. That was when I felt the slight bump on her right foot at the third metatarsal area—the ball of the foot. I couldn't see anything with the naked eye, so I used ultraviolet light and found a tiny puncture that was only a few hours old. That's the basis for my theory.

"I've seen it before. It's a rare killer who thinks to use the sole of someone's foot. Feet aren't usually that accessible. People are usually dressed and wearing shoes, and they're either standing, sitting, walking, or riding. Some are in bed, all covered up. At any rate, the feet aren't usual targets.

"Besides, the killer is usually in more of a hurry than foot poisoning would allow. However, if you know what you're doing, and you're patient, it's almost perfect."

He paused again.

"Could Angela's killer be more sophisticated than we've given him or her credit for?"

If the drug is undetectable during normal testing," Doc continued as if she hadn't spoken, "that's even better for the killer. Most of the time, the cause of death in such circumstances would be labeled *natural causes.* I believe Angela was murdered, but I doubt I'll be able to prove it. I won't be given the chance."

"Why not?"

"Someone will stop the investigation."

"Why?"

"No matter what Mrs. Allen said today, they're wealthy and, ultimately, won't want the publicity. A lawyer will tell her to shut up and let him play the game. The worst diagnosis they'll get will be suicide or accidental overdose. I don't know how much better that will make anyone feel, but it'll be better than murder."

What if they called it *undetermined?"* Hannah asked, suspecting what the answer would be.

"I don't think that'll happen."

"What do we do now?"

"Nothing for the moment. I had to tell you this. Now maybe I can get some sleep."

31

"You're right, but now I won't. Can't we discuss this with someone? Maybe Rob?"

"No. I'd like to keep this between us awhile to see how the situation changes in the next few days. My theory's too speculative. We need more evidence. When we cut her open in the morning, we'll know more. The body has a lot to tell. I have one more thing to say, then I'll let both of us get some rest."

"I'm listening."

"I can't be part of a cover-up. Like I just said, despite the mother's apparent lack of concern about appearances by accusing her own daughter of murder or about the scandal that such an accusation would bring to her family, it won't last. Eventually, I'll be asked to suppress evidence and to sign a false document. It's happened before. I didn't give in then, and I won't now. As you well know, that's an issue every law-enforcement officer has to deal with someday. It can be the toughest, most soul-searching look at our inner self we'll ever have to face."

Hannah half-listened as Doc droned on, thinking how his words would affect her investigation. He seemed unable to stop talking, to stop explaining, to stop analyzing.

"In over thirty years in forensics, I've never compromised my principles, and I won't start now. It's important that you know that."

Hannah felt cold and empty inside. "Of course you can't. I've known you a long time, Doc. You won't compromise your principles for any reason. Neither will I."

They were silent for a few minutes.

"I intend to solve this case, Doc," she said. "I want to know what really happened."

"Me, too, Han."

"We've done it before, and we'll do it again. No one will stop us. Let's take this up again after we've had some rest. We can't do anything about it at almost three in the morning."

"You're right. It's time to give up for tonight. Good night, Han."

"Good night, Doc."

Hannah hung up and tried to go back to sleep, but she didn't sleep well. She kept having nightmares about strange drugs and people trying to prick the bottoms of her feet with poisoned needles.

CHAPTER THREE

The alarm went off at six o'clock the following morning. As usual, Hannah pressed the snooze alarm twice before getting out of bed.

"I love morning," she groaned, "but why does it have to come so early?" She swung out of bed, grabbed her robe, and walked toward the shower.

Hannah always sang in the shower in the morning. It helped her wake up, and to remain current with the words to songs she loved. That morning, she began with one of her favorites, *Hard-Hearted Hannah*. That had become her theme song, according to her friends who thought she was pretty hard-hearted about men. They were probably right.

"Maybe I can't keep a guy because I keep pouring water over their heads while they're drowning." She chuckled as she recalled the words to the song.

"They'll want me to do that as a solo on Saturday. I'd better practice my vamping, which isn't easy at six-thirty in the morning."

She ate her usual English muffin with a glass of orange juice while scanning two newspapers. She reasoned that if she got both the evening and the early editions, she wouldn't miss anything.

The Allen death was mentioned in the morning paper's police beat. As usual, the four-line death notice was cold and impersonal. The only time anyone felt it personally was if he knew something about the victim. In Hannah's job, that was all too often.

Young woman, age 26, found dead in her home Wednesday evening....

Hannah felt a stronger pang of sadness than usual when she read the notice, but she knew it was important to remain objective in detective work. When an investigator gets too involved in a case, it usually has a negative impact on the investigation.

Maybe it's the twin thing, she mused. *The loss of a twin sister is tough to endure. Whatever it is, I'd better keep it under control.*

She thought of the music room at the Allen home. *I wonder who the musician is in that family? Was it Angela, or are they all musical?* She realized that was another connection to her own life. *I wonder who plays the mandolin? It's not a popular instrument. Whoever can play it must be a skilled musician.*

Somehow, she imagined Angela playing the mandolin while Gloria sat at the piano. It was a romantic image, and it fit the mental picture Hannah was creating of Angela.

What about Mariah? Is she a musician?

A chill ran down her spine.

What's that about? Suddenly cold, she wrapped her arms around herself. *Maybe it has to do with a mother accusing her own daughter of murdering her sister. What would cause a mother to do this? If she knew the child was psychotic and capable of murder, that's one thing. So, is Gloria psychotic?*

A mother's first reaction is to protect her child, guilty or not, not accuse her at the first opportunity.

A strange thought came to Hannah. *Maybe Mariah's not their real mother. What if she's an evil stepmother or a frustrated maiden aunt who was stuck raising someone else's children because she was the only one available? It could be a well-kept family secret.*

35

"OK, Hannah. Get a grip. Let's not go off the deep end," she chided herself.

After finishing her breakfast and the newspapers, she walked to her closet and stared at its contents. "Ah, yes. The daily question of what to wear was easy when I was in uniform. Now that I'm a detective, I'm back to the daily grind of choosing clothes."

Unlike her friend and occasional partner, Sharon Walker, Hannah never got into the habit of laying out her clothes the previous night.

"I'm too tired to go through that at night," she told Sharon. "I go through it in the morning."

She chose gray slacks, a pale-pink blouse, and the vest from Bloomingdale's that could be worn with anything, because it had every conceivable color in it. Hannah wore it often.

At five-feet-eleven-inches tall, Hannah was a handsome woman. She stood straight and carried herself well. Good posture had been pounded into her from childhood.

"Stand up straight and don't slouch," her mother and maternal grandmother, Grandma Finn, constantly reminded her. It paid off. She stood perfectly straight and could still balance a book on her head walking up and down stairs.

Hannah had plenty of dark-brown, naturally curly hair, which she hated, and large, dark eyes. Her features weren't perfect, but she was easy to look at, had an infectious smile, and a strong personality. She had no trouble attracting men, just keeping them. Her expectations were high. She wouldn't settle for less like many women did.

She wanted someone who cared about the same things she did, not just the ones that mattered to him. She also didn't want to have to depend on anyone for things she wanted to buy or do. She'd seen too many women begging for money for a new dress, to have lunch with a friend, or to buy shoes for a child.

"Not for me, thank you," she told friends and family members.

"Hannah, take a good look inside a guy before you fall for him," her mother said. "Give it lots of time. It's true that handsome is as handsome does. Your dad is the most wonderful, kind, generous man I know, and I don't want you to settle for less."

Hannah took her mother's advice to heart and was still looking.

Finishing the last drop of coffee and hurrying out the door, she saw her neighbor, Ben Stratton, who she saw almost every morning on her way out.

"Hi, Beautiful!" he called as he ran by, flashing his big, friendly smile.

Hannah smiled, waved, and moved on to her car parked in the driveway. She believed she could reach the couch faster going up the front walk and through the front door than through the garage, laundry room, and kitchen; and, at night, reaching the couch was her first priority.

"I'll have to time each route." She chuckled. "Just to see if I'm right or if I'm deluding myself."

Her thoughts returned to her neighbor. Ben had lived next door for two years. They shared a duplex and occasionally visited over the fence as they worked in their gardens. Hannah felt Ben liked her, and she liked him, too, but not in any special way. They were just friends, and that was fine with her.

Ben was a linguist who spoke and wrote fluently in five languages—English, Russian, French, Spanish, and Italian. He was working on Japanese.

"I've always had a love of languages," he replied when Hannah asked how he came to know so many. "When I was a child, we moved around a lot, because my father was in the diplomatic corps. I was exposed to different cultures and their languages. They just took, I guess."

When Hannah received cards or letters from a family friend in

Germany, Ben translated them for her. Another friend, studying in France, sent her a postcard, and Ben translated that, too.

Each time he translated for her, he taught her something of the language. When she offered to pay him for his services, he refused. He also encouraged her to take up languages.

"You have a natural affinity for languages, Hannah. You learn them quickly and have a good accent. That's unusual. Most people work hard to learn a new language, then slaughter it when they speak it."

"I know," she replied. "My French teacher in high school thought she spoke excellent French until she went there and discovered no one could understand her. She was devastated."

"That happens often with languages taught in classrooms in the States. There's usually little or no opportunity to talk with native speakers. If the students are lucky enough to have a native-speaking teacher, they have a much better chance of truly learning the language, its idioms, and its nuances."

At times, Ben was away for many weeks, traveling around the world, hired by Fortune 500 companies to translate documents and serve as an interpreter for employees conducting business overseas.

Benjamin Russell Stratton had never married. When the subject came up, he said, "I haven't found the right woman yet. Guess I'd better get busy. I'm not getting any younger." He chuckled.

Hannah guessed he was in his mid-forties.

There was a lot of commotion at the precinct when Hannah arrived.

"What's going on?" she asked Sharon Walker, who was walking toward her.

"You haven't heard?" Sharon's voice showed something was wrong.

"Heard what?"

"Doc died last night."

Hannah's knees buckled. It was several seconds before she could speak. "No. No...I just spoke with him a few hours ago. He can't be dead."

"He is, Hannah, believe me."

Hannah shakily reached for a chair and sank into it. "What happened?"

"Heart attack."

"When? What time?"

"Around three. They brought him to the hospital around three-thirty. He just had time to dial 911."

"No. No. It can't be. It can't."

Sharon helped Hannah stand and put an arm around her to escort her to the cafeteria. She set Hannah down with a cup of hot, freshly made coffee.

"You two were pretty close, weren't you?" Sharon asked, knowing the answer.

"He was a very good friend, someone I could always trust." Hannah felt warm tears on her cheeks. "He taught me so much. Oh, my God, what will I do?"

"Let me take you home. Take the day off. You deserve it. You work hard enough as it is. You don't need to be here today."

"Yes, I do. It's very important. Doc and I...." She stopped as more tears flowed. "We had a lot to do today. I can't do it all without him. We have a new case, a tough one. It needs his expertise and insight, but he's not here. If Doc's not on this case, someone will probably get away with murder, and we both know he wouldn't like that!" She smiled painfully.

Hannah told Sharon everything that transpired since she was first called to the Allen home along Lake Shore Drive, north of the city. She'd been leaving the office after working late on some paperwork when the call came in. Because she took the call, Hannah became the primary officer on the case.

By the time she finished, Hannah had herself under control, though her insides felt as if she'd been trampled by stampeding mules.

Sharon was dumbfounded by what she heard. "I'll get myself assigned as your partner on this one, Hannah. We'll solve it together, along with Jim Preston, who'll be taking over for Doc. He's good, reliable, and he listens. We'll be OK."

"But you have your own caseload. It's heavy, too. How will you manage?"

"There's nothing urgent. Some of it can be reassigned. What you have is far more pressing—and certainly more interesting—than anything I've got. What else do you have?"

"I just closed the Martin case, about that runaway I tracked down. I was closing that last night. The rest is just the usual, nothing urgent."

"Good. Let's see Rob. I'm sure he'll agree we should work on this together. He likes you, you know." There was a twinkle in Sharon's eye.

"Knock it off, Walker." Hannah was in no mood for sport with Detective Walker, who was forever trying to get her attached to someone, usually, their boss. "I'm not interested."

"You should be. He's a hell of a nice guy, especially for a cop. He's got a gentle side to go with his machismo."

"I don't have time."

"Everyone has time if she wants to."

"I don't want to."

"Then meet me in Rob's office in five minutes. That'll give you time to fix your face. You've got time for that, haven't you? You don't want your boss seeing you looking like you do right now."

They snarled at each other and went their separate ways. Sharon wanted to make Hannah angry enough to take her mind off Doc's death. It would be very hard for Hannah to lose her friend.

Rob looked at Hannah with affection and empathy. "I'm very sorry, Hannah. I know what he meant to you. He meant a lot to all of us. He'll be sorely missed. Sharon has asked to assist you with this case. Is that OK with you?"

"Definitely," Hannah replied. "That is, if she can stay out of my personal life."

"What?"

"Never mind, Lieutenant. She knows what I mean. I'll need all the help I can get. She's the best I could have with Doc gone." She flinched inwardly as she said that. It still didn't sound possible.

"There are some things I need to discuss with you concerning this case," she continued. "First, I need to ask a few more questions. Doc called me last night, which is why I'm so upset. I talked with him from two o'clock until almost three. He must have died right after we hung up." Tears welled in her eyes.

"I know," he said. "Sharon told me."

"I should have done something. He had trouble breathing the whole time we spoke, for almost an hour! I should have helped him!"

"How?" Sharon asked.

"Let him get off the phone and get someone there to help him."

"Hindsight, Hannah," Rob said. "You know what they say."

No one spoke for a moment.

"He had a theory. It's pretty far out in some places, and he asked me not to discuss it for a few days until I asked a few more questions and looked around. I said fine, but now I don't know what to do."

"Trust your instincts, Hannah," Rob said. "I do."

"Thanks, Boss." Hannah managed a smile.

"Thanks from me, too," Sharon said, then turned to Hannah. "Have you had anything substantial to eat this morning?"

"No. I'm not hungry."

"Well, I'm starving. All I've had is a cup of Lieutenant Dann's tasteless coffee. Let's grab a bite before we go up to Lake Shore Drive and this episode of *America's Castles.*"

CHAPTER FOUR

They arrived at the Allen estate just before ten o'clock. After they rang the chimes, a polite, gray-haired woman with a pleasant smile slowly opened the heavy oak door.

"May I help you?"

"We're here to speak with Mrs. Allen and Gloria Allen." Hannah showed her badge.

"Come in. I'll take you to Miss Allen. She's at the pool. This way, please."

Hannah wondered how long this sweet lady had worked for the Allens. *I'll bet she could shed some light on this family if she wants to,* she thought.

"This is some house," Sharon whispered as they passed through the entryway, then down a long, wide hall, around a corner, and finally out a huge sliding-glass door onto a magnificent patio.

The elderly woman pointed toward the pool in the distance, bowed slightly, and quietly left them.

"Look at this lush foliage," Sharon said as she and Hannah walked along. "I feel like I'm in the tropics. It's hot enough, that's for sure. How in the world do they keep these tropical plants so healthy in this climate?"

An avid gardener, she was enthralled by what she saw. "If this is what heaven looks like, I'm ready."

There were several magnolia trees with healthy green foliage, indicating they'd successfully been acclimated to the climate, not easy with tropical trees. Many people tried to grow them in northern climes and failed, but those plants were thriving.

A host of local perennials were planted in the area, so there was always something in bloom around the pool and beyond. To complement the perennials, almost every popular annual in the western world was on display, too. All that loveliness was tied together by rivers of hardy red, pink, and white geraniums. They surrounded the pool area and flowed in streams away from it into the estate's vast grounds, creating little pools of flowers along the way.

"Breathtaking," Hannah whispered.

"I'd like to have a chat with their gardener," Sharon said. "He or she is one talented *artiste de flora.*"

Hannah checked the layout of the pool area and the gardens and paths beyond it. She saw comfortable, expensive-looking outdoor furnishings all around. Then she noticed a young woman stretched out on a lounge chair in a string bikini and sunglasses, with a cigarette dangling from her left hand as it lay draped over the lounge's arm.

"That's Gloria," Hannah whispered as they walked forward.

Gloria didn't move until the two women stood over her. "Oh, hello. I didn't see you coming."

"Gloria," Hannah said, ignoring the obvious lie, "this is Detective Walker."

"Hello, Gloria," Sharon said.

"Hello," Gloria replied blandly. "Why are you back?" she asked with some hostility.

"We need to ask some more questions," Hannah said politely.

"Didn't you ask enough yesterday?"

"Not nearly enough. Many questions have arisen concerning your sister's death, and we need them answered." Hannah's voice wasn't as friendly as before.

The sun bore down unmercifully on them. Gloria didn't seem to notice, but, from the look of her, she was accustomed to spending a lot of time under the sun. The detectives, however, were slowly baking in the heat.

"Could we find a shady spot to talk for a while?" Sharon asked.

"I suppose."

They moved to a shaded area of the patio and sat at a large, white, wrought-iron table surrounded by three enormous cut-leaf philodendrons that swayed gently in the light breeze. With the breeze, the air was bearable, if not comfortable.

The next instant, a very young woman who seemed almost a child came out of the house carrying a large tray with three tall glasses of lemonade and a platter of petite fours and triangle sandwiches. She set the tray down without a word and left without Gloria saying, "Thank you."

"Thank you," Hannah and Sharon called.

She didn't respond.

After a brief pause, Hannah asked, "Gloria, who else was in the house at the time of Angela's death yesterday?"

"Let's see," Gloria said reluctantly. "We had a few dinner guests. Mother often has a catered dinner when the staff has their day off. They seem to think they can let their hair down a little more when busy eyes and ears aren't around."

She's forgotten what she told me yesterday, Hannah realized, *when she said she and her mother were the only ones in the house.*

"What do you mean, let their hair down?" Sharon asked.

"They act more like their obnoxious selves," Gloria said.

"Are these people frequent visitors to your home? Do you know them well?"

"One at a time, please," Gloria snapped. "Yes, they're frequent visitors and no, I don't know them well. We don't go places and do things together, if that's what you mean."

"That's what I mean," Sharon said.

When Hannah spoke, she matched her partner's tone of authority. "Where were these people when we arrived?"

"Mother sent them away the moment Angela was found. She told them Angela was ill, that she called the doctor, and they had to leave."

"We'll need their names and addresses, plus those of anyone else who might have stopped by the house yesterday afternoon for any reason," Hannah said, emphasizing the last three words.

Gloria answered reluctantly and seemed more nervous than the previous day. She was definitely less cocky.

Is she hiding something or frightened of something? Hannah wondered.

She proceeded cautiously, trying to sound more like a well-meaning friend than an authority figure. "Gloria, you seem uncomfortable. Are you frightened of something?"

Gloria immediately bristled. "I'm not afraid of anything or anyone. I've just had a terrible shock with my sister's death, and am trying to deal with it. That's all."

The detectives exchanged a look.

"When we finish talking with you," Hannah continued, "we'll need to speak with your mother again and with the staff. Would you gather the staff in the library so we can speak with them together? It won't take long."

Gloria was plainly uncomfortable. "You'll have to take that up with Mother. I don't have the authority to do that."

OK, Hannah thought. *Mama runs the show, and the girls kowtow like everyone else. Got it. I wonder what happens when the cat's away?*

Sharon looked up from where she sat and saw a figure in an upstairs window overlooking the patio and pool—Mariah Allen.

Gloria looked up, too, and then fled the scene, making no effort to camouflage her hasty exit.

"Gloria!" Hannah called. "We're not finished!"

Gloria didn't respond.

"Whoa," Sharon said softly. "That's one scared young lady. I thought she wasn't afraid of anything."

"She did the same thing yesterday when her mother entered the room. Her departure wasn't as dramatic, but she got out of there fast when Mama arrived."

They sat thoughtfully for a few seconds, then they saw Mariah leave the window and appear at the patio door, giving directions to the young woman who brought refreshments earlier.

The youngster scurried toward them. "Mrs. Allen wants to see you in the library right now!" Her high-pitched voice showed a strong Irish accent, and she was almost too terrified to speak.

"We're coming," Hannah replied.

The girl ran back toward the house.

"I want to talk to her," Hannah said softly. "She's more frightened than Gloria."

"Don't move too fast," Sharon replied. "There has to be someone who doesn't ask, 'How high?' every time that woman says, 'Jump.'"

Walking at a leisurely pace, they reached the patio door, then were greeted by the same woman who let them into the house. She seemed totally nonplussed by the hysteria around her, leading the detectives to believe it was all normal behavior in that household.

Mariah stood just inside the library doorway as the two detectives approached. "Please sit down." She made no attempt to hide her irritation.

Hannah and Sharon sat together on a black velvet divan, while Mariah sat facing them in a rose brocade wing-backed chair.

"Why are you here again today?" Mrs. Allen asked. "We're

trying to prepare for my daughter's funeral. Can't you wait to ask questions until that's over?"

"I wish we could, but I'm afraid not, Mrs. Allen," Hannah replied. "There are too many questions surrounding Angela's death. We need the answers.

"In addition to you and Gloria, we need to speak with all those who were in the house at the time Angela died as well as with the others who live here, even if they weren't in the house at the time of the death. We also need to know who might have stopped by yesterday afternoon for any reason. Actually, make that anytime yesterday."

"Gloria and I were the only ones here."

"No you weren't," Hannah said sharply. "You had a dinner party in progress, one you immediately interrupted as soon as you learned Angela was dead. You told your guests she was ill, that you called a doctor, and then asked them to leave immediately. Isn't that correct?"

Mariah, unaccustomed to being spoken to in such a manner, was taken aback. Attempting to retain control of the situation, she said indignantly, "I will not have my guests or my staff subjected to police questioning. It's unthinkable."

"I'm afraid you have no choice, Mrs. Allen. We can either visit your guests in the privacy of their homes and speak with your staff here, or we can call each of them to police headquarters and question them there. You and they have nothing to say about it. Each is not only a potential witness but a potential suspect."

She waited a few seconds to let the message sink in.

"We asked Gloria to give us the names and to arrange to have the staff meet us in here, and she was extremely unsettled by our request. She said we had to ask you, and I'm doing that right now."

Hannah spoke in such a you'd-better-cooperate-or-else manner that Mariah, who never took orders from anyone, deferred. "I'll provide the names and addresses of our guests as well as the name of the catering service. If you wait here, I'll summon the staff. You may talk with them now."

"We don't want to speak with them now," Sharon said. "We'd like to speak with you. We'll talk to the staff later."

"As you wish, but I'm a very busy woman. Let's get on with it."

"Yesterday, Mrs. Allen," Hannah said, "you told me you believed Gloria killed her sister. Did you mean that?"

With an absolutely straight face, Mariah replied, "I most certainly never said anything of the kind, Detective Bell. That statement is pure fabrication. You'd better be careful before you attempt to put words in people's mouths."

It was Hannah's turn to be taken aback. Still, she wouldn't let a bully intimidate her—or even think she could.

"Mrs. Allen," Hannah said very carefully, "you said it. It's not a fabrication. You weren't aware of it then, but I had a tape recorder in my pocket and recorded our conversation."

"Isn't that illegal?"

"No, it isn't."

"Do you have a recorder right now?"

"Yes." She took out a small tape recorder from the outside pocket of her briefcase, pressed the Record button, and set it on the table beside her. "It's in your best interests, and in Gloria's, that you cooperate with us. We have reason to believe that Angela was murdered."

She let that sink in before continuing. "Now let me be certain that I understand you correctly. Are you retracting the statement you made yesterday when you said Gloria killed Angela?"

She didn't answer.

"Mrs. Allen?"

She glanced at the tape recorder. "Yes, I am."

"You don't believe Gloria murdered her sister?"

"That's correct."

"You're aware that this statement is being recorded?"

"Yes."

"Can you explain why you accused her yesterday?"

"I was upset."

"Upset enough to accuse your own daughter of murdering her own sister?" She hoped to prick the woman's conscience, assuming she had one.

"I was angry with Gloria." Mariah was calm and composed now.

Hannah's voice oozed contempt. "Angry enough to accuse her of murdering her own sister? Do you always react so viciously when someone angers you?"

"I...I...."

Heavy silence filled the room. Mariah's confidence faltered. Then she responded with all the phony humility she could summon.

"I was wrong. I don't know why I said such an awful thing. Gloria would never hurt Angela. They cared a great deal for each other. They were twins, you know."

Hannah nodded. *She's an actress, too.* She shared a look with Sharon. *Mariah isn't stupid. That admission may serve her well later.*

"Is there anyone you can think of who'd want to hurt Angela?"

"Not a living soul. I meant what I said about her yesterday when I said people were jealous of her. That's true, but I can't think of anyone who'd truly want to hurt her, and certainly not anyone who'd want to kill her." Mariah lowered her head and wiped at her eye, but Hannah saw no tears.

"Please find the killer," Mariah said. "You have our complete cooperation. Whatever it takes, I want that killer found."

"I don't need to ask you any more questions now," Hannah said. "I know this is a difficult time." She reached into her pocket. "Here's my card. You can reach Detective Walker or me directly, or you can leave a message for us, which we'll return as soon as we can. Give yourself time to think, but please call if you think of anything that might help us locate Angela's killer. The next time we need to visit, we'll try to call first."

"Thank you. I would appreciate that. I'll call if I think of anything that will help." Her attitude softened a little.

"If you could get the names and phone numbers we need while we talk to the staff, we'd appreciate it."

"I'll do that," Mariah said coolly. "I'll send in the staff. There are six, four women and two men."

The kindly looking elderly woman entered with a tray of cookies.

"This is Anna," Mariah said. "She's the head of the staff and has been with us for many years. You may start with her." She turned toward Anna. "These detectives want to ask you a few questions about Angela."

A pained expression came to the old woman's face.

"It's all right, Anna. Answer their questions as best you can." Anna nodded.

"Please sit down," Sharon said.

"Thank you." Anna reluctantly moved toward the wing-backed chair her mistress had just vacated. She looked uncertain about sitting in it.

"You may sit down, Anna," Mariah said, motioning toward the chair before leaving.

Anna set the tray on a nearby table and sat down.

"Hello," Hannah said gently. "I'm Detective Bell, and this is Detective Walker."

"Hello," Anna replied demurely.

"How long have you worked for the Allens?" Hannah asked.

"I've worked for Miss Mariah's family since she was a girl, over forty years."

Hannah hadn't noticed before, but there was a faint Irish accent in Anna's speech. She'd been in the States long enough to lose almost all of it, but it was still there.

"So you knew Angela and Gloria since they were born?"

"No. I came to the Allen house when they returned from Europe about twenty years ago. Mariah's family was the Ryans."

"What were the Allens doing in Europe?"

"Dr. Allen studied there. He received his medical degree in England, then came home to practice. We've been in Chicago for only four years."

"Where were you before that?"

"Iowa."

"Where exactly?"

"Avon Lake, just outside Des Moines."

Sharon took notes even though the tape recorder was running.

"Where did Dr. Allen practice?" Hannah asked.

"At Mercy Hospital in Des Moines. He was head of thoracic surgery."

"How did he die?"

"A car accident. Must we talk about that?"

"Not today. What was he like to work for?"

"Very kind and gentle. He wasn't arrogant like so many doctors. He always listened and never bossed us around." Anna's voice held admiration and respect.

"And the Allen women?"

"They're like my own family. Mrs. Allen has taken good care of me over the years. She's not a warm person, but she's fair."

"Do you have a family? Any children?"

"Oh, no. I never married."

"How do Mariah and her daughters get along?"

"They're very devoted to each other."

"How so?"

"They truly care for each other."

I hear the words, Hannah thought, *but I don't see the actions.* "I have to admit I haven't seen any trace of devotion since I arrived. In fact, it seemed the opposite. I haven't seen any warmth or affection between Gloria and her mother."

Anna paused, then said slowly, "As I said before, Mrs. Allen isn't a warm or gentle person. She doesn't show much affection toward anyone. Even as a child, she kept her distance from others. She's pretty much the same as an adult and a mother, but that doesn't mean she doesn't care.

"Mr. Allen, God rest his soul, was a very warm, loving man and affectionate toward all of them, even though he received little response from his wife. The girls adored him."

"Is Mrs. Allen hard to work for?" Sharon asked.

Anna's eyes remained cast down. "Like I said, she's been fair with me."

"That's not what Detective Walker asked, Anna." Hannah didn't want to push, but she needed a better answer.

Anna didn't reply at first but then said, "She…can be difficult. I thought you were going to ask about Angela."

A quick glance passed between the detectives.

"How well did Angela get along with her mother?" Sharon asked gently.

"Fine, but in a distant way. As I said, they were devoted, but they aren't a family to share much of themselves with anyone else. They get along, but Mrs. Allen runs everything and tells everyone what to do. She runs a tight ship, as they say." She smiled at her use of the idiom.

"Tell us more about Angela," Hannah said.

"She was a little girl when I first saw her. Both girls were beautiful but different. Gloria was robust and full of energy, while Angela was fragile and much quieter. Angela was a very bright child and quietly curious about everything. She adored her father and was never the same after he died—neither was Gloria.

"In recent years, Angela withdrew further into herself. I worried about her constantly. I always hoped a prince, a man like her father, would come to take her away from here. Then they could live happily ever after. That's not very realistic, I know."

"Why do you think she needed to get away from here?"

"For one thing, she was a grown woman. She didn't belong here. Neither does Gloria." Anna spoke as if that should be obvious. "They need to get away and make their own lives. Angela especially needed warmth and the kind of love she couldn't get here. Gloria's a lot tougher." Her voice was heavy with sadness.

"Was Angela in danger here?" Sharon asked.

Anna seemed uncomfortable with the question. She chose her words carefully. "No, not physical danger, but she was in danger of totally losing herself within herself. She seemed to be fading a little more each day. I hope she didn't kill herself."

Anna spoke the final sentence with such gravity that Hannah felt the older woman's pain and sadness. *This is what you'd expect a mother to say. The housemaid shows the depth of pain you'd expect to come from the mother. How sad.*

Anna closed her eyes and lowered her head, shaking it slowly. Then she looked up with pleading eyes and asked Hannah, "Is it possible she could have died naturally?"

"It's possible. The cause of death hasn't yet been determined. Natural causes is a possibility."

When the remaining staff members arrived, Hannah noticed a man who, judging from his apparel and the tools hanging from his belt, was the gardener.

Sharon will want to talk with him, she thought. *She'll want to know the Latin name and complete history of each plant outside. We could be here for a week!* She smiled ruefully to herself.

In addition to the gardener, there were four others, including the young woman, who seemed nervous and frightened. She wrung her hands like Lady MacBeth. *I'll need to speak with her alone,* Hannah thought.

Sharon must have read her mind. "Why don't you and—what's your name?" she asked the girl.

"M…Mandy O'Brien," she said weakly.

"Mandy O'Brien. A pretty name."

"Thank you."

Sharon turned to Hannah. "Why don't you and Mandy walk outside to talk? I'll speak with the others in here."

"Sounds good." Hannah gently touched Anna's shoulder. "Thank you, Anna. You may go now." She placed a card in Anna's hand. "We may want to speak with you again about Angela. Please call if there's anything you think I should know."

Anna nodded, rose from the chair, and left the room. Hannah watched her go. Then, she turned and put her arm around Mandy, hoping to calm her. They walked out toward the gardens beyond the pool.

"Mandy, why are you so frightened?" Hanna asked as they strolled among the flowerbeds.

"Dunno."

Hannah put her arm firmly around the woman's shoulder so she couldn't run when Hannah asked, "Mandy, are you here illegally?"

The young woman stiffened and tried to pull free. Hannah grasped her shoulders firmly in her strong hands and said, "Look at me, Mandy."

The girl looked squarely into the detective's eyes. Hannah hadn't seen such fear in a long time. Mandy looked as if she expected to be shot. Her lips moved, but no sound came from her mouth.

Hannah sat her down on a nearby bench and spoke to her firmly but with compassion. "Look at me, Mandy."

It took a moment, but then two large, frightened, green eyes slowly looked into Hannah's intense dark ones.

"You've got to get yourself together, Girl. If you continue going around looking like a scared rabbit, someone will find you out— someone who can have you deported. How long have you been here?"

"Five months."

"How old are you?"

"Eighteen."

Hannah wiped perspiration from her brow. The heat was almost unbearable, but Mandy's skin felt cool to her touch. "Whew! It's hot out here." She wiped her brow again to buy more time.

"Mandy, your being here illegally is very serious business, especially if you're not eighteen. I'd say you were thirteen or fourteen. Am I right?"

The terrified girl meekly nodded. Hannah feared she might faint.

"I won't question you anymore today, but here's my card. Keep it handy. Call if you want to talk about anything at all. If you think of something that might help us learn what happened to Angela, we'd appreciate knowing it."

Mandy looked at her quizzically but didn't speak.

"There's some question about how Angela died," Hannah explained.

Mandy looked down at her hands, which were clasped tightly in her lap, and said nothing. She and Hannah remained seated for a few minutes.

"Mandy," Hannah said gently. "Call me if you need anything. I mean it. I won't tell anyone about you. You can call if you just want to talk. Can you use the house phone?"

Mandy nodded. When she spoke, she displayed a strong Irish accent. "We have a phone in the servants' quarters. I can use that one."

"I'm glad to see you've found your voice again." Hannah laughed and gave Mandy a little hug.

The young woman threw her arms around Hannah's neck, squeezed hard, then released her grip, and ran toward the house.

Hannah laughed softly to herself. *I swear, that child is as skittish as a squirrel,* she thought.

When Hannah returned to the house, Sharon was just coming out to meet her.

"How'd it go with Mandy?" Sharon asked.

"She's illegal. I told her I wouldn't tell anyone. You're not anyone."

"That explains a lot."

"My guess is the whole staff's illegal, brought in over the years to work for the family. I have no personal gripe with that unless they're being treated as indentured servants or someone is getting rich off them and their families."

"You might have something there. I didn't get much from the others, but they all have Irish accents. Some accents are stronger than others, probably depending on how long they've been here. All were reluctant to talk. I'll bet Mrs. Allen knew we wouldn't get far with them, which explains why she was so willing to let us speak with them. Think of how humiliating it would be for her if she ended up in jail for smuggling Irish nationals into the country."

Lost in thought, Hannah didn't respond.

"Can you imagine the high and mighty Mrs. Allen in jail? She'd probably handle that as badly as dear Leona Helmsly. They're cut from the same cloth."

"I'm more concerned about her staff. They'd be deported. If they went to some trouble to get here, I doubt they want to go back. Well, at least we have something on Mrs. Allen. That could be useful." A sly look came to her eye.

"You know, the staff situation might be why Gloria is so uncomfortable talking with the police."

"Could be. Sharon?"

"Yeah?"

"Did you talk to the gardener?"

"I did. He promised to send me a list of the plants in the gardens and around the pool, where they should be planted, and how to keep them healthy. He said the list even gives the Latin name and history of each plant. He keeps very complete records. That's a serious gardener! I have his name. I'll get more out of him later."

"I thought so." Hannah smiled.

"Detective Bell, did you really have a tape recorder running yesterday when Madam Allen accused Gloria of murder?"

"No. Did you get the names and addresses we need, Detective Walker?"

"Yes."

CHAPTER FIVE

The two detectives sat at a table in a nearby Wendy's going over the list Sharon had acquired. The list of guest names and addresses was short, showing only three couples and one single man. The caterer was Jolene's Fine Dining and Catering, an upscale dining establishment and catering service for Chicago's elite. Four of Jolene's personnel, two men and two women, were on the list of those who served the party at the Allen home. A florist was on the list, too, having delivered the weekly bouquets for the house.

Hmmm, Hannah thought. *The florist delivers weekly? It's every Wednesday, the same day the staff has off and when the Allens had their party.*

"I wonder how often they have these parties," Hannah said. "They said often, but not how often.

"Did you notice all the fresh floral bouquets around the house?" Sharon asked. "There were plenty of them, and they're all expensive. I wonder if it's the same deliveryman each week? It would take time to deliver the new bouquets and retrieve the old ones. Maybe he has some observations about the Allens. It would be worthwhile to ask questions of…" she consulted the list, "Mike Jones. I'll take him on."

Hannah nodded. "Why don't you take the caterer, too? I'll do the couples. You want the single guy?"

"Scardy cat!"

"No, it just evens out the work," Hannah retorted. "Six for you, eight for me. Besides, you're the one who's man crazy, not me." Since Sharon divorced her husband three years earlier, it seemed she was constantly looking for a replacement.

"I am not!" Sharon said indignantly. "I just don't want to miss a good one—if he's out there."

They chuckled and returned to their list. Suddenly, Hannah's expression turned dark.

"Oh, God. It just hit me." She pointed at the names of Mr. and Mrs. Raleigh Quigley. "I didn't catch on right away. That's got to be Judge Raleigh Quigley. There can't be that many Raleigh Quigleys in the Chicago area, especially living near Lake Shore Drive.

"I had to testify in a case he heard when I was a beat cop. He's an asshole, very pompous. He thinks he's some kind of god. An evil god, I'd say. He returned a child to his abusive parents, who later drowned him in a bathtub after sexually assaulting him. The baby was only three years old.

"He said he gave the child back because they were his natural parents." She mimicked the pompous, grossly obese magistrate's manner. "He's on my shit list. My blood boils every time I think of that case, with him sitting up there on that bench so almighty and so wrong. I couldn't eat for days after that little boy died. I woke up every night for weeks, weeping. The system can't work if the people who are supposed to make it work are incompetent, arrogant, and totally insensitive!"

"Calm down, Hannah. You're attracting attention."

"Calm down hell!" Hannah's whisper was almost a shout. "The guy's a fraud and a killer. He's as guilty of killing that child as if he'd drowned him himself. That was when I truly understood what makes normally good, decent, law-abiding people willing to kill. If I'd seen the judge during that time, I could easily have drawn my weapon and shot him without remorse."

Hannah's face was hot, her hands clammy. Her breathing came in short, pained gasps. Her words were filled with hate.

"Hannah, calm down. You're an officer of the law. You have to keep your cool. He'll get what he deserves someday."

"I hope so, but I don't have your faith. Evil deeds frequently go unpunished. Maybe he'll disgrace himself somehow with this Allen thing. That would be something."

After lunch, the two detectives went their separate ways. Jolene's was in Oak Park, thirty minutes from the precinct house in good traffic. Sharon decided to go there first. She dropped Hannah off at headquarters and drove toward the expressway.

Hannah went to speak with Detective Keys, but he was out, so she got in her car and drove to the morgue.

Dr. Jim Preston was in his office, dictating follow-up notes to an autopsy he'd just finished. Hannah stood silently in the doorway, and Jim waved to her. She stepped out of the office to wait in the hall.

As she waited, a gurney came down the hall pushed by two technicians who just arrived from a construction-site accident. From what she overheard, there were three more victims on the way.

Hannah thought as she watched them go, *They deserve a lot of credit for dealing with death every day. They see morbid scenes of mutilated bodies that were once viable human beings. Now they're nothing but dead meat to be probed and cut up like sides of beef. I couldn't do it.*

She lowered her head partly in respect for the dead and partly in admiration for those who attended to it so intimately. *I'm not allowed to touch a body at a death scene. That's against the rules. They have to. It's their job.*

"Who are you praying for?" a soft voice whispered in her ear.

Hannah jumped, then swung at the interloper. "Jim Preston, you know how skittish I am about being surprised!"

"You'd better get over it, Hannah. You'll jump into the path of a bullet someday. Come in and sit down. I know this is a rough day for you. You and Doc were close."

Hannah was ashamed of herself for forgetting about Doc's death for a few hours. She wished Jim hadn't reminded her. She slumped into the seat he offered, feeling the pain return. It was several minutes before she could speak.

"I'm sorry," Hannah said. "I'm trying to pull myself together. It's just such a shock. I was on the phone with him for almost an hour before he died last night. I feel partially responsible. If we'd talked moments longer, I might have sensed something was wrong. He seemed a little breathless, but I assumed that was due to the nature of our conversation. I never dreamed...."

With an anguished expression, she asked, "Is he here, Jim?"

"Yes."

"I don't want to see the body."

"You won't. He's put away."

Hannah winced.

"Sorry. I know that sounded cold." He looked at her with sympathy and understanding. "Hannah, he died quickly. We didn't find any evidence of prolonged occlusion. He had a generally healthy heart. A single clot got him. It was swift, which explains why he had so little time, though he managed to dial 911. He punched the numbers but was gone before he could speak."

"I loved him like a father," she said softly, then took a long, slow breath. "Have you autopsied Angela Allen yet?"

"Yes."

"What did you find?"

"A number of things. Doc took samples of her blood and found oil of tarbar in her blood. That's a death-feigning drug. There were traces in her left palm, indicating she held the pill in her hand for a while."

Just like Doc said, Hannah thought.

"Externally, we found no other wounds or lacerations. She was beautiful. As jaded as we get in this business, it's tough to see a young, beautiful woman with her life ahead of her dead. She had a small wound on the bottom of her foot, but we found nothing unusual there. She could have stepped on a needle or pin on the floor. It's not important."

Hannah went from feeling elated to crushed. *Do I tell him what Doc told me? Should I break my covenant with Doc? Doc didn't plan to die last night, and time is important.*

It didn't take long for her decision.

"Jim, I want to share with you the conversation I had with Doc last night. It was in confidence, but, under the circumstances, I feel I must trust you with what he said."

She related the conversation, telling Jim of Doc's proof, theory, and speculation. Jim sat perfectly still, listening carefully.

When Hannah finally stopped, Jim shifted positions several times, tapped his pencil on the desk, and glanced up at the ceiling before looking at her.

"I don't know how to respond to what you've just said," Jim said. "I don't believe there's any way to prove Doc's theory. There's no forensic evidence. I know he had an uncanny, almost paranormal sense about some things and was often right. We often solved crimes by following his hunches, and I believe there's something in what he told you, but I don't see how we can prove it.

"The cause of death stands right now as natural causes. It could also have been suicide, but we don't believe that was the intent. The evidence shows no overdose, and for suicide, the overdose would have had to be intentional. However it started out, something went wrong, and the girl died. We can't call it homicide, because there's no evidence. For the family's sake, we chose the most humane explanation. There's no conspiracy to cover this up."

"This is what Doc said would happen." Hannah felt sick to her stomach.

"What?"

"Nothing. Go on."

"The body will be released to the funeral home later today in preparation for burial or cremation, whichever the family wants. If you can keep the case alive, I'll do all I can to help you find a different outcome based on whatever evidence you can produce. That's all I can do. Do you understand?"

"Yes. I don't like it, but I understand." Displeasure showed in her voice.

"There's something else you might like to know."

"What's that?"

"Angela had an abortion about four or five years ago. She was in her second trimester when it was done. It wasn't done very well, but she survived."

"Oh, my God. I would never have thought...." Hannah sat silently, shaking her head.

"I would expect a girl from a family as wealthy as hers to have the best care possible in such a situation," Jim continued, "unless she did it on the sly."

"Yeah." Hannah thought about something Anna, the housekeeper said. *We've been in Chicago for about four years.*

"There's one more thing, Hannah, but this is strictly off the record. I could get in big trouble for this, so it's just between us. I'm sure, however, you'll find it interesting and possibly even helpful. You remember my daughter, Victoria?"

"I sure do. She's adorable. How old is she now? What does this have to do with Angela?"

"Vicky's eleven going on twenty-five. At the moment, she's working on a science project on the human voice. Like you, she likes singing, and she wants to know what makes the voice work.

"So, as part of her research, I told her I'd get samples of different-sized vocal cords so she could see what they looked like and study them. You know—large, thick ones for low voices, and smaller, thinner ones for high. Stuff like that.

"During Angela's autopsy, I opened her throat to remove her voice box and vocal cords. She appeared to be a perfect study for small, thin cords. What I found shocked me.

"Her cords were small all right and very thin, but they showed signs of atrophy. It wasn't major deterioration, but, from what I could determine, the atrophy came from lack of use. In other words, when she died, Angela hadn't spoken for a long time, probably years. There were no signs of disease or malfunction. She was mute by choice."

Hannah sat riveted to her chair, her mouth open, staring at Jim. "Unbelievable. That poor girl…woman…whatever she was," she muttered.

Finally, she spoke in a tone of intense frustration and mounting determination. "More and more questions keep coming up about this family, Jim. Everywhere we turn, another new set arises. I want answers!"

She rose abruptly, shook his hand, thanked him for his work and the valuable information he gave, and dashed out. She hurried down the hall, shaking her fist in the air.

"Angela, I'll find out what happened to you if it's the last thing I do!" she declared.

Sharon wheeled onto I-290 heading west to Oak Park after

sitting in a traffic jam for fifteen minutes.

"This city's impossible," she muttered furiously. *Keep your frustration to yourself, Girl. No point in getting shot by some hothead over a lousy traffic jam.*

She arrived at Jolene's at two-fifty. *Let's see what I can get out of these folks, if anything. Maybe Mrs. Allen has them terrified, too. How has she acquired her power?*

As she entered the front door, a pleasant young woman approached.

"May I help you?" she asked.

Sharon flashed her badge. "I'd like to speak with the owner or manager, someone with whom I can discuss the details of a party Jolene's catered last evening."

"You must mean the Allen party. It's terrible what happened. I've heard it on the news all day about that girl, Angela. I had no idea she was twenty-six or was Gloria's twin. They looked somewhat alike, but that was it. Angela always seemed younger."

"Were you there last night?" Sharon was glad to find someone willing to talk.

"Not last night, but I've been there many times. They have lots of parties, at least twice a month and always on Wednesday. The servants are off that day, so we fill in for a few hours."

"Have you ever seen what goes on during one of those parties?"

Just as the young woman was about to answer, a tall, strongly built woman strode heavily across the dining room. "Hello. I'm Jolene. May I help you? We're between lunch and dinner just now. We'll begin serving again at five." She turned to the young woman. "Tammy, go back and help Sandy load the truck for the party at the Smythes this evening."

"Yes, Ma'am." Tammy left.

Curses. Foiled again, Sharon thought. *We were just getting started.*

"May I help you?" Jolene asked again.

Showing her badge, Sharon identified herself. "I'd like to ask you a few questions. I'd also like to speak to the four people who served the Allen party yesterday evening."

"There isn't much to say. We've been catering parties at the Allen home for a couple years. Mrs. Allen is a regular customer who pays promptly. What more could we ask?"

"Has anyone on your staff ever spoken about anything odd going on at that house during one of the parties?"

"Nothing they've ever told me about, but then, I doubt they would." She offered a sly smile with her well-rehearsed affectation. "Something unusual *did* happen last night, though. The entire staff arrived here early, by seven o'clock. Normally, they'd just be finishing serving dinner.

"Apparently, Mrs. Allen told them just before dinner would have been served, that her daughter was ill, and everyone had to leave immediately. She asked my staff to return this morning to pick up whatever they left behind.

"I sent a couple young fellows there early this morning to pick up my equipment. I was a little perturbed, because we needed some of it for another party later last night. Mrs. Allen's request seemed a bit of an overreaction, but, under the circumstances...." Jolene shrugged and fell silent.

"When I heard about Angela's death on the radio this morning," she continued with genuine sympathy, "I was deeply saddened. What a terrible thing to happen to someone so young. The family must be devastated."

Nodding, Sharon asked, "Exactly how often did these parties occur?"

"Every first and third Wednesday of the month, as regular as clockwork. In two years of catering for Mrs. Allen, she never canceled once."

"Do you know why they hosted the parties? Were they social events, or was there business involved?"

"I have no idea. We were hired to arrive at four-thirty, set up, serve cocktails by five, dinner at six, and be out of the house by seven-thirty. The orders were very precise and were strictly enforced. Every time slot had to be on schedule—not a minute later or early.

"None of my staff were present for whatever occurred after dinner. They left enough finger food and drinks for the evening. As far as I know, the household staff was expected to clean up when they arrived in the morning. I never thought about it, to tell the truth. It was, and I hope still is, a good piece of business."

After a few more questions, Sharon asked to see the four staff members who were at the Allen home.

Jolene was very cooperative. As they talked, she seemed to lose some of her affectations. *Maybe she's fallen out of character for a while,* Sharon thought. *That's quite an act she puts on.* She smiled.

"Sandy Anderson is here, and so is Tom Phillips. You may speak with both of them. The other two are off today."

"I'll catch them later. For now, I'd like to speak with Sandy and Tom."

"Make yourself comfortable, Detective Walker. I'll send them out to you. Would you like to see one at a time?"

"Yes, thank you."

"Would you like a cup of coffee?"

"No, thanks. I just finished lunch."

They nodded politely to each other, then Jolene left for the kitchen. Sharon looked for a good place to conduct an interview. Since all the tables were empty, she chose a comfortable one near a window overlooking a small garden at the restaurant's front corner. The area was shaded, and the view in all directions was serene.

She sat where she could watch someone approach the table. She would invite the person to sit opposite her, so he'd be facing the front entrance, with its overflowing flower boxes lining the sills of the large front windows. That was as nonthreatening a setting as she could find.

Soon, a nice-looking, tall, slender lad walked through the tables until he reached her. As he drew closer, Sharon rose to shake his extended hand.

"I'm Tom Phillips, Detective Walker. Jolene said you wanted to ask me some questions about last night at the Allen estate."

Polite, with a good, solid handshake, she thought. *Makes a good impression, and probably makes oodles in tips. I wouldn't mind having him wait on my table or cater my party.*

"Detective Walker?"

"Oh, I'm sorry, Tom. I was distracted for a moment. Won't you please sit down?"

"Thank you."

"Yes, I want to ask questions about yesterday evening. What time did you arrive at the Allen estate?"

"Four-thirty sharp. We have to be on time. If we're one minute late or early—I'm not exaggerating—we hear about it from Mrs. Allen. She wants everything just so and exactly on time. She's tough to work for. Hard to please."

"You must get yelled at a lot. Most people's watches and clocks aren't in sync. You must always be a little early or late."

"Yeah. We've gotten used to it. On her happy days, as we call them, she says nothing. Otherwise, watch out." He raised his hands over his head and ducked. "I stay as far from her as I can on those days."

Sharon nodded and wrote, *Mrs. Allen is hard to please. As a mother, too?*

"Sometimes she can be quite friendly and charming. We're never sure which Mrs. Allen will meet us when we arrive. She can also turn on you in a second. Nice one minute, nasty the next."

Sharon wrote, *Volatile personality. Tough on kids growing up.* "What did you do after you arrived?"

"We set up as usual. That takes about half an hour. Twenty-five minutes to be exact. In the remaining five minutes, we double-check everything and begin serving cocktails exactly at five. Not one minute late or early. That's what we did last night."

"Who was there for cocktails?"

"The same people as always. I don't know the names of anyone except Mrs. Allen, Angela, and Gloria. I've heard the names of the others spoken a few times, but I never pay any attention. I couldn't tell you one right now."

"Was anyone missing?"

"Yes. Angela, though it made no difference. She never spoke to anyone, anyway. She just smiled, drank her cocktail, and drifted about like a little lost princess. She often went outside alone, like she didn't want to be with anyone. She sure was beautiful."

His last words sounded like those of a lovesick pup. Before she could ask another question, he continued. "She always wore long, lacy, old-fashioned dresses with high necklines and long sleeves. I never saw her in any other clothing. She almost always wore beige. The color blended perfectly with her hair. She was sooo beautiful, like a china doll with her perfect skin."

The kid was either in love or seriously infatuated, Sharon thought sadly. *Now he'll be in love with her forever. She's permanently young, perfect, and beautiful. Will anyone else be able to measure up?*

"I can't believe she's dead. Maybe she's happier now."

"What do you mean?"

"She always seemed so sad. I wondered why." Suddenly aware

70

that he was exposing his feelings, he blushed. "I...I'm sorry. I'm...kind of...nervous. I never had to talk to the police before. I mean, about something like this."

"That's all right. There's nothing to be nervous about. We're just trying to reconstruct the events of last evening so we can better determine what happened to Angela."

"What do you mean? Her mother said she was ill. Why are the police involved? She was just sick...and she died."

"She wasn't sick, Tom. That was a cover-up her mother used to get everyone out of the house. Angela was dead by the time you left, and there are some questions about how she died."

"Wow." He sat back and stared at the table, then looked up at her. "It never occurred to me that something else might have happened to her. I just assumed she was sick enough to die."

Sharon waited.

"Are you saying someone might have murdered her?"

"It's possible."

"But who'd want to hurt her? She was an angel, just like her name. Why would someone want to hurt her?" He was incredulous at the idea.

"We don't know yet that anyone did. That's what we're trying to find out. I'll give you my card. Call if you think of anything else I might need to know. You can also talk to Detective Hannah Bell. She's heading up the investigation. Her number's on the card, too."

"OK," he said so softly she barely heard him.

"One more thing, Tom. What time did you leave the Allen house?"

"Shortly after six. As soon as Mrs. Allen told us Angela was ill, and we had to leave at once, we cleared out. She told us to leave everything behind and come back for it in the morning. We didn't know if that was OK, so Bobby called Jolene on the car phone to ask. She said go ahead, so we left. We were back here by seven."

"Bobby? Was he part of your crew?"

"Yes."

"What's his last name?"

"Hill."

"Thanks. You've been very helpful. Remember, call if there's anything else you think we should know."

"I will. Would you like to talk to Sandy now?"

"Yes. Thank you."

"I'll get her."

As Tom walked away, Sharon thought, *Too bad he isn't twenty years older. The good ones are always too young, too old, or unavailable.*

Sandy corroborated Tom's story and added her own observations of the Allen parties.

"I rarely saw Angela at cocktails," Sandy said. "Gloria was always there, dressed to the teeth, as was her mother, but not Angela. She often arrived near dinnertime, or, after getting a drink, spent the rest of the cocktail hour in the garden. She always drank the same thing, plain soda water."

Sandy confirmed Angela's style of dress and that she never spoke to anyone, at least where Sandy could see or hear.

As Sharon drove back to the interstate and the precinct house, she thought, *This case gets curiouser and curiouser. I hope Hannah's there when I return. I can't wait to tell her about that not-speaking thing. That's too weird.*

CHAPTER SIX

Hannah sat at her desk in the precinct house, trying to absorb all that had happened so far that day. Her heart was filled with grief for her friend, and she was convinced there was much more to the Allen case than met the eye.

As she asked herself questions, she wrote them down, with added comments for some.

Was Angela Allen murdered? If so, why and by whom?

What was the real reason Mariah Allen accused her daughter of murder? Why did she recant the following day and insist she never said it?

Is it conceivable that Gloria killed her sister? If so, why?

Why would Gloria tell us about a conversation she had with Angela that couldn't have taken place, because Angela never spoke? She has to know we'll find out.

Was Gloria hoping the case would be closed quickly enough that no one would find out about Angela not speaking? Is she as ill-tempered and arrogant as she seems, or does her unpleasantness hide a very frightened young woman? If so, what's she afraid of? Is she in danger?

Hannah stared at the last question. It was almost as if someone else had written it. That thought hadn't occurred to her until that moment. She circled it and reread it.

When did Angela stop speaking, and why? Is there any connection with that and their arrival in Chicago four years ago and the abortion around the same time? The trauma of an abortion would be enough to damage a healthy psyche. Angela was emerging as a physically and emotionally fragile young woman. How had all the things that happened to her in her young life affected her mind? Who was the father of her aborted child?

In the margin, she added a note.

More proof that money doesn't buy happiness.

Then more questions.

What about the Allen staff? Are they all illegal, or is it just Mandy? Why is she so frightened? I can understand some of it, but she's scared beyond all reason. Has she been threatened by someone with something—return to Ireland? Is she in danger?

"So many questions. They make me tired." Her eyelids felt heavy.

What about the parties? How often do they occur? What kind of parties are they? Are they bridge parties? That doesn't seem likely. Three couples, one single male, Mariah, Angela, and Gloria Allen do not a bridge party make. The Allen women don't strike me as card players.
Board games? What about a Scrabble or Monopoly party? Are they purely social gatherings? Do they share music? Discuss politics? Plan community events? Develop and organize volunteer programs? Not likely.

As her weariness grew, Hannah set down her pen and laid her head on her arms folded on the desk. She took a deep breath and thought, I wonder....

Let's say the party group is a bunch of hoodlums who arrange to bring Irish nationals to the US illegally and then sell them as servants to wealthy families under threat of a return to Ireland if they complain. There's a lot of money to be made in that scheme, and there are plenty of people willing to pay it.

In her dream, she envisioned piles of dollars, with Mariah Allen and Judge Quigley throwing handfuls of them into the air while dancing an Irish jig.

Judge Raleigh Quigley. He'd be capable of getting involved in something like that. He has no moral core. He's also got lots of connections and the money to start such a racket. Money begets money. Greed begets greed.

Her dream was filled with more questions and strange, distorted faces floating about close to her face, clouding her vision and confusing her brain.

We need to find out about Mariah's dinner guests. Are they rich and powerful? Do they have a Celtic background? What about their households? Do they have servants? Where do they come from? How long have they been here, and how did they arrive?

What if Angela figured it out and refused to participate? Instead, she planned to turn them in. They caught wind of her plan and killed her—or had her killed?

"Wake up, Lady. You're supposed to sleep at home."

Hannah jolted awake and found herself looking into Sharon's excited face. "Ohhh. I must have dozed off. Sorry."

"I'm glad you're here. I was hoping you would be. I have something to tell you about Angela Allen. It's very interesting."

Sharon took a deep breath, then said, "Angela Allen was mute. At least, it appears that way at the moment. Both of the employees I spoke with at the caterer's today said so. Neither ever heard or saw her speak to anyone.

"One of them, a young man, was completely smitten by Angela and kept a close eye on her. He said she often walked around alone in the garden during the cocktail hour, returning to the house just before dinner. He never heard her say a word."

The fog in Hannah's mind began to clear. "Yes. I know."

"You know? How?"

"Jim Preston told me Angela's vocal cords had atrophied from lack of use. It was apparently voluntary, because there was no sign of disease or malfunction. He said it appeared she hadn't spoken for several years."

"Wow! How did he know? Her vocal cords wouldn't have been part of the autopsy unless someone suspected a problem there."

"Don't ask."

"OK. Gotcha. But why would she not want to talk to anyone? Was she that emotionally disturbed?"

"Quite possibly. She had an abortion a few years back. Jim learned that during the autopsy, too."

"Oh, boy. The poor kid. Hannah, this case gets uglier every minute."

"I know."

"What's our next move?"

"I plan to call Laine and tell her Saturday night is out of the question. I shouldn't have agreed to participate in the program in the first place. Emotionally, I'm not ready to put on a show, and besides, there won't be any practice time. I know the show must go on and all that, but it'll have to be without me."

"I'm sure she'll understand."

"She will. I'll get her to call Wanda King to fill in. If Wanda can't, she'll know someone who can." Hannah called Laine, who understood how close Hannah had been to Doc. Then Laine told Hannah something remarkable.

"A couple weeks ago, I saw a painting at a local gallery entitled Angela. It was a portrait of an enchanting young woman with long, ash-blonde hair and beautiful light-blue eyes lounging on a divan. It was all done in tones of beige with only tiny touches of color here and there, very ethereal. The plaque said it was a young local woman named Angela Allen, whom the artist used as a subject in several studies. That one was his favorite.

"The reason I remember the painting is because of the girl and the coloring. She was extraordinarily beautiful, with piercing blue eyes that struck you right in the heart. She looked like an angel without wings.

"She had a profound look of sadness, too, in her blue eyes. I never saw a portrait done in almost one color before. The only variation was in the subject's eyes and a dot of deep rose or green here and there. It was striking and very bizarre."

Laine paused to catch her breath. "After watching the news at ten last night, I kept thinking there was something familiar about the dead girl. It didn't hit me until the middle of the night. I was going to tell you when you came over. I suppose it could be another Angela Allen, but it seems worth checking out."

"What was the artist's name?" Hannah tried to hide her increasing interest, knowing Laine would sense it instantly. Then, like a bulldog, she wouldn't let go until she knew why it might be important to a case.

"Give me a minute. Ummm. Brannigan. David? Daniel? Darren. That's it. Darren Brannigan."

Hannah gasped. That was the name of the single male invited to the Allens' party. Coughing and apologizing for a sudden dryness in her throat, Hannah asked casually, "What was the name of the gallery?" She coughed again.

"Bless you, Dear. Do you need to drink something?"

"No, I'm fine. Go on."

"It's Pleasing Portraits Gallery. It's all portraits painted by Chicago-area artists. If you want a portrait painted, you can go there, tell them what you want, and have an artist paint you. It's a cool idea. While we were there, two people were being painted in the studio. You can have it painted any way you like as long as you're willing to pay. It's not cheap. They start at $20,000. I asked."

"Of course." Laine always asked the price of things, including someone's new coat or a neighbor's car. "Where is the gallery?"

"On Harrison in Oak Park. I don't remember the street number, but it's close to downtown. I'm sure it's in the phone book."

"The Mafia hung out there in the thirties, didn't they?" Hannah had a vague memory of something she'd read.

"I think so. Frank Lloyd Wright built some houses there, including one for himself, as I recall. It's a wealthy suburb. That's what you'd have to be to have a portrait done at that gallery. Twenty grand would probably get you a portrait of your cat."

"That's a bunch of money, all right. Very helpful information. Thanks. I think you've hit on something." She hoped Laine would be pleased and wouldn't ask too many questions.

"Glad to be of assistance. Maybe you'll even let me know if this leads to something."

"Maybe."

"Give me a break, Hannah. I won't tell anyone. Why can't you just let me know if my tip is a good one?"

"We'll see."

"OK. I can tell from your questions there's something to what I just told you. Otherwise, you wouldn't want to know the name of the artist and gallery, right?"

"Right."

Laine chuckled. "OK. I'm satisfied for now. See you later."

"'Bye. Break a leg Saturday."

"We'll do our best, but we'll miss you. We wanted you to do Hard-Hearted Hannah."

"Somehow, I guessed. Some other time. Good-bye." Hannah hung up.

"What is it?" Sharon asked. "What did she tell you?"

"Hang on, Sherlock. I'll tell you." She repeated Laine's story about the painting and gallery.

"Why is that significant?" Sharon asked.

"In the first place, the portrait was named Angela, and the young woman who posed for it is named Angela Allen. In addition, the dead Angela Allen had long, ash-blonde hair. I couldn't see her eyes, because they were closed, but later, when I met her mother, I saw the same light-blue eyes Laine just described. Then there are the colors in the portrait—different shades of beige. The dead girl wore those colors, and her room was decorated the same way."

"It's got potential."

"I think so." Hannah paused. "Guess the name of the artist who painted that portrait?"

"Who?"

"Darren Brannigan."

Sharon paused, then said, "That's the single guy on the list!"

"You got it."

"Whoa!"

"Get out the phone book, and we'll look for this portrait gallery in Oak Park, somewhere on Harrison. Laine didn't remember the address, but we should be able to find it. I want to go there." Hannah glanced at her watch and saw it was a few minutes before five o'clock. "Let's hope they're open late. I'd like to go right now."

They reached Pleasing Portraits Gallery quickly, and it turned out it was open late every night. It seemed their wealthy clientele enjoyed later hours. The shop opened at ten in the morning and closed at eight in the evening six days a week.

It was a fascinating place. Portraits of all kinds of people hung everywhere, showing them in poses doing many things—sitting or standing, golfing, dancing, playing a musical instrument, or painting. Some were happy, some sad. Some were beautiful, while others were grotesque. Some were very ordinary. Each portrait had only one person in it.

After giving the two women time to look around, a stately gentleman wearing an elaborate nametag that read Mr. Collingworth greeted them. "May I be of assistance?" The way his name was printed was a genteel way of telling visitors to refer to the staff in a more formal fashion than usual.

On the way to the gallery, Sharon and Hannah agreed not to identify themselves as police officers. They would pose as private citizens interested in portraits who'd heard of the gallery and wanted to look around.

"Yes, thank you, Mr. Collingworth," Sharon said. "We've heard about your unusual gallery and its portraiture. We're especially interested in seeing a portrait entitled Angela."

"Oh, yes. I know the one you mean. It's lovely, but I'm sorry. It was sold this morning."

"Sold this morning?" Hannah muttered. "To whom?"

The old man thought for a moment. "Just a moment. I'll look it up." He went to the register and checked the day's receipts. "Here it is. Mr. James Costello. I remember. Ms. Smith said he bought it for his wife as an anniversary gift. He knew exactly what he wanted when he walked in. Went right to it and paid cash." He smiled, pleased.

Hannah and Sharon exchanged glances. Costello was another name from the list.

Cash? they mouthed to each other, rolling their eyes.

"Just out of curiosity," Hannah asked, "how much would a portrait like that cost?"

"He paid $75,000 for it. The artist put a high price on it, saying that anyone who wanted it would have to pay that much for it. Won't he be surprised?"

"I'm sure."

"May I ask the artist's name?" Hannah asked.

"Yes. Mr. Darren Brannigan. He has several paintings here. I'd be happy to show you some of his other work.

Hannah hesitated.

"Yes, thank you," Sharon said. "We'd like to see them."

They walked through the gallery. Mr. Collingworth showed them six other paintings by Darren. All were of very young women, none older than twenty-five. Each portrait was distinctive. Hannah noted they all used plenty of color, unlike Angela's monochrome scheme.

Mr. Brannigan appeared to be an excellent artist, judging by the way looking at his portraits made the viewer feel. His subjects looked right through someone and bewitched each with their charms. Hannah and Sharon were mesmerized.

"Hannah, look at this one," Sharon said. "Mr. Collingworth, who is this gorgeous man? This is another Brannigan, but there's no bio like the others."

"That's a self-portrait of Mr. Brannigan." Mr. Collingworth spoke with pride, as if he'd created the portrait himself. "It's a considerable likeness."

Oh, my, Sharon thought. I could eat him alive. "Very nice." Her voice showed the proper amount of decorum.

So that's what he looks like, Hannah thought approvingly, as the blood involuntarily rushed up her neck, to her cheeks and over her ears. She turned her head away in hopes her partner wouldn't notice and make some embarrassing comment. She said softly, "I wonder what he's like on the inside?

"Are you ladies looking to add to your collection?" the salesman asked.

"Not just now, thank you," Hannah said.

"I don't have the wall space for one of these. They're huge. They're wonderful, though. I'd love to have them all."

The three of them exchanged smiles.

"Mr. Collingworth, did you know the young woman who posed for the Angela portrait? Have you ever met her?"

"No. Mr. Brannigan was very fond of her. When he brought that one in, we all marveled at it, but he was especially proud. He said she was special to him."

"Really?" Hannah felt an unexpected pang of jealousy. "Thank you for your time. We're glad to know you're here. We'll be back when we have a little more wall space." She smiled.

As they walked to the car, Hannah suggested Sharon spend the night at her place so they could discuss the case and make plans for the next day. In the morning, they'd start out to interview the people on the guest list. Sharon agreed.

"We'll call headquarters in the morning and let them know what we're up to," Hannah added.

"Sounds like a plan. Wasn't he the most scrumptious thing you ever saw?"

"Who?"

"Don't give me that. You know exactly who I mean. I saw your face when you looked at the portrait. You tried to hide it, but you were blushing."

"I was not."

"Yes, you were. What's the matter with you? Can't you at least admit a guy's good looking? That doesn't mean you want to marry him, for heaven's sake."

After a short pause, Hannah nodded. "OK, so I thought he was cute. I don't want you to bug me about it. You're always trying to fix me up, and I don't want that. I'll do my own fixing."

"When?"

"When I'm ready."

"You're not getting any younger, Kiddo."

"Would you have me copy what you did, marry someone, decide I don't like him, and divorce him? I don't want to do that."

"You think I planned to get a divorce? How was I to know he'd turn out to be a jerk?"

"You knew it before you married him, and so did I. Just about everyone you know knew it, too, but you went ahead. Lots of women do that, but I refuse. Now you spend most of your time looking for another one. I won't do that, either."

Neither spoke on the drive back to Sharon's home. She ran inside to pick up a few things, then they continued to Hannah's. When they pulled up in front of Hannah's duplex, Hannah said, "I'm sorry. I had no right to say that. I know you mean well. Someday, I hope we both find Mr. Right."

Sharon sighed. "No, Hannah. You're right. Why do women always think they need a guy, anyway?"

"Because that's the way nature intended it," Hannah said philosophically.

CHAPTER SEVEN

As the detectives sat at Hannah's kitchen table, reviewing the day's events and sharing information, they were particularly interested in the purchase of the Angela portrait from the gallery.

"Why today?" Hannah asked. "Why so much money? Is there a connection with Angela's death?"

"The problem with this case, Hannah, is we keep coming up with more questions and never find any answers. Do we have any answers yet?"

Hannah looked at her list. "Nope. Not one."

"Tell me again the name of the third couple on that list. I know we've got the Quigleys and the Costellos. Who else?"

"Let's see." Hannah sifted through the papers on the table. "Reilly."

"That's it. I know that Reilly, Quigley, and Brannigan are Irish, but Costello sounds Italian. Is it?"

"I don't know. I have a book of Irish surnames. I'll look it up. What are you getting at?"

"I was just thinking about the Irish connection. There is the Irish staff at the Allens, then the names Brannigan, Quigley, and Reilly on the guest list."

Hannah took a book down from her living room bookcase and opened it to the index. "Hmmm. I didn't know Allen was Irish."

"Oh, yeah? That's another connection. What about Costello?"

Hannah eyed the list. "I'll be darned. It's Irish, too. I never would have guessed. I thought it was Italian."

"Maybe it's both. You know the Irish are a pretty mixed bag. Just about everybody's been there at one time or another. The Romans were in Ireland for a long time. It makes sense that their surnames would be passed down the generations. We should dub this case the Irish Connection."

"You know what, Sharon? This makes the purchase of the portrait by Mr. Costello more interesting than ever. What does that portrait have to do with a group of Irish-heritage guests who visit the Allen home twice a month? Why did one of those guests rush out to buy the portrait the day after Angela died, and for so much cash? It smells fishy."

"To me, too." Sharon furiously typed Hannah's latest rash of questions into Hannah's computer. "Why was it hanging in the gallery in the first place? Why wasn't it in the Allens' home or that of the artist, especially if he was so fond of it? Seems to me that would have been more appropriate."

Sharon paused. "I'd like to know just how long that thing hung in the gallery."

"Yeah." Hannah knew where Sharon was headed. "A gallery makes a great hiding place. But, why hide the painting? I'll call Mr. Collingworth in the morning and find out how long the portrait was there. I also want to know the exact time it was purchased."

"Good morning, Pleasing Portraits Gallery."

"Good morning. This is Detective Hannah Bell from the Chicago Police Department. We understand a gentleman bought a portrait from you yesterday entitled Angela. Do you know of it?"

"Oh, yes. I sold it to him. Is there a problem?"

"Are you Ms. Smith?"

"Yes, I'm Diane Smith."

"There's no problem, Ms. Smith. We just need to know what

time he purchased it. We know it was in the morning, but we need a more exact time. Can you tell me?"

"Sure. I usually come in early, at eight, to finish some paperwork before we open at ten. The gentleman was waiting for me. I told him we weren't open yet, but he was very persistent, so I let him in. He wasn't here more than ten minutes. He knew which portrait he wanted and paid cash. He wouldn't even let me wrap it. He was in a big hurry."

"Did he say why he wanted it?"

"He said it was for his wife for their anniversary, which was why he was in such a hurry. The anniversary was the previous day, and he'd forgotten. His wife had seen the portrait and fallen in love with it, so he wanted to buy it for her."

For seventy-five grand? Hannah wondered. Now that's a loving husband…or a guilty one. "Ms. Smith, how long was the portrait in your gallery?"

"About one year. Mr. Brannigan, the artist, brought it in last summer."

"Thank you. You've been very helpful. If you think of anything else we might need to know, please call our 800 number and ask to speak to Detective Hannah Bell or leave a message on my voice mail."

"I will. Good-bye."

"Good-bye."

"Costello's a liar." Hannah hung up and explained what she'd learned.

"This case gets stranger by the minute," Sharon said.

"It sure does."

"It's especially strange since Gloria said Angela was about to commission a portrait of herself for herself. Apparently, there was one already. Why isn't that one hanging over Angela's bed."

"I don't want to go off on a tangent here, but I have a hunch

Angela's death, all these Irish folk, and the portrait are connected."

"The Irish Connection," Sharon said, swallowing her last sip of coffee. "I'm off to visit the infamous Judge Quigley and intimidate the hell out of him."

"Be careful," Hannah called as Sharon rushed out.

"I will. See you at the precinct at four."

Hannah sat quietly, drinking another cup of coffee in peace. She was going back to the Allen house to have it out with Gloria. I'll threaten her with a murder charge if I have to, she thought. She was the last person to see her sister alive, and she's the best suspect we have.

Then she remembered how Jim Preston said they'd probably handle the cause of death. I'd better talk to Jim first. Once the family is told death came from natural causes, they'll stop cooperating. Gloria might not know yet. So, I better go see her first. I'll check with Jim later.

"Hello, Anna," Hannah said as the friendly older woman opened the door to the Allen estate.

"Hello, Detective. I'm sorry, but I've forgotten your name."

"Bell."

"Please come in, Detective Bell. I'll get Mrs. Allen."

"I don't wish to speak with her. I want to see Gloria, please."

"I'll take you to her."

Does she spend time anywhere but at the pool? Hannah wondered as Anna led her outside again.

When Gloria saw Hannah coming, she jumped up from the lounge and yelled, "What are you doing here? Don't you have any respect for the dead?"

"Just how are you showing respect for the dead?" Hannah asked. "Sit down."

Shocked, Gloria gave her an angry look.

"Sit. I want to talk with you. We can do it here or go downtown. It makes no difference to me. You do have clothes, don't you? And don't run away if you see your mother. If you attempt to do that, I'll drag you downtown by your hair to make sure we have some privacy."

Gloria was so stunned to be spoken to in such a manner that she sat down immediately.

"Let me tell you what I know and what I want to know," Hannah continued. "You were the last one to see Angela alive. You said so. You also said you had a conversation with Angela Wednesday afternoon. Since Angela hasn't spoken in years, that's not possible. Did you think we wouldn't find out?"

Gloria opened her mouth to answer, but Hannah kept talking.

"I want to know what you know about the portrait of Angela that already exists—in addition to the one you said she planned to commission—painted by one of your party guests, Mr. Darren Brannigan. I also want to know why you think Mr. James Costello, another of your guests, was so eager to possess that painting that he rushed out to buy it early in the morning on the day after Angela's death. He paid $75,000 for it."

Gloria attempted to speak.

"I also know Angela had an abortion a few years ago, and I want to know every detail of that unfortunate incident. I also want you to tell me every detail about your daily life in this miserable household. I want to know about the parties that go on here two Wednesdays a month. What's their purpose? What goes on during them? Don't forget anything.

"I'm ready to book you for murder, so be careful what you say. Every word had better be the truth."

Gloria burst into tears under the barrage. "I can't talk to you here. I can't."

"Put on your wrap and sandals. We'll go for a ride."

As they left the house, Mariah saw them and called, "Where are you going?"

Neither woman answered.

"Gloria! Where are you going? Come back here!"

Hannah held tightly onto Gloria's arm and forced her to keep walking. Once in the car, Hannah asked Gloria in a softer voice, "Are you weeping because you were caught lying, or are you afraid of something—or someone?"

There was no answer, just more crying into the shaking hands Gloria held over her face.

Sharon drove to Judge Raleigh Quigley's estate. The driveway was long and twisting, and she didn't see the oncoming car until it was too late. She swerved, missed the car, and sideswiped an enormous oak that caved in the passenger side of her car. The speeding car never stopped.

For a time she was dazed but still conscious. Her head pounded, and she checked herself for broken bones. All she found were some bruises and her head was bleeding.

"What the hell are you doing?" she shouted at the long-vanished vehicle. "You almost killed me, you son of a bitch!"

After regaining her wits, she called in the accident and gave her location. Then, opening the driver's door, she stepped out and immediately collapsed.

Then she felt the pain in her right leg. My God. It's broken, she thought as everything went black.

Hannah, hearing the accident report on her car radio, felt very uneasy once she heard the location. She called in and asked who the injured officer was.

"Detective Sharon Walker," the dispatcher said.

"How bad is she?" Hannah felt her stomach move to her throat.

Please, God, not another one, she prayed.

"Don't know. She called in the report herself. That's a good sign. We don't know the extent of her injuries yet."

"I'm on my way."

With Gloria Allen in tow, Hannah arrived at the precinct. She gave instructions to the sergeant regarding preparation of the witness for questioning. "I'll be right back."

She walked quickly to the dispatcher's office to learn where Sharon had been taken. As soon as she was satisfied that her partner was stable, she returned to the interrogation room and found Gloria, calmer but still weepy.

"Gloria, I don't know yet what's going on at your house, but we're going to find out. We're willing to protect you if you need it, but we can't help you if you don't tell us the truth. The death of your sister has raised many questions, not only concerning her death but about the importation of illegal aliens from Ireland. We don't know if there are more violations beyond that, but we'll find out. If you know anything about this, we need your cooperation."

Gloria's weeping stopped, and true terror set in. Hannah watched as Gloria stared back in stunned silence.

"Gloria, I'll make you an offer. I expect that going back home right now isn't very appealing. Am I right?"

Gloria nodded.

"OK." Hannah exchanged glances with the officer who witnessed the session. "For your own protection, you'll stay here at the police station. You won't be charged. You'll be under protective custody. This is a common practice when we need to protect a witness."

The look of fear remained, and Gloria didn't reply.

Then Hannah did an extraordinary thing. She made an offer she'd never made before and never expected she would. It was against regulations, so she knew she might be in trouble for doing it.

"If it would make you feel more at ease, you can stay with me at my house while you and I sort this out. No one will know where you are except this officer, my boss, my partner, and me. What do you say?"

What have I done? Hannah wondered. Too late now. Let's see how she reacts. The lieutenant will hit the roof over this.

For the first time since they left the Allen estate, Gloria looked as if she might survive another day. She nodded.

"I'll go with you," she said weakly.

"Let me make this clear. If you stay with me, you'll talk to me and tell me the truth. If I find you're lying, I'll charge you with murder as promised. I have enough evidence for that. I could also send you back home."

Fear returned to her eyes. "They'll kill me, too," she said in a terrified whisper.

The two officers looked at each other, realizing the significance of what Gloria said.

"We won't let them," Hannah said. "Who are they?"

Gloria's terror returned, and she shook her head, refusing to speak.

"OK. We'll discuss that later. I have some matters to attend to now. This is Officer McCabe. She'll make you comfortable in a private cell until I return for you." She looked at the other officer. "See that she gets something to eat."

"We'll take good care of her, Hannah. Come with me, Gloria."

Gloria stood and reluctantly followed the officer.

They'll kill me, too. The words reverberated in Hannah's head. I knew it. Something's rotten at the Allen estate. That's good news to share with Sharon. We're finally getting somewhere. I hope she's OK.

She gathered her briefcase and hurried to St. Mary's Hospital.

Sharon was sitting up in bed, her leg in traction, when Hannah arrived.

"I'm glad to see you alive, Friend," Hannah said. "You gave me quite a scare for a while there."

"You were scared? I thought it was all over when I saw that car right in front of me. I'm lucky to be here."

"Did you see the driver?"

"All I saw was a blur of red. That son of a bitch didn't even stop."

"Did you hit the car?"

"No. I swerved and hit a tree instead. A couple more inches, and I wouldn't be here. He could have at least stopped to see if I was OK."

"Thank God for small favors. You're still here and can still swear."

Sharon smiled. "Yeah, I can."

"I'll go out there and see what I can learn about the accident and the murder. I'm not so sure I want to meet Judge Quigley, but it's my job."

"Maybe you'd better leave your gun behind," Sharon suggested.

"Very funny. He's not worth the cost of a bullet. We'll get him another way."

"Good girl."

"Take care of yourself while I'm away."

"Can't get into much trouble here."

Throwing a handful of paperback books on the bed that she'd picked up on the way to the hospital, Hannah said, "Here's some reading material. These will keep you busy."

"This is all I need, a bunch of romance novels to keep me up nights dreaming. Say, I like Ailene Humphrey's books. Thanks."

"You're welcome. Oh. I almost forgot. I have Gloria in custody, and she's terrified out of her mind. She'll stay with me for a couple of days. I plan to question her gently but ruthlessly until I find out what I need to know. When I issued the invitation and told her what it would entail, she accepted. She's a bit over a barrel—scared to death of jail and just as scared to go home."

"Have you told Rob about this yet?"

"No. I, well, I don't think he'll be too happy. After indicating she'd stay with me, she said, 'They'll kill me, too.' Can you believe it?"

"Wow. That's it, then. Well, almost. Keep working on her. You're on the right track."

"She knows plenty. I'm sure of it. If she doesn't tell us the truth now, she knows she'll end up in jail on a murder charge. It's quite possible she knows who killed Angela, or, at least, suspects someone.

"She doesn't know the official cause of death yet, which is another reason I wanted to keep her away from home and the police station until I find out what I need to know. Once she knows the official cause of death, she'll probably clam up. I have the weekend to break her down. Angela's memorial service is Monday afternoon. Unfortunately, she's already been cremated."

"That eliminates any further analysis of the body," Sharon said gravely. "That could be costly to the investigation."

"That's why we need Gloria to talk."

"Good luck. You'd better get going."

"Get well fast. I need you."

Sharon knew what that meant. There would be little rest for either of them now that Hannah had the scent. "I get a walking cast tomorrow morning. I'm supposed to be out of here soon after that."

"Great. Give me a call when they're ready to discharge you,

and we'll pick you up—Me and My Shadow." Hannah walked out humming the old tune.

As Hannah carefully drove along the Quigley driveway, she was extra vigilant for oncoming vehicles. She passed the tree Sharon hit and winced. "Another foot, and she would have hit it head-on. Thank You, God."

Upon reaching the house safely, Hannah was impressed. The three-story mansion was faced with Cambrian brick and had eight enormous white pillars across the front. The windows at all three levels looked as if they were two stories high. Each was surrounded by immense green shutters encompassing the white trim of the windows themselves.

The entire structure was topped off with a large cupola, complete with widow's walk. A circle drive took Hannah to the mammoth front entrance, where she parked and walked up the marble steps to the broad stone porch. Before she could knock, a distinguished-looking gentleman opened the door.

"Good afternoon, Ma'am."

"Good afternoon, Sir. I'm Detective Hannah Bell of the Chicago Police Department. I'm here to speak with Judge Quigley. Is he in?" She hoped he wasn't.

"He's not in at the moment."

Hannah felt relieved, then a voice spoke from the distance.

"May I help you?"

Looking past the man facing her, Hannah saw a small, extremely thin woman walking toward them quickly but unsteadily.

"Good afternoon, Ma'am," Hannah said loudly enough to be heard over the clicking of the woman's shoes on the Italian tiles on the foyer floor. "I'm looking for Judge or Mrs. Raleigh Quigley."

As the woman stopped in front of her, Hannah saw she was drunk. It wasn't even noon yet, but she was well on her way to a good afternoon buzz. Her breath reeked of alcohol, and she had trouble maintaining her equilibrium. A whiskey glass rested in her hand.

"I'm Kathleen Quigley. What can I do for you?" she asked sluggishly.

"I'm Detective Hannah Bell from the Chicago Police Department." She showed Mrs. Quigley her badge. "I'd like to ask you a few questions.

Trying to sober up quickly, Kathleen said, "Oh, yes. We're so sorry about the accident this morning. My husband already spoke with some officers. I don't think I can help. If I've told that boy once, I've told him a hundred times, he drives too fast out of this driveway. It's a wonder it's taken so long for something to happen."

"Who was he?"

"My son. He's been visiting a couple weeks this summer. I'm so glad no one was hurt."

"No one was hurt? Mrs. Quigley, a police officer was hurt. She has a nasty bump on her head, several cuts, and a broken leg. She's in the hospital."

"Oh! No one said that. They said no one was hurt."

"Who said it?"

"My husband and son."

"They were lying, Mrs. Quigley." Contempt showed in Hannah's voice.

"They were probably trying to spare me some anxiety. My husband and son are always doing that." She looked somewhat puzzled, as if wondering why they acted that way.

The elderly gentleman looked at the two women with a distant, confused expression.

Kathleen turned to him. "Henry, you may go now. I'll speak with the detective."

"Yes, Ma'am." He shuffled off.

"Henry's too old for this work, but it's all he knows. Nevertheless, I'll have to retire him soon."

I wonder how they'll do that? Hannah wondered. With a little cyanide? This place gives me the creeps. It's beautiful, but it has a sinister air.

"I need to ask you some questions, Mrs. Quigley," Hannah said. "Perhaps we could find a comfortable place to sit and talk for a few minutes."

"I don't think I can help you. I don't know anything about the accident. I was asleep when it happened."

"Not that. Something else. It's about the death of Angela Allen Wednesday evening."

"I can't help with that, either," she said uneasily.

"You were at the Allen house that evening, weren't you?"

"Why, yes, we were, but we left when Mariah said Angela was ill."

"Is there a comfortable place to sit? I have a number of questions to ask."

"Certainly, but I won't be of much help. I really don't know anything."

"Sometimes even small things are a major help for us. That's what I'm looking for."

They walked into a vast library. Hannah had never seen such a huge room in a private residence in her life. There was a set of mobile stairs for reaching the higher shelves, just like the law library at the university where she finished her undergraduate work.

"This room must be fifteen hundred square feet!" she said. "My entire duplex would fit in here, and then some."

Mrs. Quigley didn't hear the comment, but she saw Hannah's amazed expression. "Are you a book lover, Detective?"

Without waiting for an answer, she continued, "My husband is. He reads constantly, and every book and magazine he's read since the day I met him forty years ago, is in this room."

"Amazing. He must know a lot about many things."

"He does. Ask him anything, and he knows the answer." There was a touch of acrimony in her voice.

Then Hannah saw a portrait hanging above the fireplace mantel at the far end of the room. It showed Kathleen looking radiant, beautiful, and very stylish.

"Is that you, Mrs. Quigley?"

"That's me," she said indifferently.

"That's gorgeous."

"Thank you."

"When was it done?"

"About three years ago."

"You should be very proud of the likeness."

Hannah was impressed that the artist was able to work beyond the self-inflicted destruction of the woman and show her truly exquisite physical beauty. "Who painted it?"

"Mr. Darren Brannigan. He's a friend of ours and has remarkable talent."

Hannah heard pride in the woman's voice, but it was for the artist, not herself.

"The gown you're wearing in that portrait is the most ravishing I've ever seen. What an honor to have your portrait hanging in such a grand room."

"Yes, but then, it's the only place it would fit." Kathleen chuckled.

Hannah looked at her and smiled. "It's truly a work of art."

"Thank you again. I'm pleased you're so taken with it. Won't you have a seat?" She gestured toward a nearby French divan.

"Thank you." Hannah sat at one end, while her hostess sat at the other. "Can you tell me about the parties at the Allen house on the first and third Wednesdays of the month? What are they for? Do you always attend?"

"The parties are primarily social. We've known each other for years, and for many of those years, we lived many miles apart. Since we now live closer together, we try to see each other as often as possible."

"Does that include Mr. Darren Brannigan?"

"Oh, no. He's a new friend for about the past three years, if that."

"I see. You said you see each other—the group, I mean—as often as possible. Does that mean you get together outside the parties?"

"We occasionally go to the opera together or travel, like a cruise or something like that."

"All of you, including the Allen women and Mr. Brannigan?"

"No, no. Just the Reillys, the Costellos, and us. Mariah always refuses, so we've stopped asking. Mr. Brannigan, well, he has a different kind of life. We're not that close. He's mostly Mariah's friend."

"What about the girls?"

"Oh, he's friendly with them, too." A note of finality crept into her voice.

"Tell me more about the parties, Mrs. Quigley. What time do you arrive? What do you have for cocktails and dinner? Who serves? What happens after dinner?'

Kathleen happily obliged with a little slurring of her words on occasion and having to search her mind for an answer as she sipped from the tumbler in her hand. Hannah's interest rose when the woman discussed the meetings that took place after dinner on each occasion. She was a little annoyed, because Mariah always attended those, but none of the other women were permitted in the room with the men.

"Mariah says it's necessary for her to serve as their hostess, while her daughters are hostesses to the rest of us. To my mind, we should alternate, but it never happens. Mariah's always with the men, and the girls are with the women.

"Anyway, we usually go to the music library and play the piano and sing. We love that. I'm sure we have more fun than the men. Who wants to talk business, anyhow?"

"They talk about business? What business?"

"I have no idea, since I've never been there, and Raleigh never tells me. You know, Angela was an excellent musician. She played the piano and the mandolin very well. She even wrote songs that she played for us, but she never sang. We always hoped that someday she'd break her silence, but she never did."

"Do you know why she didn't speak?"

"No. It was never discussed. I always had the feeling it was taboo to ask."

"I wonder why?" Hannah asked softly.

Mrs. Quigley didn't reply.

"Did anyone else play the piano or mandolin?"

"Gloria and Anne Reilly played duets on the piano. They were very good. We always told them they should go on the road." She laughed. "As if they needed money. It would have been a hoot, though."

They smiled at the thought.

"Mrs. Quigley, on the evening Angela died, did you see her at all?"

"No. She was napping. Gloria told us. Just before dinner, Gloria went upstairs to fetch Angela. Then Mariah told us Angela was very ill, and we had to leave."

"What time did Gloria tell you that Angela was napping? Was it just as cocktails began, during cocktails, or before she went to wake her?"

"Hmmm. Let me see. I'd just sipped my first drink when she came to the judge and me and told us, making the proper excuses. That would have been shortly after we arrived at five o'clock sharp. Mariah doesn't like people arriving early or late, so we always knock right at five, even if we've been out front for a few minutes.

"It's funny, actually. There we were, all of us, knocking on the door like a flock of sheep seeking our master." She laughed.

Hannah smiled. "Did Angela usually come to cocktails?"

"Not really. I mean, she might have come long enough to get a drink—water, I imagine—but then she usually went into the garden. She didn't mix with us very much.

"She had such a sorrowful look about her. I tried talking with her when we first attended the parties, but I finally gave up. The only time she seemed truly happy was when she was playing the piano or the mandolin. Then she almost glowed. She was full of music."

Mrs. Quigley stopped to wipe a tear from her eye. "I wish I knew what was wrong with her, but it didn't seem that anyone knew. At least, no one outside the family."

"What do you know about Darren Brannigan and Angela?"

"Oh, he was smitten with her, but, as far as I know, he never got anywhere. She mostly ignored him."

"You never saw the two of them together?"

"No."

"Did they share a certain look between them? Across the room, maybe?" Hannah's heart beat faster, and she hoped she wouldn't blush. Why did Darren make her feel that way? It was very unsettling.

"Not that I ever saw."

Hannah's heartbeat slowed.

"Are you almost finished asking questions?" Kathleen was weary of the grilling. "Angela Allen took ill and died. Why is this necessary?"

"We think it possible that she was murdered."

Mrs. Quigley dropped her glass and it shattered against the coffee table. She stared at Hannah open-mouthed.

"Are you all right, Mrs. Quigley?" Hannah checked to see that the woman hadn't been cut.

"I must have had a little too much to drink. I'm fine. Are you all right? Did any of the glass hit you? I'll have Henry come and clean up this mess right away."

"I'm fine," Hannah answered.

Mrs. Quigley shouted for Henry, who must have been waiting right outside the door. "Henry, come clean this up, and get me another drink." Turning back to Hannah, she asked, "Would you like something to drink, Detective Bell?"

"No, thank you."

Henry bowed and left on his errands. Hannah hoped he could remember them.

"Who would want to kill Angela?" Kathleen asked in disbelief. "She was a dear little thing, a perfect lady, always so meek. I can't imagine her having an enemy in the world."

"As hard as that might be to believe, she must have had at least one."

"I can't believe it." Kathleen shook her head.

"I have just a couple more questions. How long do the Allen parties last?"

"We usually leave at ten. At nine, we have dessert—cookies, cakes, and herbal tea, something like that."

"Who serves the dessert?"

"No one. The caterer leaves it for us. We just gather in the main dining room, have dessert, visit a bit, and go home. It's always a good time."

"I'd like to speak with your staff. Can you arrange that?"

"Why would you want to do that? I don't see a need to talk with them. They didn't know Angela."

"It's just routine." Hannah tried to sound authoritative and hoped it would work.

"I'm afraid Henry's the only one here right now. My husband dismissed them all for the day this morning. I don't know why. He just said it would be nice to give them a little extra time off."

"I see. Is he in the habit of doing that?" She tried not to sound annoyed.

"No. In fact, quite the contrary. He usually complains when they take their regular time off. I don't understand it." She looked around. "Where is Henry with my drink?" She suddenly became aware that she'd been empty-handed too long.

"Could you at least give me their names?" Hannah found herself hoping that Kathleen's lucid moment hadn't passed.

"Sure. I can tell you from memory."

It took a few minutes and some restarts, but Hannah was able to compile a list.

Henry Nolan and his wife, Maude, run the household.
Brian White is the gardener.
Ray McDonnell tends to things other than the garden.
Shannon and Sherri Reid are the maids, upstairs and down, respectively.

"You may speak with the staff, but it'll have to be another time, unless you want to speak with Henry," Kathleen said.

"His wife went out with the others?"

"Actually, she's visiting her sister in Boston and will be back on Sunday."

"I might want to speak with Mrs. Nolan. I don't know how much help Henry would be. I'll contact Mrs. Nolan when she returns." Wanting to move on, Hannah asked, "Are all your staff of Irish extraction?"

"Why, yes. How'd you know?"

"Just a wild guess. I'm Irish, too."

"Of course. Bell's an Irish name. How many generations have your people been here?"

"As far as I know, three."

"Then you're very much an American, aren't you?"

"Very much. And you?"

"Oh, yes, though we maintain our ties with the homeland. We go to Ireland every other year to visit family and friends."

"Did the members of your staff come directly from there?"

"Mostly, yes. Raleigh brought Henry and Maude back with him thirty years ago. They were the first. They're like members of the family."

"And the others?"

"Let's see…."

Again, Hannah slowly learned the information she wanted. Brian was hired through the Bristol Agency in Boston, which handled many Irish immigrants looking for work. Ray turned up on the doorstep one day ten years earlier. The girls were fairly new, having worked at the mansion for the past two years. The Quigleys learned of them from some friends out East, and those friends brought the girls to Chicago.

"Are any of them citizens yet?"

"My, yes. Henry and Maude have been for years. Brian and Ray for about five years. I'm not sure exactly. All have become good American citizens. The girls are studying to become citizens, but have a way to go. We're very proud of them. "

"Their papers are in order, I trust?"

"Of course. My husband handles all that sort of thing. He would make sure the papers were in order."

"I'm sure he would." Hannah hoped her sarcastic tone wouldn't be noticeable to the intoxicated woman sitting beside her. It wasn't. "Thank you for your help, Mrs. Quigley. If I need to speak with any of your staff, can I reach them here? What's their usual day off?"

"Thursday. Please feel free to call anytime." Annoyed, she looked around. "Where is that Henry? You'd think I'd sent him to Siberia or something."

"All right. I'll be on my way. Please call me if you think of anything else that might be helpful. By the way, where's the judge?"

"He spends most of his time golfing these days. Since he retired, I see him less than before."

"Is that what he's doing today?"

"Probably. He has an early morning tee-off each morning except Sunday. We go to church on Sundays. Then he plays golf the rest of Sunday, too.

"On weekdays, he plays eighteen holes before lunch, then he lunches with his cronies at the club and plays another round, sometimes two. At least that's what he tells me. He comes home in time for supper at eight." Her voice held a hint of mistrust.

"I'm a classic golf widow," she said bitterly. "It's worse than another woman. At least then, the man's home occasionally." The pain of many lonely years showed in the lines of her face, although she was still pretty. Her husband's addictions had left her neglected for a long time. The latest one happened to be a sport—any excuse to be away from home.

No wonder she drinks, Hannah thought. "When did he leave

this morning?"

"Early. I don't know the exact time. He usually tees off at six o'clock. That's the middle of the night to me. I'm still asleep then. I'm a night person, he's a day person. That's another reason we don't see each other."

He didn't tee off at six this morning, Hannah thought. Not if he knew about the accident. Sharon didn't leave my place until after eight, and didn't Mrs. Quigley say her husband told her about it? She must have seen him this morning.

Is she as witless as she sounds, or is she covering up something? If so, what is it and why?

Hannah decided not to pursue the discrepancy for the moment but made a mental note of it. "Thank you again for your time and courtesy, Mrs. Quigley. I appreciate your cooperation."

"You're welcome, Detective Bell. It's nice to have someone to talk to. If Angela was murdered, I hope you find out who did it and hang him by his thumbnails. She was a sweet girl who didn't deserve such an awful fate. I felt a kind of kinship with her. She was lonely, too."

"We'll do our best, Mrs. Quigley." Hannah smiled and nodded. "Good-bye." She had the urge to reach out and give the pathetic woman a hug. Instead, she turned to leave.

As she did, Henry arrived with a fresh drink for his mistress and a broom and dustpan to clean up the broken glass on the floor and coffee table.

"Good-bye, Detective Bell," Mrs. Quigley said warmly, sipping from her drink so fast she choked softly.

I'll have a tough time getting back in here without a warrant, Hannah thought, once the judge learns I was here. Oh, well. I learned a lot. I'll have to be satisfied with what I have for now.

It was after noon, and Hannah was hungry, but she was eager

to return to the precinct and make a few calls. She grabbed some Greek takeout and drove toward work. Before settling into making her calls, Hannah cornered Rob Keys, told him the latest developments, including her concern about Mandy O'Brien's illegal status in the country and her interest in gaining Mandy and Gloria's confidence.

She explained about Gloria's situation for the weekend. After lecturing her on the inappropriateness of such an offer and telling her she was on her own if the department came down on her for breaking regulations, he added his secret approval.

"Don't tell anyone except Walker," he said. "She'll have to know that I know. Tape everything."

He advised her how to handle the situation so her evidence wouldn't be thrown out of court.

As they parted, he said, "We'll both catch hell for this."

Hannah went to her office and called Maggie Costello and Anne Reilly. Both were cordial, if a bit reluctant to talk at first. They answered Hannah's questions politely, and, Hannah believed, truthfully. Jim Costello turned out to be a bank president, while Mr. Reilly was a patent attorney. Their wives were proud of their husbands' success and reputations. While their husbands were busy with their careers, Maggie and Anne raised ten children between them. Both were good Irish-Catholic families.

They were proud of their heritage and talked easily about their families and their emigration from Ireland. They weren't concerned when Hannah asked about the nationality of their household staff and how they came to the States. Most of the staff were now US citizens, and the two women were proud of that.

They explained how they and their husbands wanted to help other Irish nationals find better lives. They were proud of their efforts. However, like Kathleen Quigley, they knew nothing of the details concerning how their staff members actually came to America. They just graciously received them when they arrived.

They also didn't understand why Mariah Allen spent part of their social evenings with the men. They eventually concluded that was just Mariah's way. She felt more important being with the men than the women.

When the women asked their husbands questions about what they discussed in the library, the men never answered. They said it wasn't important, nothing to be concerned about.

Old-fashioned patriarchal marriages, Hannah thought. That wouldn't fly with most women today.

The women said they enjoyed the musical adventures with Kathleen, Angela, and Gloria, so they were happy with the arrangement. They also confirmed Mariah's coldness. Hannah found it interesting that none of the women in the group seemed to care much for Mariah, though none were impolite enough to say so.

Kathleen, Maggie, and Anne often went shopping together and socialized. Mariah was never included. She never expressed any interest in joining them, either. It seemed the only contact the so-called friends had with each other was at Mariah's parties.

Both women, however, were fond of Angela and Gloria but felt they were incomplete people who seemed much younger than their years. They believed the girls had been greatly overprotected and dominated by their mother. The highest compliment they could give was that they had good table manners and were very musical.

According to Maggie, the girls rarely left the house. She invited them individually or together to her home more than once, but they never came. She also invited them to a few fashion shows and to join her in learning how to play golf, but nothing came of that, either. They didn't seem to have any outside friends. Angela didn't talk, making it difficult to learn more about her, but Gloria's contributions at the dinner table were limited to insipid laughter and uneasy banter about nothing. The women couldn't think of a single conversation of substance with Gloria.

What they did have were their times together after dinner at the parties when all five women gathered in the music library. The girls were very happy, and all five of the women enjoyed themselves, but there was never anything more. More than once the women invited the girls to attend a musical theater production of some kind, thinking they'd be excited at the possibility, but the invitations were always refused. After a while, the older women stopped asking.

Maggie and Anne were deeply saddened by Angela's death and confirmed much of what Hannah had already learned about her. They, too, couldn't understand why anyone would want to hurt Angela, nor could they add anything to the circumstances surrounding her death.

"I honestly believe their mother has kept them prisoners in the mansion," Anne said emphatically. "I'll bet the farthest Angela or Gloria ever got from the house without Mariah was the garden beyond the pool." Her voice filled with sadness. "How dreadful it will be for Gloria with Angela gone. At least they had each other."

An interesting thing occurred when Hannah spoke with Maggie. She congratulated the woman on her recent anniversary and said she'd seen the wonderful portrait her husband bought to give her.

There was an uncomfortable silence on the phone, then Maggie said in a stilted but gracious voice, "Our anniversary is in April, and I received no gift recently. I didn't even know there was any portrait of Angela in existence."

"I'm sorry, Mrs. Costello," Hannah said. "I must have my information wrong. Thank you for your time."

She hung up and smiled. With her detailed notes and having Diane Smith as a corroborative witness, they'd have Mr. Costello on that one if the need ever arose.

Hannah's final call of the day was to Darren Brannigan. She found her breathing increasing and her heartbeat quickening as she dialed his number. She felt the same way when she'd been a teenager calling to ask a boy to the Sadie Hawkins Day dance at high school. She wasn't able to ask a boy to his face. On the telephone, she had a sense of distance if he refused. No one ever refused her invitations, but she never got over the nerves.

This is a perfect stranger, she admonished herself. Get a grip, Girl. He's probably a jerk. Don't waste your nerves on him.

That line of reasoning didn't work, of course.

When she heard an answering machine, she felt relieved—a bit. She didn't leave a message, intending to call from home later that evening.

Before Hannah left for the day, she called Jim Preston to see if he knew of any funeral or memorial plans for Doc. No one in her department seemed to know anything.

"I released his body to his nephew this morning," Jim said. "He said Doc asked that no funeral or memorial service be held upon his death. He wanted to be cremated and have the ashes spread over Lake Michigan."

"That sounds like Doc. Who's tossing the ashes?"

"His nephew."

"So the rest of us don't get to say good-bye?"

"Nope."

"I guess I can see Doc wanting it that way. It's easier in some ways. We can all remember him as he was."

"I prefer that," Jim said quietly.

"Me, too. Thanks, Jim. I'll tell the others."

CHAPTER EIGHT

"I remember very little about the Quigleys," Gloria said. "I was very young the last time I saw them before we moved to Chicago, and my mother renewed their friendship.

"We visited them in England when Angela and I were five years old. My parents knew them during my father's studies there. I don't remember Mrs. Quigley much except for how she smelled. She smelled strongly of English lavender, and she kept hugging me. It made me sick to my stomach. I've never liked that fragrance since.

"What I remember about the judge, who wasn't a judge then, was that he was a lawyer, or a barrister in the English legal system. Anyway, he had a collection of live frogs. Some were even poisonous. I thought they were pretty neat. Angela hated them, but I liked them. That's all I remember."

She smiled at the memory. It was good to see her brighten up, even if it was for only a little while.

Hannah and Gloria were on their way to Hannah's duplex when Hannah asked about the Quigleys, Costellos, and Reillys. Somehow, the conversation turned to the early days of their acquaintance, and Gloria shared memories of her parents when she was young. She didn't know any of the couples well. Her parents and the three couples met while they lived in Europe. They established friendships then, though for years they were separated by distance, work, and the business of raising their families.

"I remember nothing of the Costellos and the Reillys, only what I've learned since the parties began," Gloria continued. "I always feel so awkward at dinner and very much out of place. They talk way over my head, so I don't say much and feel foolish when I try. Since Angela didn't talk, that made it more awkward for me. There was no one for me to talk with.

"The gatherings in the music library were the whole thing for Angela and me. Mrs. Costello and Mrs. Reilly were fun, and they're talented musicians, too. Both play the piano, although Mrs. Costello is too shy to perform anywhere. She only plays at home when no one else is around, or so she says. We're still trying to get her to play with us. She draws, too. Mrs. Quigley's pretty quiet most of the time."

Barely taking a breath, Gloria continued, "Often while we're playing, she sits and draws caricatures of us."

"Who does?" Hannah asked.

"Mrs. Costello."

"I thought you were talking about Mrs. Quigley."

"Nooo. Mrs. Q usually has a buzz on before we even get to the music library. She sits there and grins. I guess she's enjoying herself.

"Anyway, as I was saying, Mrs. Costello draws great caricatures." She emphasized the words Mrs. Costello and looked at Hannah to make sure she heard her. "They're funny, too. You should ask her to show them to you."

Hannah had the feeling Gloria rarely, if ever, reminisced or talked to anyone about anything. At that moment, she seemed lost in her own little word, talking to herself and being prompted occasionally by Hannah's questions. Hannah enjoyed the young woman's banter and was pleased she found something to be happy about.

As Hannah listened to Gloria with one half of her mind, the other half wondered how the sheltered, socially unsophisticated young woman would handle a night on the town in Chicago. I might gain more insight into what makes her tick, too, she thought.

When she finally had the chance to speak, Hannah tried to use an enthusiastic, positive tone that invited a similar response.

"It's Friday night, Gloria. What do you say we go out for dinner and hit a club or two? Chicago's a terrific town, especially at night."

Gloria immediately became uneasy.

Hannah sensed that a night on the town would be a new experience for Gloria. "Don't worry. It'll be OK. We'll have a good time. There's nothing to be afraid of. I've probably got something to fit you in my closet. If not, we'll do a little shopping."

Gloria relaxed a bit. Perhaps she was beginning to trust Hannah. She certainly needed to trust someone. Hannah wasn't sure she should be the one, but she was willing to risk it.

I just hope this doesn't backfire on me, she thought, driving toward the city on a steamy summer evening. Traffic was heavy, and Hannah, after driving in it for so many years, could have made a good cab driver. She darted in and out of places where there didn't seem to be any space at all.

After a few moments of silence, Gloria asked, "How close are we to Bloomingdale's or Nordstrom's?"

"Not far. Let's go." Hannah pulled off at the next exit and headed for the Miracle Mile, one of her favorite places.

Gloria looked stunning in the black silk jumpsuit and black pumps she bought. She had good taste and knew what she looked good in. She bought several items at Bloomingdale's, including a black Gucci evening bag that cost $500.

I don't spend that much on an entire wardrobe, Hannah mused.

Of course, I rarely shop at Bloomingdale's, either. TJ Maxx is more my speed.

Hannah watched as Gloria bought more than enough clothes to last a month without wearing anything twice. She kept saying, "I'll take that and that and that…."

The sales people who knew her waited on her eagerly.

That's what lots of money does, Hannah thought.

"I've always wanted to do this," Gloria said excitedly, acting like a kid in a candy store. "I've never been here without my mother, and I always have to buy what she says. Sometimes, I call and have them send things to the house. Mother gets angry, but she never stops me from doing it. Of course, Angela never got yelled at, because she always bought prissy stuff, like lace dresses with high collars, long sleeves, and long skirts. That's not my style."

Gloria wanted to eat dinner at the Hard Rock Café, but Hannah talked her out of it.

"It's so loud in there, you can barely hear yourself think. We won't be able to talk," Hannah explained. "Let's try the Signature Room on the ninety-fifth floor of the John Hancock Building."

Gloria became excited. "I've always wanted to go there. My mother's been there many times, but Angela and I never…." A sad look crossed her face.

They were silent for a moment. Then Gloria said, "after dinner I want to go to Planet Hollywood. That's another place Angela and I always wanted to visit. I'll pretend Angela's here with us, and all three of us are going."

"It's Friday night," Hannah said. "It'll be busy and very loud. Is that OK?"

"Sure."

The twenty-six-year-old woman-child was blossoming before Hannah's eyes. She hoped Gloria's present comfort level would continue, and she'd talk freely. Hannah planned to ask some very tough, direct questions as the weekend progressed. Taping their conversations would certainly affect Gloria's current positive attitude, but Hannah would deal with that when the time came.

They walked across Michigan Avenue from Bloomingdale's to the John Hancock Building and took an elevator to the ninety-fifth floor.

When the elevator stopped, Gloria said, "That's the fastest ride I've ever taken."

"I've often debated with myself whether or not I'd like to see how fast it moves. Everything would probably be a blur."

"I'm just as happy not to see it. Having my ears pop twice on the way up is enough for me, thank you."

Their dinner conversation was very enlightening. Hannah learned a lot about Gloria's childhood. She and Angela loved their father and feared their mother—not the respectful fear children should have for their parents but the kind of fear that grows when they never know what kind of parent they have. Mariah was OK at times, never great, but then she'd turn ugly, although she never struck her daughters.

"Punishment usually meant being locked in a closet in a remote area of the house for hours," Gloria said. "That was terrifying." She paused. "My mother uses people. When they're used up, she throws them away, like my dad. Angela and I have always thought she killed him."

Hannah almost choked on her London broil. "Why do you think that? Wasn't he killed in a car accident?"

"Yes, but he wasn't well for several days before he died, and Dad was never sick. He seemed tired and had no appetite. He was working too many hours at the hospital, too. He might have died in a car accident, but Angela and I thought he had help."

"That's a serious accusation to make against your mother. Have you ever shared your feelings about your father's death with anyone?"

"No one would have believed us, nor will they now. They'd just pooh-pooh whatever we said. We were only nine when Daddy died, and my mother is a great actress. Many people thought she was the perfect wife and mother, because that's how she always acted when people were around. We lived with her and knew different. She often threatened us with great bodily harm if we told anyone, especially our father, that she locked us in the closet."

Keeping in mind Gloria's earlier statement concerning her own safety, Hannah gingerly asked, "Do you think your mother had anything to do with Angela's death?"

Gloria set down her fork and stared at her hands without speaking.

"Gloria, I want you to trust me. I can help, but you need to tell me everything that you think is going on, even if you're not sure. That's the only way we can look into the things that will help us find out what happened to Angela and why. I want whoever killed her to be put away forever. Don't you?"

"Yes," she said weakly, "but I don't want to die, too."

"We can protect you, Gloria. Please let us help."

They sat in silence for a few minutes.

As they sat there, Hannah saw a tall, handsome man walking toward their table. He looked vaguely familiar, but she didn't know him. Suddenly, he stopped beside Hannah, nodded politely, and looked at Gloria, who stared at her plate.

"Hello, Gloria," he said in a deep, resonant voice.

Gloria's head jerked up, and she almost jumped to her feet. "Darren! Hi!" Then she stared at him.

Hannah felt the crimson tide rising from her neck to her cheeks and up to the top of her head. Darren Brannigan. *Why does this man, whom I don't even know, do this to me?* She felt disgusted with herself.

Darren took Gloria's trembling hand. "I'm so sorry about Angela. I didn't know until I heard it on the news. I called the house this afternoon to see how you were getting along, but your mother said you'd been kidnapped. When I asked what she meant, she said you left with a detective. This is quite a surprise. Are you all right?"

Gloria nodded.

He looked at Hannah and asked, "Are you the kidnapper?"

Finally, Gloria found her tongue. "Darren, this is Detective Bell from the Chicago Police Department. I'll be staying with her for a few days. She didn't kidnap me. I needed to get away from that miserable place for a while. Mother's taking care of the memorial arrangements for Angela, and I can't stand being in that awful house right now. Detective Bell offered me a place to go. That's all."

"I understand. Is there anything I can do for you? I know I can't do anything for Mariah. She won't let anyone help her. I'm available if you need me."

Again, Gloria seemed at a loss for words. The way she looked at Darren told Hannah that the young woman was possibly in love with the man and couldn't talk to him easily.

Very interesting, Hannah thought. If she's in love with Darren, is he in love with her, or was he in love with Angela?

Hannah pondered the dynamics of the trio. Is it possible that Gloria loved Darren, but he loved Angela, so Gloria killed Angela to get her out of the way?

Then a very attractive young woman came along, hooked her arm through Darren's, and said in a friendly voice, "Hello."

"Hello," Hannah and Gloria replied.

"Ladies," Darren said, "this is Savannah Nelson. Savannah, this is Gloria Allen and her friend, Detective Bell. Detective Bell, what's your first name?"

"Hannah."

"My mother's name was Hannah, with an H on the end."

Hannah laughed. "Me, too." She hoped her crimson complexion wasn't too obvious.

"How do you do?" Savannah asked, and they replied.

It was easy to see that Savannah was very fond of Darren, although he remained calm, cool, and in control of himself. The young woman on his arm was very beautiful, with long, lush wavy blonde hair that fell loosely about her shoulders. She had medium blue eyes and a slender figure that looked great in the blue jumpsuit she was wearing.

Looking straight at Hannah, Darren said, "We must be on our way. Take good care of Gloria, Detective. She needs a little tender, loving care. If I can help—in any way at all—call me at my studio. Here's my card."

He handed her a card. "If I'm not there, leave a message, and I'll get back to you. It was nice to meet you. I look forward to speaking with you again."

Hannah was glad she didn't have to stand up. She didn't know if her legs would support her. "Thank you, Mr. Brannigan. I'll do that."

"Please call me Darren," he said with a smile.

Hannah replied with a cool nod.

After saying a round of polite good-byes, Darren and Savannah walked away.

Gloria said nothing.

"Are you upset, overjoyed, or what?" Hannah asked.

There was no reply.

"I'm just trying to understand your silences. I can't tell if this is a happy one or a sad one. Can you give me a clue?" She made her voice light as she asked.

"I had no idea we'd run into him tonight," Gloria said softly.

"Did seeing him upset you?"

"Not seeing him, but I could have done without seeing her."

"Who is she?"

"I don't know. One of his friends."

"I see. Are you in love with Darren?"

"I'm not in love with anyone," she said quickly.

"OK. Enough of that. What do you think about dessert?"

"I'd like some ice cream."

After leaving the restaurant, Hannah and Gloria hit the town, stopping first at Planet Hollywood. It was busy, but Gloria found it exhilarating and acted like a kid out of school. She laughed and chatted with people, although it was more like a shouting match, but she didn't seem to mind. She was having the time of her life.

After a while, she asked Hannah if they could visit some other nightspots she'd heard of.

Their final destination was a piano bar on Ontario, appropriately called the Redhead Piano Bar. Customers sat around the piano, or stood, mostly, because the place was crowded, and took turns singing their favorite songs.

That night, the place was packed, with barely enough room to wiggle through the crowd. There were plenty of regulars in places like that, and they each took turns singing.

Gloria turned to Hannah and asked, "Do you like to sing?"

"Do I?" Hannah smiled. "I do a bit of that occasionally."

"Let's do one together. What do you know?"

"You and I probably don't sing the same kinds of songs, Gloria. Why don't you pick one you like?"

"Oh, no. I'm not ready for that yet. If we do one together, maybe I'll have the courage."

They named several songs, but none worked out. Then Hannah

said, "I know one that has great harmony, is fun to sing, and people always like it."

"What's that?"

"Beyond the Blue Horizon."

"Perfect! You're right. That's a fun one. Once on the radio I heard a DJ do that with people who called in. They had to sing the melody while he sang the harmony. It was pretty funny. Most of the people couldn't sing, but they sure had fun. Let's do it."

"Which part do you want?"

"I can do either. How about you?"

"Either."

"OK. What's your voice?"

"Mezzo."

"OK. You do the harmony, I'll do the melody."

They waded through the crowd toward the piano bar to position themselves for a moment in the limelight. While they waited, they whispered the words back and forth, making sure they knew them all. Then they were ready.

When their turn came, they were a hit. It was obvious both women were natural performers. Their voices blended well, and the crowd gave them a thunderous round of applause.

"More! More!"

"Now what?" Gloria whispered to Hannah.

"Just smile and bow."

When Gloria looked at her again, Hannah said, "Let's go. Maybe we can come up with an encore. Otherwise, I'd rather leave them hungry."

"We'll be back!" Gloria called to their admirers.

That brought more applause.

"This is great!" Gloria shouted as they waded through the crowd to someplace they could hear themselves talk. They were besieged with pats on the back along the way, mixed with shouts of, "You guys were great!"

"That was fun," Hannah agreed. "It'll be a tough act to follow if you really want to try. I'd rather enjoy what we've accomplished and not risk spoiling our moment."

"Aw, come on. Where's your sense of adventure? Let's see if we can at least come up with something."

Once again, they recited lists of songs to each other, trying to find one they could sing together.

"Why don't you try a solo?" Hannah suggested.

"Not yet."

Then Hannah remembered a duet version of Danny Boy she heard once. She went home and figured out the harmony, writing it down so she could learn it.

"Do you know Danny Boy?" Hannah asked.

"Do I know it? Anyone who doesn't know that song has lived a more sheltered life than I have, and that's hard to believe. Sure, I know it, but isn't it usually a solo?"

"Usually, but I know a harmony part. That's the only song I can think of that could possibly follow what we just sang. It's probably the most beloved song in the world. The only way it'll go wrong is if we butcher it. Let's find a quiet place, perhaps the ladies' room, and go over it to find the right key."

"OK. I'm right behind you." Gloria was thrilled they had another song to sing.

When the two women returned to the piano, there was tumultuous applause, then they were ready.

"Key of D, please," Hannah told the pianist.

He nodded, and they were off.

When they finished, the room was amazingly quiet. Hannah sensed that the room had never been quieter than at this moment. Although there were many wet cheeks around her, there was absolutely no sound.

Hannah and Gloria stood transfixed in their places, knowing they'd done something extraordinary. Finally, they bowed their heads and stepped back from the piano.

A few seconds later, it sounded as if the roof was being blown off the building. The walls rattled with applause and shouts of, "Bravo!" and, "More!"

After bowing profusely and thanking their fans, Hannah put her arm around Gloria's waist and dragged her out of the building.

"What are you doing?" Gloria demanded.

"We just did something very special in there. There's no way we could improve on it. They saw and heard us, and I know we'll be welcome back anytime. That'll be a very tough act to follow, and I wouldn't want to try that right now. Let it settle into their souls—and ours."

Gloria sighed deeply. "You're right. You know, I've never had a night like this in my life. I never had a moment like this. I'll always remember it."

"Me, too."

They walked in silence for a few minutes.

"You're a very special lady, Detective." Gloria's eyes were filled with tears of admiration and affection. "You made a miserable life happy, even if it's just for a little while." She took Hannah's arm and walked with her.

They reached the corner, then Gloria laughed and exclaimed, "Oh, my God! People will think we're gay!" She broke free and ran across the street.

Hannah, laughing and shaking her head, crossed the street, and they continued walking side-by-side the remaining block and a half toward her car. As they walked, it began to rain, falling heavier with each step. Soon, they were running.

As a police officer, Hannah had a special license plate that allowed her to park in restricted zones. Though she seldom used it for personal reasons, she was grateful for it that night.

CHAPTER NINE

"I haven't been out that late socially in years," Hannah said the following morning. "It's sure a lot more fun than a stakeout, and much less boring."

They sat in Hannah's little breakfast nook, drinking coffee and orange juice and eating English muffins.

"I've never been out until three ever in my life," Gloria said. "Why are we up so early?"

"Early? It's nine o'clock. I'm usually on the street by now. You could have slept in."

"No. Actually, I'm an early riser, too, but I'm usually in bed by eleven."

"Well, I practically had to undress you and put you to bed. You bombed out on the way home."

"When I got up to go to the bathroom, I didn't know where I was. Then I saw you passed out on the couch. At least you were familiar, so I figured it must be OK, wherever we were."

"It was good to see you having such a good time, Gloria."

"It was good to have a good time."

"We have a lot of talking to do today," Hannah said seriously.

"I know," Gloria said softly.

"The same conditions still apply, even though we've enjoyed many light moments since I kidnapped you yesterday."

"I know. Just let me savor this a little while. It's so nice to sit in a friendly, sunny room with a friendly, sunny companion and enjoy the early part of the day."

Hannah agreed. They sat together, reading the paper, discussing unimportant things, and enjoying the fragrance of the bouquet of pink roses Hannah received a few days earlier from a secret admirer.

"Where'd these come from?" Gloria asked. "Those are the biggest, pinkest roses I've ever seen. Even Stewart's roses aren't that big."

"Who's Stewart?"

"Our gardener."

"Oh. Sharon's buddy."

"What?"

"Nothing. I don't know who sent them. They were at my door the other night when I arrived home from work—vase and all. They're lovely, aren't they?" Hannah asked thoughtfully.

"Yes, and the vase is worth many times the price of the roses. Did you know that?"

"No. How'd you know?"

"One thing we Allen women learn about is crystal, china, silver, and really important stuff like that. Mother Mariah would pay you plenty for that vase. It's worth several thousand dollars and quite possibly more, if someone really wanted it. It's Lalique, and it's an antique, besides. I knew that the moment I saw it."

"Why would someone deliver flowers to me in a vase that valuable?" Hannah wondered. "There's no florist card. I don't think it came from a business."

"Well, then, it could be your admirer doesn't know the value of the vase. Lots of times people have stuff like that around and don't know its value."

"Could be." Hannah felt relieved to think so.

"It would be cool, though, if he knew the value."

"I don't know how cool that would be, Gloria. It would make

me very nervous. It would be totally inappropriate, to say the least."

"At least try to enjoy the flowers. They're pretty sensational. Somebody admires you a lot."

"That's what worries me." Hannah frowned.

"Just enjoy them," Gloria said enviously. "I sure would if someone sent them to me."

The phone rang, and Hannah answered. "Hi, Sharon," she said, glad to hear her partner's voice. "How are you?"

"I'm doing OK. I'll be released at eleven-thirty. Can you pick me up?"

"Sure. We'll be there at eleven and will wait for you."

"Who's we?"

"Gloria Allen and I. Remember?"

"Oh, yeah. Is she right there?"

"Yes."

"You can tell me how it's going later."

"I'll do that."

"Where's Gloria?" Sharon asked as she and Hannah left the hospital.

"She's basking by the pool at the apartment," Hannah replied.

"No surprise. You trust her there alone?"

"Why not? She has no wheels and seems far more interested in cultivating skin cancer than in running away. She wanted to stay behind so I let her."

"How have things gone with her? Have you learned anything important—or at least interesting?"

"Quite a few things. She talked pretty freely about her family last night. She seems well aware that they're seriously dysfunctional, and she actually had a sense of humor about it. At least, that was how it appeared.

"We also ran into Darren Brannigan at dinner. Gloria was unnerved by the fact that he was with another woman, a very beautiful one, I might add. I think Gloria's in love with him."

"Did you blush all over the place?"

"No. I'll have you know I did not. I kept my cool very well. I hate to admit it, but he is handsome. His portrait, as good as it is, doesn't do him justice. He's the type to stay away from, though. He's incredibly charming and must know of his affect on women. I wouldn't want to be involved with someone like that. It's too risky. As the song goes, 'easy on the eyes, hard on the heart.'"

"Maybe. I wouldn't mind giving it a try."

"Be my guest. You seem to be doing pretty well with the cast. How do you feel?"

"Pretty good. I'm still sore, but it's good to be out of there. I don't like hospitals. They give me the creeps."

"Let's head to my place. Why don't you stay overnight so I can look after you? If you feel up to it, we can all go to the concert tonight. If not, you can stay home and keep an eye on our charge."

"That's right. Tonight's the concert near your place, right?"

"Yeah."

"I'd like to go. Is there a pharmacy nearby where I could fill a prescription?"

"Just one block from my place."

While Gloria sat in the sun by the pool, Hannah and Sharon sat in the shade, sipping iced tea and discussing recent events and Hannah's interrogation of Gloria.

"Won't it be tough to continue your conversation with Gloria if I'm hanging around?" Sharon asked. "She might feel we're ganging up on her, and she'll shut up fast." She glanced toward Gloria, whose sunny location was many feet away.

"We talked a lot this morning before I came to pick you up. A little at a time is best. We'll have another chance.

"She said that she and Angela became aware that something strange was going on at the so-called parties at their house. They were curious about what happened in the main library while they were in the music library. Several times when their mother was out of the house, they searched the library for clues without any luck.

"Everything was locked, down to all the desk drawers and cabinet doors. They were also hindered by the fact that they didn't know what they were looking for—just anything odd, apparently.

"Eventually, they discovered a secret passageway off the main room. They accidentally triggered a hidden button. It took them a while to figure it out, and Gloria didn't want to tell me yet. Anyway, the passageway led to a hidden door into the garden, an obvious escape passage to the outside.

"There was another passageway that led to a hidden door in the pantry beside the kitchen. They had fun exploring the hidden passages and were intrigued by their history, but they didn't dare ask any questions.

"Angela entered the passageway many times during cocktails on the evenings of the parties when she was alone in the garden. Nobody paid any attention, and why should they? She wasn't going to talk to them, so they left her alone."

Sharon, listening intently, nodded.

"Anyway, they tried to figure out how they could listen in on the meetings in the main library without arousing suspicion.

"They finally decided that Angela would leave the music library with the excuse she didn't feel well. She was the best candidate for the job, because it was less likely anyone would ask her any questions, since she wouldn't answer. Since she wasn't as robust as Gloria, she could more easily fake an illness or emotional frailty. She was so sweet and meek, no one would ever think she was capable of anything covert.

"She would return sometime later feeling better, so she could be present for dessert and final good-byes. Gloria and Angela felt the women in the group were unaware of any shenanigans going on. There would be plenty of time to ask Angela if she felt all right before they rejoined the others later in the evening.

"The girls were right. The subject of Angela's occasional disappearances from the music library never came up during dessert or any other time. Gloria believed that if the women had mentioned Angela's disappearances to their husbands, the girls would have heard about it, because their mother would want to know what was going on. She knew Angela wasn't ill, and she would insist on learning the truth.

"Gloria said her mother is a very suspicious person, with good reason. She's apparently very dishonest herself and thinks everyone else is the same."

"So the girls can think for themselves," Sharon said, feeling impressed. "Apparently, they're not as unworldly as we thought."

Hannah nodded. "I wonder sometimes if that unworldly business is an act. In fact, I worry about it a lot. From what I've seen in the past twenty-four hours, Gloria's got a lot on the ball. Part of me wants to be very careful around her."

"That's because you're a cop. You're supposed to be suspicious. It's your job."

"Well, anyway, one evening four months ago, sometime in April, Angela excused herself from the group, went into the garden, and entered the secret passage. She was attempting to hear what was going on in the main library when she heard a commotion down the tunnel.

"She was terrified of being caught, so she ran as fast as she could toward the opening into the kitchen. That meant she was running toward the sounds she heard. She felt certain she'd be caught and frantically tried to think of an excuse as to why she was there or how she even knew about the tunnels.

"Fortunately, she wore a long, dark, hooded cape over her Victorian dress, because it was cold that night. Being a bit delicate and knowing the passageway was cold, she'd gotten into the habit of putting on the cape to stay warm.

"That paid off when she realized she wouldn't reach the corridor to the kitchen. She found a small alcove, ducked in, covered her hair and face with the hood, and tried to become invisible. She was so terrified, she felt she'd die of fright. Her heart was pounding so loudly, she imagined going deaf before she died. She shook so badly she thought they would hear her knees knocking. It was an effort to become still."

"That took guts, especially for a meek young lady." Sharon smiled. "It would seem she was tougher than anyone suspected, even herself."

Hannah nodded. "Moments after she found the alcove, the first of the intruders came by. It was Judge Quigley. Angela recognized his voice, but she couldn't understand him, because he was speaking Gaelic. From his tone, she guessed he was telling the others to be quiet. She heard lots of Gaelic but no English. There were sporadic beams of light from a flashlight, and she was certain someone would see her. It seemed like an eternity before they passed."

Hannah stopped for a few seconds. When she spoke again, her voice lowered to a whisper.

"Then Gloria told me the most extraordinary story. While Angela was in the alcove, she began mentally reciting the Lord's Prayer. Praying wasn't her custom, but she continued praying until the last person was gone and it was safe for her to step out again.

"Later that night, when the girls were alone in Angela's room before bed, Angela wrote down the words to the prayer to share with Gloria. The following day, she couldn't remember a word of the prayer, much less what happened in the passageway.

"The kicker is, neither of the girls had ever learned the Lord's Prayer."

After a moment of silence, Sharon said, "That just goes to show you what a moment of terror can do for one's spirituality no matter how we try to deny its existence. Angela heard that prayer somewhere, and it stuck without her knowing it."

They looked at each other in wonder.

"After the group passed," Hannah continued, "Angela dashed down the passageway to the corridor leading to the kitchen. It took her a long time to recover, and she was afraid she wouldn't make it back to the music library before dessert time. If worse came to worst, she'd go back to her room and pretend to be sick in bed. She wanted to take the easy way out, but she decided to rejoin the others if she could, because that would be best."

"Another show of inner fortitude."

Hannah nodded. "Gloria says she remembers that night well. Angela came into the music library looking paler than usual. The other women didn't notice. They were enjoying the music. But, Gloria knew something was wrong. She told me Angela should have received an Academy Award for her performance the rest of the evening.

"After dessert, when everyone left, and the two girls went upstairs, Angela collapsed on her bed, sobbing uncontrollably and shaking. That scared Gloria. She thought her sister was having a nervous breakdown.

"Then Angela got up off the bed, sat at her writing table, and began writing down what happened. It took several days before Gloria understood it all. Then, unfortunately, the girls destroyed the writing so no one could find it.

"At first, they had no idea why all those people were entering their house through a secret passage, or why Judge Quigley was with them. Then it dawned on them that they were smuggling Irish nationals into the States. The Gaelic Angela overheard was a good clue. Bringing in Irish nationals didn't seem like a bad idea. Doing it illegally wasn't so good, but Gloria said they'd rather see those poor people smuggled into the States than be killed in Ireland.

"They kept wondering why the adults were doing it. None of them were moral crusaders of any kind. The girls decided it had to be about money. Were the adults doing what others did in Mexico, China, and other countries, charging those unfortunates thousands of dollars to bring them to another country with a promise of work, a better life, freedom, safety, and then selling them into slavery or abandoning them?

"That was hard to contemplate. Could their mother be involved in such a thing? Even though they knew she was selfish and unethical, it was tough to think of their own mother taking advantage of desperate people.

"They had to find out, but how? They didn't want to involve the police if they didn't have to, and they couldn't let any of the staff know. What were they to do?"

Hannah stopped as Gloria walked toward them.

"Don't you guys want to get some color?" she asked.

"No, thanks," the two women answered.

"How about a glass of iced tea?" Sharon offered.

"That's what I came over here for. It looks great. Thanks."

"Would you like to go to a concert tonight featuring the Sweet Adelines?" Hannah asked.

"Sure. I've never seen a group of them live. I've heard some recordings, but that's all. That would be great."

"The concert's at eight, and it's just a couple blocks away. We can walk. We'll leave at seven-fifteen so we can find good seats."

"What about Detective Walker's leg?"

"It'll be fine," Sharon said. "It's a short walk. It'll do me good."

"I'll haul out my little red wagon and give you a ride," Hannah teased.

"Won't you be a picture of grace, Detective," Gloria said, glancing at the full length cast.

"Very funny," Sharon said. "I'll have you know I'm an experienced runner. A walking cast won't even slow me down."

"It's tuna salad sandwiches," Hannah interrupted, "with fruit and iced tea for supper. I hope you're OK with that."

"We are," Gloria and Sharon chorused.

Gloria sauntered to her lounge chair, set down her glass on the concrete, and dived into the pool.

"I never saw her go in before," Hannah commented. "I'm glad to know she can actually swim."

The pool was empty except for Gloria, who swam like a champion back and forth, changing strokes with ease and diving frequently.

"She's quite a swimmer," Sharon said. "She looks like a dolphin."

"Our young friend is full of surprises, isn't she?" Hannah asked.

They watched Gloria swim for a few minutes, then Hannah returned to her story.

"The only way the girls could find out what was going on in the main library was to position themselves within earshot of the room or find a way to tape record the conversation. Taping would probably increase their chances of being caught, so they decided to try the passageway again. Once they decided, they also decided to wait awhile. If Angela left the group too often, it would attract attention.

"While they waited, Gloria somehow acquired some modern listening equipment that would allow Angela to listen through the passageway door."

"How'd she do that?" Sharon asked.

"When I asked how she came by the equipment, she said a friend found it for her. I didn't want to risk alienating her, so I let it go. We'll pursue that later if necessary.

"Anyway, they sneaked into the main library after each party to see if any clues were left behind, thinking someone must eventually drop something, but they found nothing. The room was always clean.

"Then, last month, they tried the passageway again. Angela tucked herself into an alcove near the kitchen entrance and waited for the intruders to pass. She crept down the corridor to the main library, prepared to rush back to the alcove if she had to, and stood near the hinged door in case it opened.

"With her equipment ready, she listened. All she heard were muffled voices, including her mother's. The device wasn't powerful enough to pick up clear sounds through the door. Angela started to wonder what the door was made of. It was thick, but what was the material? She had assumed it was wood."

"It must have had lead in it," Sharon said.

"Probably. After a while, the door opened, and the intruders came out, led by Judge Quigley. Hiding behind the door, Angela felt certain she'd be caught, but the group kept going. No one turned back even when the door shut heavily behind them.

"As soon as the passageway was clear, she ran for the kitchen corridor. As she neared it, she heard footsteps coming back up the main passageway from the outside, so she ran as fast as she could into the kitchen corridor and then into the kitchen. She was sure whoever was back there, probably Judge Quigley rejoining the others in the main library, must have glimpsed her or heard her footsteps.

"At dessert that evening, the group from the main library was unusually quiet, and Mariah kept looking suspiciously at her daughters as if trying to see something that might betray them. The judge looked at them intently, too, but his gaze was primarily on Gloria. He probably thought Angela was incapable of such an escapade.

"Of course, they didn't dare say anything to the girls for fear of giving themselves away, or so the girls thought. The girls behaved normally and enjoyed their dessert.

"Gloria said the idea of their being suspects might have been only in their imaginations, because they knew what they'd done. Maybe no one suspected after all."

"I know that feeling," Sharon said. "I was in trouble more often than not when I was a kid, because my face gave me away."

"Me, too," Hannah interjected. "Whatever I did was always on my face. I couldn't get away with anything."

"You still can't, Friend." Sharon chuckled. "You're getting better, though."

"Thanks."

"Back to the story—Gloria said it was kind of funny, because the music group was chatting away happily about their evening together and smiling, while the other group was unusually quiet and unresponsive.

"At one point Kathleen Quigley asked her husband, 'Raleigh, you look as if you'd just lost a round of golf. What's the matter?'

"Gloria took the opportunity to giggle and say something insipid to distract everyone. The evening ended earlier than usual, just after dessert. There were no last-minute jokes or long good-byes. The girls excused themselves as soon as the last guest left and went to their rooms. They feared their mother might come up to question them, but she didn't, nor did she later.

"The next eventful thing that happened was the dinner party this past Wednesday night when Angela died." Hannah paused to sip her tea. "This might explain why there was such a strain between Mariah and Gloria.

"Gloria thinks her mother is involved in a seriously illegal and immoral act, while Mariah, who may think Gloria knows, hasn't said anything, because she doesn't want to risk exposing herself to her daughter—in case Gloria doesn't know anything after all.

"It might also explain Gloria's comment about being killed, too. She has reason to think that one of the main library group killed her sister and might intend the same for her. Worse, she wonders if it's her mother."

Sharon thought about that. "Do you really think Mariah would kill her own daughter even if she thought Angela knew what she was doing?"

"I just don't know. She might be capable of that. If the group feared the girls were on to them and might expose them, they might have decided the girls had to die, and Mariah had to do it."

"If so, then Gloria really is in danger."

There was a brief silence.

"Maybe Judge Quigley or one of the others in the group went to Angela's room and killed her," Sharon suggested.

"It's possible but not likely. I don't know how any of them could have gotten upstairs during cocktails without being seen by Gloria or one of the wives. From what the witnesses said, the party guests tend to walk about freely during that time. Someone other than Mariah or Gloria going upstairs, however, would have appeared too forward and would have caused comment.

"Mariah could have done it easily. No one would suspect her if she went upstairs in her own house during cocktails. She probably would have used the back stairs off the kitchen. No one would see her."

"The caterers are out," Sharon said slowly. "There isn't anything there. The household staff wasn't present. We haven't spoken with the florist yet, though I doubt we'll learn much there, either. It also seems unlikely it was a guest. So, unless someone else came into the house and killed Angela while the others were walking about, we're right back where we started."

"We know a lot more than we did a few days ago."

"Yes, but most of what we've learned just raises more questions."

"Before I came to pick you up, and after Gloria left for the pool, I called Rob at home and told him of my conversation with Gloria. I have it all on tape. He'll put together an investigative team and get immigration involved in the people-smuggling aspect of the case. The slave trade isn't our territory."

"The makeup of the group is interesting. We have a judge, a banker, a patent lawyer, an artist, and a wealthy matron. Each has a very specific role to play in this little enterprise.

"They have someone who knows and can interpret law, someone who can act upon it, someone who can acquire and launder money, someone who can create counterfeit documents, and an attractive woman to charm, distract, and provide cover for them. Quite a resplendent group."

"Resplendent?" Hannah chuckled. "That's one way to put it." Seeing Gloria walking toward them again, Hannah summed up their discussion and stood to gather her things. She caught Gloria's eye to signal it was time to leave.

"We have to get ready for tonight," Hannah said. "With three women and one shower, it'll take extra time."

CHAPTER TEN

The detectives and their charge arrived back at Hannah's place at four-thirty. Hannah checked her messages and found an urgent call from headquarters. When she called in, she reached Sergeant Languille.

"Mariah Allen was found dead at her estate earlier this afternoon," Languille announced.

"What happened and why?" Hannah moved away from the others.

"They found her in the garden room beside the pool at two-fifteen. She had choked to death."

"Choked? On what?"

"She was eating lunch when it happened. Apparently, she choked on something she was eating."

"Was she alone?"

"I guess."

"What's the estimated time of death?"

"Shortly after noon."

Hannah rang off and called Jim Preston at the morgue. As she did, she walked down the hall toward the bedrooms.

"Hello," Jim said.

"Jim? Hannah Bell here. What's up with Mariah Allen?"

"You've heard?"

"Yeah."

"She simply choked to death on her lunch. She was eating a

chicken salad sandwich and some fruit. From the evidence, it appears she'd taken a bite out of the sandwich and then took a piece of fruit. We removed a piece of fruit from her throat at the scene. The food and her plate were on the floor when we arrived. Apparently, no one noticed her slumped over the table until a guest arrived. The maid and a guest found her."

"Who was the guest?"

"A family friend named Brannigan. The friend came to check on the family."

Hannah flinched. "You have the body?"

"Yes."

"Is anyone still at the scene?"

"I don't know. I left an assistant there, and she hasn't returned yet. You may want to head out there to check the situation out yourself."

"She was dead for about two hours when they found her?"

"Right. Rigor mortis hadn't begun to set in, so she wasn't dead long."

"Thanks. I'm on my way out there."

After hanging up, Hannah took a moment to collect herself before walking to the living room where her guests were chatting and laughing. She walked over to where Gloria sat on the couch, then sat beside her and took her hand.

"Gloria, I have some very bad news," Hannah said gently. "Your mother has been found dead at home."

Gloria closed her eyes for a moment, then opened them and stared out the window before looking back at Hannah. "Not the invincible Mariah," she said with remarkable calm. "How did she die?"

"She choked to death."

"Choked? Oh, my God, how awful. How in the world...?" Her voice trailed off.

"She was eating lunch when it happened."

"No one was there?"

"Apparently not. At least, not at the time it happened."

There was silence for a few moments, then Hannah touched Gloria's arm. "Gloria, I need to go out there. Do you want to come with me, or would you rather stay with Detective Walker?"

"I'll go," she said solemnly.

"Who found her?" Sharon asked.

"One of the maids, probably Anna, and Darren Brannigan."

"Darren?" Gloria gasped. "What was he doing there?"

"He stopped to check on you and your mother. Of course, he must have known you weren't there after last night."

Gloria seemed unnerved. Her face flushed, and she excused herself quickly.

"What's that about?" Sharon asked after Gloria left.

Hannah shrugged. "Detective Walker, are you up to conducting an interview?"

"It depends."

"Darren Brannigan?"

"I can handle that."

When Gloria returned, Hannah said, "Detective Walker will talk to Mr. Brannigan to get his story."

Gloria's eyes instantly turned dark and brooding.

Is every woman on earth a threat to Gloria when it comes to that man? Hannah wondered.

"Come on," Hannah said. "Let's go to your house. Detective Walker can visit Mr. Brannigan." She handed Sharon the card Darren gave her the previous evening.

Gloria glared at the card as it passed between the two women.

Hannah called a cab for Sharon, and they waited for it to arrive. Sharon washed her face and put on fresh makeup, while Gloria, clearly agitated, watched.

The change in Gloria was startling. After being friendly and open with both detectives, she sudden became sullen and brooding. Her apparent intense jealousy at the thought of another woman in Darren's company was frightening. Hannah wondered what Gloria was capable of while in that state of mind.

No tears for her mother, but intense anger at the thought of any woman interacting with Darren, Hannah thought.

As Sharon got into her cab, Hannah leaned close and asked softly, "You sure you want to do this? This guy could be a killer."

"Call me reckless, but I doubt it," Sharon said confidently. "If he tries anything, I'll kick him with my cast."

"Just be careful."

"I will. Maybe I'll get a ride home."

"In a cab! Just come back here, OK? I still think it's best for you to spend the night here. I'll take you home tomorrow. If you want, you can come with us to my folks' house for the usual Sunday-night gathering."

"OK. I'll come back here. I'd love to see your folks. We'll talk about that when I return. I'm off."

Hannah and Gloria waited for the cab to pull away, then walked toward Hannah's car. As they drove, Gloria continued brooding.

"Gloria, are you all right?"

"I'm fine." Her previous insolence was back.

"Are you jealous that Detective Walker is visiting Darren Brannigan?"

Gloria gave her a look that made Hannah draw away. Determined to do whatever was necessary to learn what was going on with the younger woman, Hannah suddenly pulled onto the shoulder and parked. She looked hard at Gloria and repeated her question.

"Are you jealous that Detective Walker is visiting Darren Brannigan?"

"No. Why should I be?" came the adolescent, chip-on-the-shoulder reply.

"That's what I'm asking. You've been delightful for the whole day, and now you're moody and nasty again. You should see your face. You look like the devil."

Watching Gloria carefully, Hannah saw her change personality as if she understood Hannah's words and wanted to gather herself.

That's remarkable, Hannah thought. It's like she's conjuring another personality.

After a moment, Gloria said, "I'm sorry, Detective. I didn't mean to be so rude. I do like Darren Brannigan, and I have a problem with jealousy. Please forgive me."

"You're forgiven." Hannah felt shaken by what she'd just witnessed. What is this girl capable of? Is she a victim or a demon?

"Let's go," Gloria said.

As Sharon's cab pulled slowly into the driveway of Darren Brannigan's home, a gold Jaguar was coming out. The driver was more sensible than the one Sharon met barely twenty-four hours earlier, approaching at a reasonable speed and staying on her side of the road. Still, Sharon felt momentarily ill at ease. She saw the driver was an attractive young woman with long, blonde hair, who looked hard at Sharon as if trying to memorize her features. Sharon gave a friendly smile and wave as the two vehicles passed.

A few moments later, as she left the cab, the Jaguar pulled up, and the young woman got out.

"Who are you?" The woman walked up so close to Sharon that she almost lost her balance.

"I'm Detective Walker of the Chicago Police Department." She moved backward and held up her badge.

"What are you doing here?"

"I'm here to speak with Mr. Darren Brannigan." Sharon didn't like the woman's manner. "Are you related to him?"

"No. I'm a friend. What do you want to talk with him about?"

"I'm sorry, Miss, but that's none of your business." She walked around the young woman and moved toward the house.

"I'll bet you're not a detective." The woman stepped in front of Sharon, blocking her way.

Suddenly, the front door opened, and Darren stepped out. "What's going on, Jennifer? I thought you left." He sounded annoyed.

"I was leaving when I saw this woman coming up the driveway. I'm curious about her business here."

"Don't you think that's my business?" He spoke to her as if she were a child. "Run along. I'll see you Monday."

Jennifer reluctantly walked back to her car and got in. She gave Sharon a threatening look as she drove off, but Sharon pretended not to notice.

Darren turned to Sharon. "I'm very sorry about that. Who are you?"

"I'm Detective Walker of the Chicago Police Department." Sharon flashed her badge. "I'd like to talk to you about Mrs. Mariah Allen's death."

"Certainly. Please come in. I'll be glad to tell you what little I know." He eyed her cast and bruised eye and cheek. "What happened to you? You look like you came out on the wrong end of a dog fight."

"A minor car accident yesterday."

"A minor accident that broke your leg and left you all banged up? That doesn't seem minor to me. Are you sure you should be traipsing about the countryside one day after an accident?"

"I'd rather be traipsing about than sitting about."

Darren smiled.

Sharon felt herself becoming more infatuated than ever. Watch it, Girl. She agreed with Hannah that Darren's portrait didn't do him justice. He was very charming, and that incredible, deep, rich voice…. I could still eat him alive, she thought.

As they entered the house, Darren summoned a maid. "Please bring us iced tea on the patio. The maid nodded and left them."

They walked through the house to a cool, shaded patio surrounded by a large, oddly shaped pool. Sharon looked at it a moment before realizing it was the shape of an artist's palette with a little island where the thumb hole belonged.

"Clever," she said.

"Excuse me?"

"Oh, I was just commenting on the shape of the pool. Very clever. Very cool."

"Thank you. It's new, a dream of mine. As a kid I dreamed about having a pool someday. Not just any pool, a pool shaped like an artist's palette. Then I would know I'd finally made it."

"Your painting is going well?"

"Very well, thank you, especially since I started the portraits. I can't keep up with the demand. The young lady you had the pleasure of meeting when you arrived is a client, although she tries to act like my keeper. Sometimes, the young ones think that once an artist paints them, they have an intimate relationship. Learning to handle that has been a challenge."

"I thought you did very well with your words and tone. Whether she understood you is another matter."

"I doubt she fully got the message. It's happened before. Oh, well. Let's move to the subject of your visit. First question."

"What was your relationship with Angela Allen?"

The maid arrived with a large tray that held two glasses of iced tea, a pitcher of tea, and a plate of cookies.

"Thank you, Molly," Darren said. "That will be all."

"You're welcome, Mr. Brannigan." She curtsied gracefully and spoke with a distinct Irish accent. An attractive young woman with a turned-up nose, she had short reddish-brown hair, brown eyes, and a freckled face. By the way she looked at her employer, it was clear she felt genuine respect and admiration for him. It was also obvious she'd been well taught. Tall and lanky, she carried herself gracefully and had a very professional air for one so young. Sharon guessed she was in her early twenties.

"Molly's from Ireland, isn't she?" Sharon asked.

"Yes. She's been here three years. She's reliable, works hard, and is a pleasure to have around."

"How many household staff do you have, Mr. Brannigan?"

"Please, call me Darren. I have three. There's Molly, a gardener who doesn't live here, and Mrs. Hennessey. She looks after Molly and heads the house. Mrs. Hennessey and Molly live here."

"Is your entire staff Irish?"

"Yes. That was a vow my family took long ago. We promised to help Irish nationals find employment in the States so they could live here."

"That's very admirable. All their papers are in order, I trust?"

"They certainly are. The last thing any of them needs is trouble with the law. None want to return to Ireland. It's sad." His expression was honest and open. "Back to Angela. What was your question again?"

"I asked about your relationship with Angela."

"I was extremely fond of her and very concerned about her. She was very sweet and gentle, as angelic as her name implied, but also disturbed, or so I believed. She wasn't insane or anything, just, well, deeply disturbed and very unhappy.

"Anyone who suddenly stops speaking one day and never speaks for years afterward is obviously disturbed about something. I tried to talk with her about it, but I failed. She wouldn't listen and thwarted all attempts to help her.

"I know she was raped several years ago. Her mother told me that much. Angela stopped talking around that time. According to Mariah, Angela began avoiding men after the rape. I wanted to change that, to restore at least some trust in men, but Angela would have none of it."

He stopped and took a deep breath, then stared into the distance beyond the pool. "I guess it doesn't matter anymore." He gave an anguished sigh. "At least she's at peace."

Sharon waited.

Turning to look at her, Darren said, "I seriously considered proposing to her just to get her away from that house. She never would have accepted, and that wasn't what I envisioned for my own life. But she deserved better than she was getting. Some kind of happiness. Some warmth. Mariah was, for the most part, a frigid, heartless woman who used people and threw them away when she finished with them. I learned that early on, though she never had the chance to use me, because I wouldn't let her."

"Were you in love with Angela?" Sharon asked gently.

"Not the way I'd like to be in love someday. I just cared for her and wanted to do something to make her happy. I would have married her for that reason. Perhaps love would have come later."

There was a brief silence.

"What about Gloria?" Sharon asked.

"What about her? She's scary. One minute, she's congenial, upbeat, and nice—one could almost use the word sweet to describe her. The next minute, she's a disciple of the devil—irritable, mean, and uses language that would make a sailor blush. Like her mother, you never know just what you'll get.

"Mariah could be affable on occasion, which was very bizarre, because it seemed so out of character. I never knew how to read her, either. I was most uncomfortable during the rare times she was actually cordial.

"Angela was different from both. She seemed to have inherited her father's goodness and nothing from her mother except those incredible blue eyes. Gloria, on the other hand, inherited her mother's ill temper and very little of her father's grace and goodness, if any. I understand he was a special man."

"How do you know that?"

"From Anna. She talks about him all the time. It's strange, because he's been dead almost twenty years, but she still remembers him well. Her memories of him are always in the forefront of her mind."

"Is Gloria in love with you?"

Darren gave her an uneasy look and appeared to be thinking how best to reply. "I don't think Gloria is capable of loving anyone but herself, although I think she genuinely cared for her sister. She's attracted to me, but that's far from being in love. She's a lot like Jennifer, the young woman...."

"I know who you mean," the detective said, interrupting.

Darren continued. She'd like to think she owns me, and I've never even painted her portrait."

"Why not?"

"Good question. I don't know. The subject never came up. Mariah asked me to paint Angela, and I continued to use her as a model, but she never asked me to paint Gloria. Perhaps she planned to someday. I don't know. I don't ask people if I can paint them. They ask me."

A little ego showing, Sharon thought with a smile.

"Anyway, Angela was the perfect subject. Her long, blonde hair, blue eyes, innocent countenance, and Victorian look made her an ideal subject. I imagine a portrait of Gloria would be very different. It would probably resemble Satan, complete with horns and pitchfork. She scares me, and there aren't many women who do."

"Why does she scare you?"

"I really don't know. Perhaps it's because she's such an unknown. I really haven't figured out why. There's just something about her."

"Tell me what happened the night of the party."

"I was a guest in the Allen home along with several others. We were just about to sit down to dinner when Mariah walked into the room where we were having cocktails and said Angela was very sick, and that we had to leave at once, so we did. None of us had any idea Angela was ill. She hadn't come down for cocktails, but that was no surprise. She rarely stayed with the group, anyway, usually taking solitary walks in the garden. That night, she didn't come down at all."

"Was that unusual? Were there other times when she didn't show up at all, or was she always there physically if not socially?"

"Yes. She was usually physically present at some time during cocktails. She was always around by the time we were ready to sit down to dinner."

"Were you aware that she was napping while you had cocktails on the night she died?"

"No one said anything to us about that. There'd be no particular reason to do so."

"Did you go home after you left the Allens?"

"I did. I rarely have unscheduled time, so I took advantage of it to sit down with a good book and read all evening. It was memorable, because it was so rare."

"When did you learn that Angela had died?"

"On the radio the following morning. I was stunned. I called the house right away to confirm it. Mariah answered, as usual, and confirmed. She didn't seem very upset about it and was rather matter-of-fact, but then, that was Mariah—no show of emotion, if, indeed, she ever felt any.

"I've stopped by twice since Angela died to see what I could do, but there wasn't anything. Mariah handled all the arrangements for Angela's memorial. I wonder who'll do that for Mariah? I can't imagine Gloria doing it. This time when I stopped to visit, Mariah was dead."

Suddenly, he stopped and drank from his iced tea. "I don't think Angela died of natural causes. Even though the forensic people say Mariah choked to death, I find her death odd, too. She was a slow, meticulous eater. She took forever to chew her food. I find it hard to believe she could choke to death."

"Who would have killed her?"

"I don't know. The only people I know that the Allen women associated with, other than their household staff, were those who attended the small parties. I can't imagine it being one of them. What would be the motive?"

"Perhaps we can come up with one." She glanced at him from the corner of her eye. "Did everyone get along? Were there any petty jealousies?"

"None that I knew of. As parties went, they were more comfortable than most, with very little pretense. It was just a congenial evening with friends."

Either he's telling the truth, or he's a hell of an actor, Sharon thought.

"Darren, we understand that the Allens have the same group of people over twice a month on Wednesdays, and that you're a member of that group. We also understand that after the dinner, the party splits into two parts. One group retires to the music library, the other goes into the main library. Can you explain that?"

"It's a little different, I admit. The judge, Jim Costello, Liam Reilly, and I like to play cards. None of the wives do. They like music, so they, along with Angela and Gloria, both of whom were very musical, entertain themselves in the music library, while we head for the main library."

Cards? Who's he trying to kid? I can't buy that. Sharon continued smiling.

"Mariah acts as our hostess, or so she says, but she doesn't do anything. She doesn't need to be there, but I suspect she prefers being with us than with the other women. She's not a woman's woman. She reads or gets into heated discussions with the judge over politics.

"That's another thing. We're all into discussing world affairs, and the other women have no interest in that. As a result, somewhere along the line, the groups separated according to interest. It works quite well, actually, but it began before my time.

"I came into the picture later, after the arrangement had already been made. I also like music and sometimes wanted to join the women in the music library, but suggestions to that effect brought harsh looks from the others. I figured I could live with that for two nights a month. Overall, it's a good time."

"How'd you join the group?"

"Mariah stopped by the gallery where I was painting. After talking with her awhile, she asked if I'd paint a portrait of Angela. That was how it began. When she invited me to one of her parties, I accepted."

If Sharon hadn't already heard the story about secret passageways, Gaelic voices chattering as people moved along them, and listening devices, she would have found Darren's explanation totally acceptable, although a bit odd. However, knowing what she did, she felt distressed about Darren's character.

Was he lying? If so, was it to protect himself or someone else? Part of what he said could be true, and the situation might have progressed from innocent card games to smuggling Irish nationals, but that just didn't feel right.

Sharon didn't want to believe Darren was involved in anything illegal or corrupt, but, if he were, she didn't want to raise his suspicions. Rob Keys was already setting up an investigative team, and she didn't want to compromise that effort.

She fought back the increasingly strong desire to bluntly ask, "So how many Irish nationals have you smuggled into the States since you joined the group? How much money did that racket make for you? Did that money pay for your pool?"

She refrained and changed the subject. "What are your thoughts about Mariah's death?"

"As I just said, it's hard to believe she choked to death. Maybe she had help."

"How do you help someone choke to death? That's generally considered strangulation."

"Don't help them." He looked at her for a moment. "She was disliked by almost all who met her, but I wouldn't think they wanted her dead, so it had to be something else. She was worth a lot of money. I once overheard her discussing leaving a large chunk of money to a conservancy. Another time, she talked about leaving her money to a convent. I heard her threaten the girls with statements like that. If her threats were real, maybe someone wanted her behest sooner rather than later."

"That sounds like a veiled accusation against Gloria, Darren."

"In reality, who gains the most from Mariah's death? Probably Gloria. She certainly had a volatile relationship with her mother. With her temper, I can see her killing Mariah in a fit of rage over some issue, but Mariah didn't die violently. More importantly, Gloria was nowhere near when her mother died.

"Gloria's a clever girl, but I don't think she's figured out a way to be in more than one place at a time."

"Do you think Gloria is capable of hiring someone to kill her mother or her sister?" Sharon asked.

Darren looked intently at her, then pondered the question before saying, "I hadn't thought of that. It's possible except for the fact that her circle of acquaintances is very small, and I don't believe she has any friends. I don't see how she could have made the kind of contact she would need to have someone killed. How could she go about it?"

Sharon didn't answer.

"Perhaps the fact that she wasn't home when it happened is convenient, especially since she's almost always home. The girls rarely went out. The fact that Gloria was with a police detective makes it a very good alibi. She told me she was staying with the detective for a few days. That's about the best alibi she could have."

"That detective is my partner," Sharon said. "Gloria's been with Detective Bell since yesterday afternoon."

"So it seems she couldn't have killed her mother, unless she hired it done, and I find that a pretty big stretch."

"When you arrived at the house, who was there?"

"I don't know who all was there. Anna opened the door and took me to Mariah. That was when we found her. Anna hadn't been back to the garden room since she served Mariah promptly at noon. Mariah was a creature of habit. She had to eat at noon each day, and there was hell to pay if lunch was late. I was there once when that happened, and I know."

"What time did you arrive?"

"A little after two. I wanted to see how Mariah was getting along with the memorial arrangements and with Gloria being away. I was actually more curious than anything over how Gloria got out of the house. It was quite a surprise to see her out the previous night. As far as I know, that never happened before."

"Did you notice anything unusual when you found Mrs. Allen?"

"The fact that she was dead was highly unusual. She looked a little disheveled, very unlike Mariah, as if she struggled some.

Her head was on the table, her arms dangling toward the floor. She was sitting on the edge of her chair, and her plate had been knocked to the floor. Apparently, no one paid any attention to her after she was served lunch. Since she didn't call any of the servants, they left her alone.

"It's kind of sad to think that she ended up dying alone in a physical struggle with herself."

Sharon nodded and glanced at her watch. It was almost eight. She took out a business card and handed it to Darren. "That's all the questions for tonight, Darren. Thank you for being so cooperative. Please call either Detective Bell or me if you think of anything we should know. I'm sure we'll be in touch again. I hope you don't plan to leave town anytime soon."

"Nope. I have too much work to do."

"Could you call a cab for me? I'm not driving at the moment."

"I'll do even better than that, Detective. I'll take you home."

Sharon's heart lurched, and she had to pause before she felt ready to speak. "Thank you. I accept. I'm staying with my partner tonight, so you may take me there. It's closer, anyway."

As they drove toward Hannah's home, the conversation became more personal.

"I take it you don't have a family yet?" Darren asked.

"I was married for a short time, but it didn't work out. Fortunately, we had no children, so we just ended it. How about you?"

"No. I've never been married. I'm still looking for the right girl. My friends say I'm too fussy, but I don't want to screw it up. I've seen too many people do that."

"Have you ever been close to getting married, besides trying to save Angela?"

"Once. The woman ended up marrying my best friend. After we broke up, they became closer. Three years later, they married.

Now they have four kids and are very happy."

"Four? That's a lot these days."

Darren laughed. Sharon thought even his laugh was beautiful. She had never met such a gorgeous man in her life, and, at the moment, he seemed totally natural—no pretense, bravado, or overblown ego. He was a regular guy with a little more self-assurance than most.

Can he be for real? she wondered. Is this just an act? He seems too good to be true. When you know it can't be so…. She stared out the window at the clear night with millions of stars that were hidden by the city lights.

"Someday," she said softly, "I want to live where I can see the stars at night."

He didn't reply.

"I want to live in a big house on ten acres of land with a small lake on the property, raise a couple horses, plant plenty of flowers, and have spare time to spend at home with someone to come home too."

"That's a wonderful dream. If you really want it, you can have it."

Sharon gave him a slightly embarrassed smile. "I'll have to win the lottery first. It'll never happen on a detective's salary."

They were silent for a while.

"Detective," Darren said, "despite all the uncertainty about how it was done, I think Gloria is somehow responsible for her mother's death, maybe Angela's too. I don't like the idea, but it seems right. I can't think of anyone else who had a reason to kill them or have them killed. I've thought about this a lot, and Gloria always comes out as my prime suspect.

"She was insanely jealous of Angela. Has anyone mentioned that? She hated her mother, too. Now she's the mistress of the Allen estate and stands to inherit millions of dollars and an enormous piece of property. I think that somehow, some way, she planned the whole thing."

"Whoa, Nelly! Where'd that come from? You've been waltzing around that all evening, haven't you, but you couldn't come out and say it, could you? What changed things?"

"I had to get it off my chest."

"We might have a tough time proving it, especially in Mariah's case, but I agree she's a likely suspect. To prove she killed her mother, we'd have to prove she left Detective Bell's home, went to her own home, caused her mother to choke to death or just happened to arrive as Mariah was choking and didn't help, then returned to Detective Bell's home."

Sharon stopped. There was a poignant silence.

Could that be possible? She wondered. Hannah was away for quite a while when she came to pick me up at the hospital, but Gloria had no car. I need to discuss this with Hannah.

She felt electrified, as if she'd discovered something. She noticed Darren looking at her intently while trying to drive.

"Where are you?" he asked.

"Just thinking."

"I don't know how she might have done it, but I still think she could have."

"If she did it, she's a very dangerous young woman."

"Yep."

"You follow directions very well, Darren. We're here. You can park in front of Hannah's garage."

Hannah and Gloria arrived at the Allen home. Instead of ringing the bell and waiting for Anna, Gloria took some keys from her bag, unlocked the door, and they stepped in.

I don't remember her having keys when we left, Hannah thought. Hmmm.

"Anna?" Gloria called.

Anna hurried into the foyer. "Oh, Miss Gloria!" She burst into tears, and it was clear she'd been crying before they arrived. "I'm so sorry. I can't believe it."

"It's all right, Anna. I'm here now. Everything will be fine."

"Anna, may I speak with you for a few minutes?" Hannah asked.

"Do you think that's a good idea?" Gloria asked. "She seems too upset to talk right now."

"Yes, Gloria, it's necessary to speak with her now." Hannah gave her a look to remind her who was in charge. "Why don't you check the rest of the staff? You can make sure they're OK while I talk with Anna."

"Oh, all right." Gloria walked off.

"Let's find a comfortable place where we can talk without being disturbed for a few minutes," Hannah said.

Anna led her toward the music library.

"Would it be all right if we talked in the main library?" Hannah asked. "I've seen it in passing and have been very curious about it."

"Miss Mariah doesn't like people in that room," Anna replied.

"She's not here, Anna."

Anna, remembering, cried again.

Hannah waited till she pulled herself together. A few moments later, Anna led the way to the main library. They entered the room, and Hannah saw it clearly for the first time. While not as large as Judge Quigley's library, it was still enormous. Hannah looked around to see if she could find the hidden door. She couldn't.

"Have a seat, please, Detective." Anna motioned toward two large, overstuffed, wing-backed chairs.

"Thank you." Hannah walked to one and sat down. "Anna, what happened here today?"

It took a few minutes for Anna to regain her composure, but Hannah was patient. It was a very difficult time for Anna, who must have wondered what would happen to her and the others.

Gloria's in charge now, Hannah thought. She'll take care of them if she can.

"I served Miss Mariah lunch, right at noon, in the garden room beside the pool. Then I left her alone, which is the custom. I noticed her still in the room sometime later. I thought that a bit unusual, but I was pleased to think she might be relaxing a bit, maybe even enjoying the flowers." Anna smiled hopefully.

The eternal optimist, Hannah thought, always hoping for improvement in another human being.

"I've known Mariah Ryan Allen all her life. It's like losing my own child. She was far from perfect, but she mattered a lot to me. She went through a lot in life. It seemed she could survive any adversity, perhaps not in the best way, but she still survived."

"What kinds of adversity?"

"She was the youngest child of seven in a very wealthy family. Her mother didn't want more children, so, when Mariah was born, she all but gave her away. She ignored Mariah most of the time. Her brothers and sisters were much older and either didn't have time for her or didn't want to make time.

"I took care of her and became almost her mother. She even called me Mama when she was little, which upset her mother," Anna said sadly. "She didn't want the child, but she wanted the honor of being called Mother. I had to break Mariah of that habit before I was fired. Then she would have had no one.

"Mariah was never a happy child, though she was a beautiful one. People stopped us in the grocery store just to look at her. I was warned not to turn my back on her, or she'd be gone. It seemed she learned to use her beauty early to get what she wanted. She grew up harsh and cold. I was probably the only person she ever truly loved, except for Jamie."

"Who was Jamie?"

"Jamie Allen, the older brother of Bernard, Mariah's husband. Mariah was crazy about Jamie, but Jamie loved her sister, Beth, but Beth loved Bernie. They were even engaged once, but Bernie really loved Mariah, who was just a child. It was all mixed up like a soap opera.

"Then, suddenly, Bernie and Mariah married. Shortly afterward, they left for England so Bernie could finish his medical studies there. Mariah was only seventeen and poorly prepared for life in the outside world."

"That sounds like the way she raised her girls, leaving them unprepared for life outside."

"Yes, unfortunately. I tried to tell her, but she didn't want to listen to anyone, even me."

"Why did Mariah marry Bernie?"

"Out of spite. In her twisted mind, she thought that would hurt Jamie and Beth. In Beth's case, it worked. Her heart was broken, and she never recovered or married. She killed herself when she was thirty-five. It was very sad."

"How did Mariah react to her sister's death?"

"She didn't, really. She said it was too bad, and that was it. She and Bernie were visiting in Europe at the time and didn't come home for the funeral."

"Were the Allens a happy couple?"

"As you might expect, there were problems. Mariah was very demanding. Bernie existed to serve her, although he seemed willing. She indulged the girls but didn't take any interest in teaching them anything, including manners. Again, I did most of that, though Mariah was more attentive to her girls than her mother had been to her.

"It was a terrible blow to the girls when they lost their father.

He was the joy in their lives. He was a good-natured man who loved them dearly. He taught them how to ride horses, how to fly fish, and how to sail. He also taught them how to handle money. He was good at everything he did and always told the girls they could do anything they wanted if they set their minds to it.

"All that ended when he died. Mariah wrapped the girls in a cocoon, and it's been like that ever since."

"Did Mariah have any friends?"

"Not really, even when she was a little girl. There were a few acquaintances, but nothing solid or lasting. The relationships she has now—had, I mean—were very superficial. Each one existed for a particular reason that would advance Mariah's purpose somehow. The people she was closest to in recent years were the men in the Wednesday-night group. She was closer to them than anyone, although they weren't really friends."

"Enemies?" Hannah saw Anna beginning to tire, and she didn't want to alienate her, because she needed her help. Anna might be the only link to the truth behind the Allen affair.

Anna gave a deep, melancholy sigh. "As you might suspect, she had enemies. Most of the people she dealt with disliked her intensely. She drove a harsh bargain in business and also used her money to threaten people.

"I've always felt that the reason the staff wasn't here for the Wednesday-night parties was because there was something going on they didn't want us to know about. It had to involve lots of money. I don't have any proof, but that's what I think."

"What goes on at those parties?"

"I have no idea, but there's something, and I doubt it's good. I have a bad feeling about the secrecy of the whole business, including how the parties always happened when the staff was away. Wouldn't you think that the staff would be needed for such occasions?"

"It would seem so."

"It's possible one of them might have killed Mariah for some reason."

Hannah had an uncomfortable thought. What if someone in the group thinks about how much Anna might know? Is she in danger? If so, how can I protect her without raising suspicion among the people who might wish to harm her?

Gloria entered the room. "Detective, you've talked with Anna long enough. She needs to rest now."

Hannah was amazed at how much Gloria suddenly resembled her mother. Even her countenance was the same. It was clear she'd taken over Mariah's role.

"I agree, Gloria," Hannah said. "How is the rest of the staff? Are they OK?"

"Yes. Quite. I won't be returning with you tonight. The staff needs me to be here, and I have to start making arrangements for my mother's funeral."

Hannah wasn't surprised. She'd felt that coming on the ride to the house. "Please be careful, Gloria. You may not be safe here."

"I'm not worried," Gloria said confidently. "No one here now would hurt me." She turned and put an arm around Anna. "We'll be fine, won't we, Anna?"

She's on stage and is the star now, Hannah thought. Lord, help us. "I'll call tomorrow to see if everything is all right. Can you handle your sister's and your mother's arrangements by yourself?"

"Yes. Anna can tell me what's been done for Angela, and I'll take it from here for Mother. I might delay Angela's service so we can do them together. I'll think about it. I'll send someone around tomorrow for my things. I enjoyed our time together, Detective." For a moment, Gloria showed genuine pleasure and affection.

"So did I. I'll be out most of tomorrow, but someone can come around in the evening. Call first to make sure I'm home. Take care of yourselves."

"We will," Gloria replied.

On the way home, Hannah wondered about the future of the Allen household. The head of the house was gone, and the only one left to run it was a bit unstable. I hope they all live through the night, she thought.

Then she saw the car parked in front of her garage. "What the...? Oh, I get it. That's a message from Sharon that we have company—Mr. Darren Brannigan, I suspect."

CHAPTER ELEVEN

"Welcome home, Detective," Sharon said, opening the door for her friend.

"Thank you so much," Hannah replied with exaggerated courtesy.

"We have a guest," Sharon whispered.

"I noticed. Thanks for the warning. How long has he been here?"

"We arrived five minutes ago. I had him park in your driveway to let you know someone was here. I knew you'd figure out who it was."

"Sharon, this is a little dangerous. What if he's the murderer? Now he knows where I live."

"I don't think he's the murderer."

"A lot of people didn't believe Ted Bundy was a murderer, either."

"You're moving out of here pretty soon, anyway."

"It'll be at least six months before my condo is ready, my dear. I could be dead by then. You're taking a pretty cavalier approach to my safety."

"Hannah, I really don't think he's the killer. He's probably mixed up in the Irish business. I can't see any way out of that, but I sincerely doubt he's the murderer. You can determine that for yourself. We'd better return to the living room. We mustn't be rude to our guest by leaving him sitting in there alone."

They walked from the small foyer to where Darren sat looking at a current copy of People magazine. Princess Di was on the cover – again.

As they approached, Darren rose to greet them, extending his hand to Hannah. "It's nice to see you again, Detective." He looked behind her. "Where's your charge?"

"She stayed behind at the estate."

"Is that a good idea?"

"I'm not sure, but she's an adult. Unless I arrest her, she can stay where she wants. Right now, she wants to be home." She turned to Sharon. "Her mother's dead. We have to regroup. I learned a lot last night and today. We've made some progress."

Sharon nodded.

Darren, staring intently at Hannah, seemed transfixed. After a moment, he said, "You're much taller than I would have thought from our meeting last night, but then, you were sitting down. I'm impressed that for such a tall woman, you stand so straight. It's very becoming."

Not knowing how to respond to such a blunt compliment, Hannah knew what would happen—the dreaded blush. Blood rushed up her neck onto her cheeks and continued toward the top of her head. She wanted to run, but where?

"Thank you, Mr. Brannigan," she said as calmly as she could.

He looked at her without expression. "Please call me Darren."

"All right. Please have a seat, Darren."

Darren sat back down on the couch, and Hannah sat opposite him in a chair. Sharon sat at the other end of the couch from their guest, placing her leg with the cast on cushions and looking at Hannah with a Cheshire-cat grin.

"Are you aware, Darren, of Gloria Allen's intense feelings for you?" Hannah asked professionally, then wondered why she'd asked.

"I'm aware of her attraction for me, but, as I told Detective Walker, I doubt it's anything more than an infatuation. I doubt Gloria can feel genuine affection for anyone."

"That's a pretty strong statement, Mr...Darren."

"It comes from observing her for a long period of time. I certainly have no feelings for her other than those of an interested friend of the family. The Allen women are...were.... Gosh. There's only one left, isn't there? Anyway, Detective Walker can fill you in on our conversation regarding Gloria."

"I'd like to see your studio, Darren," Hannah said, wondering why she asked or where she would go with the information.

"Anytime. How about Monday? I'll be there all day, except for Angela's memorial service."

"That might be postponed," Hannah said. "Gloria may want to have her sister's and her mother's services combined. At least, that's what she said this evening."

"That seems reasonable." Darren nodded. "That means Monday is entirely open. How about letting me paint you?"

Sharon suddenly lurched forward, choking and clutching her chest. She writhed in apparent agony for a few seconds before regaining her composure.

Hannah and Darren were instantly at her side to offer aid. As they rushed toward Sharon, they collided. In the next second, Darren grabbed for Hannah to keep her from falling, then lost his own balance. Both ended up on the floor in a heap.

By then, the not-so-stricken detective was laughing and pointing at them, rocking on the couch, her broken leg still propped on its cushions. "You two make quite a picture there on the floor. I wish I had a camera."

Hannah was furious but took great pains to conceal it. "What in the world was that all about, Sharon?" She calmly collected herself and got up off the floor with Darren's help, who was already standing.

"A piece of candy was caught in my throat.""Oh, really? Where'd you get it?"

"From the dish." She pointed to an empty candy dish on the end table. "I guess it was the last piece."

"Uh-huh." Hannah turned toward her guest. "I'm sorry, Darren. Are you OK?"

"I'm fine. I'd better leave now. Detective Walker needs her rest," he said with obviously feigned concern. "She's had a rough couple of days. Her injuries are beginning to take their toll."

"I might take my own toll," Hannah muttered.

Turning to Hannah, he handed her a card. "I look forward to seeing you on Monday. If you come at noon, I'll have more time to talk, because there won't be any clients. Perhaps you'd like to have lunch with me?"

"Thanks. I'll plan on it."

"Good."

Darren said good-bye and left. Hannah counted to ten after closing the door, then she darted into the living room where Sharon was still sitting. Hannah put her hands around her friend's neck and started squeezing.

"OK, OK! I get the message!" Sharon pulled away from Hannah's grasp.

"You can be so annoying!" Hannah shouted. "What's the matter with you?"

"Hannah, he barely took his eyes off you the whole time he was here after you arrived. I spent almost two hours with him at his house, in his car, and here, and he never looked at me like that. How often do you suppose he asks to paint someone?"

"I have no idea."

"Never. He told me so. He made a point of it, adding that people asked him, not the other way around. He likes you, Hannah!"

"So what? Why do you have to act like such a child? That was humiliating!"

"I'm sorry. I couldn't help it. It was so obvious. I couldn't believe it when he asked to paint you." Her tone became more serious. "He's beautiful, and he's a perfect gentleman. The whole time I interviewed him, he was polite and cooperative.

"He was very forthright in his answers. He thinks Gloria was responsible for Mariah's death, and, possibly, Angela's. He talked around it at first, then he made it a bold statement and let it drop. He's certain that Gloria is involved somehow."

"And he calls himself a family friend?"

"Even a family friend can see the trees in the forest. Besides, his real feelings were for Angela."

"What do you mean?" Hannah asked quickly.

"Oh? Is the ice block melting a bit?"

"Knock it off." Hannah tried to sound tough. "You're already in trouble."

"He wasn't in love with Angela, at least not that way. He said so. He added that he considered proposing to her just to get her out of that house and away from her mother."

"Pity isn't a very good reason to marry someone, but it's certainly noble."

"He said Gloria was insanely jealous of Angela, but he also said he thought Angela was the one person Gloria cared for."

"He sounds just as mystified as the rest of us about those three women. I'm getting a search warrant in the morning. Oh. Tomorrow's Sunday. I'll have to get a judge out of bed or, more likely, off the golf course.

"We need a closer look at that house. Maybe we'll find something a disturbed young woman might use to kill her sister, and, possibly, her mother. Besides, I want to see that secret passage."

"What about Immigration's investigation?"

"I'll check with Rob first. I'm sure he'll agree. We'll be careful not to raise suspicions about the Irish thing. We'll concentrate on the two deaths.

"We'll need to keep a close eye on Gloria, but I doubt we have to worry about the staff. Nevertheless, let's be cautious around them, too. They might even help. I hope to catch a glimpse of Mandy and see how she's doing."

Hannah thought hard for a few minutes. "What if Darren and Gloria planned the whole thing? What if they were in love and decided to get rid of Angela and Mariah so they could have each other and all that money?"

"So why would Darren accuse Gloria of murder?"

"Part of the cover. Essentially, he says he doesn't like her and accuses her of being responsible for her mother's death, maybe even her sister's. That helps cover up their love affair. He vacillates a little so he won't appear too eager to condemn her, but he leads us to thinking she did it. She, however, gives the impression that she's infatuated with a man who seems beyond her reach."

"Where does it say he's beyond her reach? Seems to me Gloria believes she can have anything she wants."

"I don't think so. Not with men, anyway. She acts awkward around him, like a silly schoolgirl, knowing all the while everyone knows guys like him wouldn't be attracted to her."

Hannah paused to allow her partner to comment, but Sharon didn't speak.

"Have you seen the movie Malice?" Hannah asked.

"With Alec Baldwin and Nicole Kidman? Yeah. That was one grotesque story."

"When did it hit you that there was something really evil going on in that movie?"

Sharon pondered the question. "When Bill Pullman—Andy—

found out his wife's mother wasn't dead as he'd been told. Then he visits Mama, and she gives him an earful about what her daughter is really like. That makes the first connection with the doctor."

"I was dumbfounded. I had no idea the story would go in that direction. It was downhill all the way for me after that, a ride to hell."

"Tracy seemed so sweet, wanting children and all."

"That's the point. Tracy wasn't what she seemed to be."

"It was only a movie."

"Movie, my foot. There's nothing stranger than real life. Movies can't compare to what people really do. Somewhere in this world is a person like Tracy, probably several.

"That movie really got to me," Hannah continued. "I still think about it. The evil characters were so good at their craft, especially Tracy. The doctor at least had a line he wouldn't cross, but not her. She was 100% evil, and a completely different person than the public image she gave, especially to her husband. Can you imagine what he must have felt when he realized how depraved his wife was and how cruelly he'd been duped?

"Evil people pull off their depraved stuff, because the rest of us are incapable of thinking like they do. We don't have the mind for it. The closest we come is an occasional thought of how we'll pay someone back for a real or imagined wrong. That's usually the end of it. Most of the time, we can't even carry out a well-deserved payback.

"There are times, as a cop, I'd like to bash in some guy's head, and he probably deserves it. The world would be better off without him, but I can't do it."

"We both know cops who can."

"Yes, we do," Hannah said. "They walk a narrow line between good and evil."

They were silent awhile.

"What do you think?" Hannah asked. "Is it possible that Brannigan and Gloria planned this?"

"They could have, but it seems pretty far-fetched."

"Let's take a look at where we stand right now. Angela and Mariah are dead with no proof of foul play so far. If Brannigan or Gloria killed or arranged the deaths, they probably have gotten away with it.

"Gloria is now in the house. I wonder if she was planning to kill her mother or have her killed while she was buying all those clothes yesterday? That's her coming-out wardrobe in a way.

"Now they just need to let time pass. After Angela and Mariah are buried, Brannigan can court Gloria, which would be natural for a friend of the family. In a while, they marry. The deed is done, and they live the good life on Mariah's money."

"You really don't want to like him, do you?" Sharon asked.

"What?"

"You're trying awfully hard to make him into a bad guy."

Hannah looked away.

"We're just assuming Gloria is the beneficiary, right? What if it turns out Mariah didn't leave her money to Gloria? What if it went to an institution or something else? According to Darren, she threatened to do that more than once."

"That would make it a whole different story." Hannah sighed, then took a deep breath. "Let's get off this case for a while and think about something else."

"How about a video? We need something to make us laugh."

"OK. I have quite a collection."

"Have you got *Caddyshack*?"

CHAPTER TWELVE

Hannah intended to take the whole day off so she could spend more time with her parents. Instead, she found herself, search warrant in hand, at the Allen estate.

"What's this all about, Detective?" Gloria asked curtly. "This is Sunday." She greeted the group in the entryway as Anna let them in.

Hannah was astonished at the change in Gloria. It's incredible, she thought.

It was like looking at a redheaded, brown-eyed Mariah. Gloria was dressed to the nines. She stood before her guests exactly as Mariah once stood, and she looked much older and definitely in charge. Her voice was a little gentler, so she didn't sound as cold as her mother, and she appeared less hostile.

Maybe our relationship, whatever it is, affected her positively, Hannah thought. I hope so.

"Are you on your way to church?" Sharon asked.

"No."

"So our being here shouldn't inconvenience you," Sharon said with an edge to her voice.

"We need to search the house, Gloria," Hannah said, handing her the warrant. "There are some things we need to look for. Perhaps you can help."

"Perhaps I can." Gloria seemed confident in her new role. "Where would you like to begin?"

"The officers have their assignments and know where to go. How many bathrooms in the house?"

"Six full baths and two half baths."

"Do they all have storage areas?"

"Yes."

"Let's begin with your bathroom. I assume that's off your bedroom, correct? Does each bedroom have a private bath?"

"Yes to both questions," Gloria said coolly.

"Six bedrooms, then?"

"Yes."

Hannah turned to Anna. "Detective Walker will accompany you to the kitchen." She turned back to Gloria and told her where the other officers were headed and that she expected everyone's full cooperation. She nodded to the others, and they walked off to their assignments.

"Gloria, where's Mandy today?" Hannah asked.

"She's at church right now. It's St. Luke's, just a couple blocks away. She walks."

"When do you expect her back?"

"Shortly after eleven. Services are from ten to eleven."

"I want to speak with her when she returns."

"Certainly."

"Shall we begin?"

The two women walked toward the stairs.

As Anna and Sharon walked toward the kitchen, Anna became slightly agitated, which seemed out of character, but then, a lot had happened since Sharon first met the woman.

"Are you all right?" Sharon asked.

"I'm worried."

"About what?"

"I don't know. That's just it. Something very wrong is going on in this house. First Angela dies, then Mariah. People are talking about murder, and Gloria has taken over the whole household. I guess that's to be expected, but, the way she's been acting, it seems like she's been preparing for it for some time."

"We've been wondering the same thing."

"I don't like to think what that might mean."

"Anna, we're having a hard time proving Angela was murdered, even though we believe that's what happened. Gloria is our prime suspect, only because she was the last to see her sister alive. Mariah was also high on the list, but she's gone now. If it turns out she killed Angela, she has paid the price. We need proof to support our theories before we can arrest anyone. If you can help us, please do."

Anna didn't answer.

"Are you afraid of Gloria?"

"No. I'm more worried about her than frightened of her. I'm afraid she'll turn into another Mariah. We don't need any more of that around here. She ran an efficient household, which was good, but she was very difficult to deal with even for those who loved her."

"I'll let you in on a little secret," Sharon said. "Maybe this will trigger your memory. One of our forensic specialists believes Angela was poisoned by being pricked on the bottom of her foot with a poisoned needle. The poison used can't be detected through normal testing. It takes a special series of tests, but we need to know what to look for in order to test for it. Do you know of any poisons in the house or on the grounds?"

"Well, the gardener has some poisons to keep pests off the property and to kill weeds."

They reached the huge kitchen, a room big enough to hold a small apartment.

"Where's the pantry, Anna?" Sharon asked. "I'd like to start there. We need to remove everything from the shelves. It's a good time to take inventory, eh?"

She took a large notepad from her bag and followed Anna to the pantry. "I'll be a bit clumsy with this cast, but together, we'll be done in an hour or so. If you have to answer the door, go ahead. I'll keep working."

The very large pantry had enough dry goods to last a long time. Everything was in perfect order, making their job easier.

"This is very well organized, Anna," Sharon said. "Is that your doing?"

"Yes, Ma'am."

It took over an hour to complete the pantry inventory, but they found nothing unusual. There were a handful of household poisons in a box on the near-top shelf, well away from foodstuffs.

"Where are the refrigerator and freezer?" Sharon asked.

"This way." Anna walked to the other side of the room to a mammoth, double-door refrigerator that occupied an entire wall.

"We'd better look in there. Does anyone else use the kitchen besides you? Do the Allen women ever come in here?"

"Mariah did quite often. She always made sure the kitchen was in top shape, and she knew where everything was."

Sharon opened one of the refrigerator doors and scrutinized the contents. She started with a section that held a miscellaneous collection of items, like most refrigerator doors. Then she noticed a small plastic bag tucked behind several bottles of salad dressing. One corner of the bag stuck out between two bottles.

"What's this?" Sharon pulled out the bag.

"I don't recognize it," Anna said.

"It's not marked." She looked at the bag carefully. "There's a small vial with some liquid in it. I'd better take this with me and determine what it is." She reached into her bag and took out a miniature ice bag, dropping the vial inside.

Anna laughed. "I wonder what all you've got in that bag, Detective. Next thing I know, you'll pull out a grocery cart."

Sharon smiled and took a contraption out of her bag made of collapsed metal rods with small wheels attached. When she pulled the pieces a certain way, she suddenly had a portable cart.

Anna was astonished. "Modern technology! It's beyond me." She shook her head and chuckled.

"It's made of a very lightweight alloy and can carry up to fifty pounds. They're standard equipment these days when we carry out a search. Every officer has one in his bag."

"Each officer has his bag of tricks," Anna quipped.

They finished with the refrigerator/freezer and returned to the foyer. When they arrived, they found a small group waiting in the library off the foyer and joined them.

It was almost eleven-thirty, and the search had been underway for two hours. All the others in the team were waiting—Hubbard, Barhydt, Dolan, Hansen, Rader, Hannah, and now Sharon and Anna. Gloria and Mandy were there, too.

Only a few items had been confiscated so far, but the five auxiliary officers were preparing to search additional areas of the house and estate.

Hannah explained to a very unhappy Gloria that all items would be returned as soon as possible, and some of the officers would remain until the search was finished. More items might be temporarily confiscated.

"This is robbery," Gloria said.

"We'll take very good care of them, Gloria. You'll have all of them back within twenty-four hours unless there's something we need to examine further or hold as evidence."

"Evidence? Of what?"

"You know what, Gloria."

"You'll never be able to prove anything, Detective. My sister died of natural causes, and my mother choked to death. That's all there is to it."

Hannah wondered if Gloria had just admitted her guilt. "We'll see."

Hannah turned to Mandy. "Would you walk in the garden with me for a couple of minutes?"

Mandy nodded nervously and left with Hannah.

"How are you doing?" Hannah asked. "You seem less frightened than the last time I saw you."

"Not really. I'm just getting better at hiding it. This house is a scary place. I've been here only a few months, and two people die within one week. If it weren't for Anna, I'd be out of my mind, and even she's beginning to crack. I sure would like to get away from here."

"Is there anyplace you can go, perhaps relatives or friends?"

"No. I have no one here. Besides, I'm not allowed to leave the premises alone. They'd never let me go. Someone even goes to church with me."

Hannah shook her head. "How'd you come here?"

"I was brought."

"By whom?"

"My mother received a letter saying there was work in this country for me, and my passage would be free. It seemed like a dream come true. I was very eager to come, although I was sad to leave my family.

"I took a ship, a plane, and then I arrived in Chicago. We were picked up at the airport and taken someplace. We had to put on blindfolds when we got into the van. That was the first time I was scared. I didn't know why they asked us to do that.

"We were in the van a long time, or so it seemed. When we stopped and got out, we were led through a tunnel. I could tell, because it was cold and very dark. Then we entered a room through a heavy door. I sensed it was a big room, and there were other people there, but only one spoke.

"I heard paper shuffling. I was scared and wanted to cry, but I didn't. We were handed envelopes and taken away in the van again. They said the blindfolds and secrecy had something to do with our safety. They must have thought we were stupid. I wasn't so sure I wanted to be in America anymore." A tear ran down her cheek.

When she continued, her voice sank to a whisper. "I think we were here. It feels like it. When I told Anna that, she made me shut up and told me not to mention it again. That made me certain we were here.

"That was when they told us we owed them money for our passage and expenses, and payment would come from our wages. The letter originally said passage was free and never mentioned expenses."

Mandy's voice rose. "Detective, they said we owed them $20,000 apiece! I'll never be able to repay that with what I make here, and I don't want to spend the rest of my life in this awful place." She shivered.

"It's all right, Mandy. We'll fix it. Your papers are fake?"

Mandy winced. "I…I guess they must be."

"How'd you get them?"

"They were in the envelope. They also took our fingerprints. I felt like a criminal."

"Who brought you to this house to begin your job?"

"A man. I hadn't seen him before or heard his voice, and I haven't seen him since."

"What did he look like?"

"He was short and thin, bald and probably in his fifties. He was very quiet and said less than ten words to me on the way."

"Do you know where any of the others who were with you are

now?"

"No. I wish I did. I'd like to talk to someone. I wonder if any of them are as scared and disappointed as I am."

"I'm sure they are. I hope you won't judge all Americans by those people."

"If most Americans are like you, then I know there are good people here." She smiled.

Hannah put her arm gently around Mandy's shoulders. "To your knowledge, have you had any contact with any of the people in that room since you've been in this house? I know you couldn't see anyone, but you said one person spoke."

"Oh, yes. I recognized his voice and his smell. People have their own scent, you know. When you're blindfolded, you can smell better." She smiled. "He's been here a couple of times to see Mrs. Allen. When I told her I recognized his voice, she became angry and said if I wanted to keep a roof over my head, I would never mention it again to anyone, and I was never to speak to the gentleman. That's what she called him, but I have another name for him!"

She shook her head. "She also told me not to speak so much American English. I thought she'd be pleased with how quickly I learned it, but she wasn't. She said British high English has more class and less slang. She didn't like slang. She…."

"Mandy, can you describe the gentleman for me?"

"Oh, yes. He's a very big man, tall and heavy with lots of white hair that he combs across his head to cover a bald spot. He also combs it over the tops of his ears. It looks very strange. His face is bright red, his eyes are blue, and, for a man, his voice is too high."

Sounds like the judge, Hannah thought, remembering that he combed hair over the tops of his ears. She'd heard he lost part of an ear in a brawl years earlier. He also tried to hide his bald spot.

So Mandy can identify the judge? This is very good. I have to keep her safe. Hannah felt excitement rising in her.

"What do you think happened to Angela?"

With some hesitation, Mandy said, "I think…I think she might have killed herself. I know that's a terrible thing to say, and it's against God's law, but she was the saddest person I ever met. I don't know what made her that way. I never saw her smile. Her mother was cold and distant, but it was more than that with Miss Angela. She was sooo sad."

She looked at Hannah with longing in her eyes. "My own mother doesn't show her feelings much. That's the way of Irish women. Their lives are hard. I think the men cry more than the women, but that doesn't mean she doesn't love us. It just means that's the way she is. We were poor but happy growing up. It's easier to be happy than sad. Something else made Miss Angela so unhappy. I just keep wondering who'll be next. I'd really like to get out of here."

"There's one way you can."

When Mandy and Hannah reached the main library, the only people still there were Sharon and Gloria. When they saw the two walk in, Gloria gasped, while Sharon merely raised her eyebrows.

Mandy was in handcuffs.

"What's the meaning of this?" Gloria demanded furiously.

"I've arrested Mandy for the murder of Angela Allen," Hannah announced. "She confessed."

After checking in at the precinct, Hannah spent some time with Mandy to assure her she'd be well treated. Hannah asked the duty officer to check on Mandy regularly to see that she was all right.

Hannah set up an appointment to interview Mandy with Lieutenant Keys present in the morning. They'd work out a way to keep Mandy safely locked up for a few days. The fact that she could identify a major player in the smuggling ring would allow them to keep her in protective custody for a while. During that time, they might learn more.

We're getting there, Hannah thought, dialing her parents' home. She told them she was running late but would be there within ninety minutes if all went well. Hannah's visits meant a lot to her parents. She was all they had, and they loved her dearly.

They were also very proud of her, though neither had been happy when she first announced she wanted to go into police work, especially her mother. "Women shouldn't be police officers," she said. She had a host of reasons, from women not being strong enough physically to them being too emotional in stressful situations. Eventually, they accepted her decision, though it wouldn't have mattered. As Hannah told them, she'd heard the call, and nothing would change her mind.

Mr. and Mrs. Bell had lived in Waukegan, Illinois, forty miles north of Chicago, for thirty-five years, ever since Hannah and her twin sister, Heather, were one year old. Her father ran a small, successful corner drugstore. The family wasn't wealthy, but they were comfortable.

Hannah's parents wanted her to work for the Waukegan Police Department, because they felt that would be safer, but, as Hannah explained, she wasn't looking for safety. She wanted to work where she felt she could do the most good and affect the most people. Also, Hannah wanted the excitement of a big city. Waukegan was a very stable community, and Hannah didn't feel it would provide enough of a challenge.

"Stable communities need good officers, too," her mother said. "Why do you think we're so stable? It's because we not only have good people, we have a good police department."

Hannah couldn't argue with that, but she wanted more, so she headed for Chicago and big-city life. She enjoyed all the city had to offer—its culture, frenetic pace, and people. She visited museums, operas, and even joined a civic theater group, but eventually, her work took over her life, and her parents became concerned.

"Hannah, there's more to life than being a policewoman," her father said. "You would make a wonderful wife and mother, too."

Just the previous week, her father added, "You need to think of your later years. At the rate you're going, you'll spend them alone. Is that what you want?"

"Of course not, Dad, but I'm happy with what I'm doing right now. I'll settle down eventually."

Her father returned to the newspaper he'd been reading. He didn't talk very much, having never recovered from the loss of his daughter, Heather. The fact that she was never found was hard on the entire family, but it was particularly hard on him. For some reason, he blamed himself, but Hannah and her mother never understood why. The situation saddened them greatly.

Freeman Bell was a good man, a kind and loving husband and father. He deserved the happy life he worked so hard to provide for his family, yet he suffered excruciating emotional pain for over twenty-five years—pain he wasn't able to overcome or share.

Hannah's mother coped better, but then, she was an extraordinarily strong woman, emotionally. With a name like George, she had to be.

Lena Cusick Bell's given name was George Alena Cusick, but everyone called her Lena. Her father already had three sons when she was born, but, since he wanted another, he gave his new daughter a boy's name. Along with everything else in life, Lena took that in stride.

She had certainly suffered many painful losses over her lifetime, not the least of which was the death of her older brother when she was twelve. John was nineteen and confined to a wheelchair from the results of polio, but he died of pneumonia. Lena's mother and sister became ill simultaneously, shortly after John's death and almost died, too. Lena had to take on the responsibility for running the household.

In those days, fathers rarely took on household responsibilities but let them fall onto the remaining female no matter how young or capable she was. Lena's mother and sister lived, but Lena remained the family's caretaker until she married and left home. Even then, she was its bulwark, the strong one everyone turned to in time of trouble.

CHAPTER THIRTEEN

Just as Hannah left the precinct, the duty officer called, "Detective? You might want to see this." She waved a piece of paper.

Hannah, who wanted to ignore it, couldn't. "OK, Sergeant. I'll be right there."

When she reached her desk, Hannah saw the sergeant wore a rather odd expression.

"Hannah, why don't you sit down?" She spoke with enough firmness to make Hannah obey without question.

The sergeant handed her the paper. It was a universal police wire from the Harbor Springs, Michigan, Police Department.

Remains of a young female found in makeshift grave alongside M119 north of Harbor Springs, Michigan, at 4:00 PM Saturday. A preliminary exam determines the remains to be of a young girl between the ages of 10 and 12. The estimate for the time the remains have been buried is 20-25 years. DNA tests will be conducted to determine the victim's identity and age. Some clothing material is still intact. It also appears that bones from a small animal were in the same grave. Those remains are also being studied.

Hannah, turning pale, stared at the piece of paper, feeling hope and terror well within her. Could this be Heather at last? she wondered.

When she could finally speak, she repeated, "Oh, my God," several times.

The duty officer, Sergeant Linda Wilson, gave her time to absorb the impact of what she'd just read, then asked, "Isn't that near the area where your sister disappeared?"

"Yes," Hannah choked out, barely able to breathe, move, or speak.

Sergeant Wilson walked to the water cooler and brought back a cup of water for Hannah.

The long-awaited, terrible day has come, Hannah thought, reaching for the cup without being aware of it. I have to tell Mom and Dad. Can I handle this? Oh, Heather....

She began to cry. "Heather, Heather, Heather," she said through her tears. "I didn't want it to turn out this way. No. No. No."

The years of pain and waiting completely overcame her, and she convulsed in tears. Sergeant Wilson gently took Hannah's arm, made her stand, and led her to a couch in the officer's lounge. She sat Hannah down, fluffed up some pillows, and laid the grief-stricken woman against them before covering her with the afghan hanging over the back of the couch.

Hannah didn't protest or say a word. She was incapable of independent movement, her mind in turmoil.

Two officers in the lounge watched in wonder without speaking. Sergeant Wilson's eyes told the story. They all knew about Heather Bell's disappearance and were on the lookout for any information regarding her.

"I have to get back to my desk," Wilson told the others. "Keep an eye on her, will you? Don't leave her alone. Either call me or find another officer to sit with her until she pulls herself together."

Somewhere through the fog clouding Hannah's mind, she heard the officers' voices, but she couldn't understand their words. The voices were simultaneously loud, soft, and strangely distorted, and that frightened her.

Still, she couldn't move. She drifted into deeper mindlessness, a kind of waking sleep, and dreamed of her sister.

"Gotcha last!" Heather shouted, tagging her sister on the way out the front door.

"I'll get you!" Hannah shouted through the closed door. "You just wait."

They loved spending their summers in northern Michigan. It was beautiful at their cottage in Bay View, a summer music school set on the terraced slopes of Little Traverse Bay. Bay View was settled in the 1870s by a group of spiritual leaders and their followers who wanted to escape the intolerable heat of Chicago, southern Michigan, Indiana, and Ohio. They also sought a more Godlike setting in which to worship.

The Bay View Association was made up of late nineteenth century cottages surrounding a central campus that included a huge auditorium, college and faculty dorms, and buildings with classrooms and rehearsal halls for the faculty and students. Summers there were idyllic, and the girls never wanted to return home when it was time.

Since both girls were musical, they especially enjoyed the Sunday night vesper concerts in the John M. Hall auditorium. Those concerts were originally religious in nature, but became more secular over the years. However, the high quality of music and the professionalism of the musicians attracted people from across the country to that little slice of paradise for eight weeks each summer.

The girls were on their way to the beach to meet their friends and swim in the refreshing, frigid bay water. As usual, Heather ran ahead of Hannah to get a head start. Even at eleven, Hannah was fast—faster than kids two or three years her senior. Hannah wanted to participate in track in high school, so she prepared herself early.

Hannah didn't take long to catch up to her little sister, as she called her. Being three minutes older, she felt that gave her the right.

"OK, Little Sister, I've got you!" She grabbed the strap of Heather's tank top and stopped her cold.

"I'm not your little sister! We're twins, remember?"

"Must I always remind you which of us is older?" Hannah assumed an exalted air.

"Every day!" Heather stuck out her tongue.

"You know Mom doesn't like that."

"So what? She's not here to see it." She stuck out her tongue even farther.

Hannah grabbed the tongue and yanked.

"Ow!" Heather hit Hannah's stomach as hard as she could.

Hannah released the tongue and held onto her stomach. "You're such a brat."

"Takes one to know one."

With an exasperated shrug, Hannah walked toward the beach. She did her best to ignore her pesky sister, although, with Heather tagging her and yelling, "Gotcha last!" it was difficult.

The two girls were very different. Heather was a bundle of energy, silly and very verbal. Hannah had plenty of energy but was much quieter, more thoughtful, and, according to Hannah, more mature. She loved to read, ponder things, sing, and run. She ran everywhere.

At the moment, she wanted to run away from Heather but couldn't. Their mother admonished them to stay together.

"It's called the buddy system, Girls," she said. "Stay together and make sure you always know where the other one is."

At the moment, Hannah wanted to lose her sister, but she knew it wouldn't be worth the effort. Heather was like a shadow, always hanging around.

"What time will Laine get here?" Heather asked.

"Mom said around seven o'clock."

"Will she bring her puppy?"

"No. Muppet will stay home with Laine's grandparents."

"Darn." Heather pouted, something she was very good at. "I love Muppet. She's so cute."

"It's hard to travel with a dog, Heather," Hannah replied matter-of-factly.

"I guess."

They walked to the beach and swam with their friends for a couple of hours. Then it was time to go home for supper and wait for company to arrive.

They certainly arrived on time, too. Laine's dad was a stickler for being somewhere when he said he would. If he said seven o'clock, that was exactly when he arrived.

They spent a fun-filled evening together, going to the movie at the auditorium and then to Juilleret's in Harbor Springs for ice cream. They talked about the picnic they'd have at Burt Lake the following day, where they'd visit Freeman Bell's army buddy, Gus Wilkins, and his family at their cottage.

The two men served together in Germany during the Vietnam conflict before it became a full-fledged war. They had different personalities and backgrounds, though, and would never have become friends in the regular world. The shared experiences of Army life and the loss of mutual friends in a distant land gave them common ground. They made an effort to see each other at least once a year in northern Michigan.

Gus and his wife, Micky, had no children, but they had two cats and a dog. The girls were crazy about the animals, especially

Bess, the long-haired dachshund. Bess thought she was a human princess, and the girls were happy to oblige. Every summer, they dressed Bess up in an old white summer slipdress Micky gave them and a crown made from construction paper and tin foil. Heather particularly loved that dog.

The day was all they expected. Burt Lake was a typical northern Michigan lake—clean, clear, and uncrowded. They swam, water skied, played volleyball and badminton, and grilled hamburgers. Gus played guitar while everyone sang songs. Gus even let Heather play the guitar.

"Someday, I want to play the guitar," she said.

"Then you will."

They laughed at his comment, because they all knew Heather's dogged determination to do whatever she decided. If she wanted to learn the guitar, she would. No one doubted her.

The Bell party returned to the cottage at midnight. Feeling tired, they went to bed and agreed to sleep in the following day.

Laine and Hannah were to sleep in the girls' room, while Heather slept in the little bedroom at the top of the back stairs that their father usually used for short afternoon naps. It was cool and comfortable, and the girls felt very grown up when allowed to sleep there. Laine's parents slept in the guestroom that faced the lake with windows across the front. That was their favorite room in the house.

No one rose before nine o'clock the following morning. The adults had coffee and talked on the front porch while letting the girls sleep in. At ten o'clock, Hannah and Laine came downstairs.

"Where's Heather?" her mother asked.

"She must still be asleep," Laine said.

"Lazy bones," Hannah teased.

"Then leave her alone," her mother said. "She'll be up soon

enough."

An hour later, Hannah's mother told her and Laine to rouse Heather. "This is very unlike her," she said. "She's usually the first one up. I hope she's not ill or anything."

Hannah and Laine, climbing the back stairs, entered the bedroom only to find Heather absent.

"Heather?" Hannah called. "Come on. Quit hiding."

There was no answer.

"Where could she be?" Laine asked.

"Let's check the other bedrooms. She probably heard Mom tell us to come get her, so she's hiding someplace."

They checked all the bedrooms and bathrooms, but there was no trace of Heather. They returned to the kitchen.

"We can't find her, Mom," Hannah said. "Did she come downstairs?"

"No. She's not here."

"She wouldn't have gotten up early and gone somewhere, would she?" Mrs. Yahr, Laine's mother, asked.

"You never know with Heather," Hannah said, frowning. "Still, it's not like her to do that without telling me." She started worrying. Her stomach was queasy, and her hands trembled as she took a banana from the fruit bowl on the table. She put the banana back, not really wanting it.

"Mom, where do you think she is?" Hannah asked.

"I don't know, Honey, but don't worry. She's around somewhere. Go ask your dad and Mr. Yahr if they've seen her."

The girls ran to find their fathers.

"Dad?" they asked in unison, seeing both fathers on the front porch, looking at the bay.

"Yes?" the two men replied.

"Have you seen Heather?" Hannah asked.

"She's not in her bed or anywhere else in the house," Laine

added.

"She's around somewhere," Mr. Bell said. "She's probably hiding from you two. Did you check the basement?"

"No!" Hannah said loudly. "I didn't think of that. I'll bet that's where she is."

As Hannah and Laine walked back toward the kitchen and the basement steps, Hannah said, "I'll crown her when I find her for scaring us like this."

The fathers smiled while watching the girls go.

"It starts young, doesn't it?" Mr. Yahr asked.

"What starts young, Gene?"

"Trying to understand women."

"Yeah, it sure does."

Hannah and Laine scampered down the basement steps, shouting, "Heather? Come on out! We know you're down here."

There was no reply.

"Heather," Hannah said impatiently, "we're getting tired of this. Come on. We're going to Five Mile Point, and we have to leave without you in a minute." She turned to Laine and whispered, "That'll get her for sure. She wouldn't miss Five Mile Point for anything."

After a few moments' silence, however, Hannah called upstairs, "Mom? She's not down here, either."

"She has to be somewhere." Mrs. Bell tried to hide her rising concern.

"No, she isn't," Hannah whined. "I have a bad feeling, Mom." She paused, then blurted, "Someone kidnapped her." She clapped a hand over her mouth when she realized what she'd just said.

"Is that wishful thinking?" Mrs. Bell teased.

"I'm serious, Mom." Fear showed on her face. She ran up the steps with Laine right behind her. "Heather has never done anything like this. She'd never go away without telling me. She just wouldn't."

Hannah was becoming frightened. The twins were close even though they fought like most siblings. Hannah's fear infected her mother and their guests.

"Hannah," Laine asked, alarm showing in her voice, "you really think someone kidnapped her?"

"I don't know!" Hannah started crying. "This isn't like my sister."

Mrs. Bell put an arm around Hannah and held her close. "Please don't be frightened. She'll turn up soon."

Hannah pulled away. "No, she won't, Mom. We have to call the police."

"First we'll call everyone we can think of where she might have gone to visit, then we'll call the police," Mrs. Bell said, forcing her voice to remain calm.

Mr. Bell and Mr. Yahr walked the campus while Mrs. Bell called the neighbors. When there was no sign of Heather, Mr. Bell, frightened now, called the police, and the real search began.

"Hannah? Are you all right?"

Hannah heard a distant voice that sounded like Sergeant Wilson. It faded, then returned.

"Hannah, look at me. Are you all right?"

Hannah looked into Sergeant Wilson's wide brown eyes and saw how worried she was.

"Let me take you home," Sergeant Wilson said.

"No," Hannah heard herself say. "I'm OK. I have to see my folks. They're waiting."

"I called them a little while ago and said you'd be late because of an emergency. I promised you'd call when you could."

"Thanks, Linda. I'm all right now." Hannah stood and

straightened her clothes. "It's just such a shock, that's all. I've waited so long for something, and now it's here, and it's still a shock. It might not even be her." Her voice lowered. "It might not, but I want it to be her. I want it to be over. She can't be alive after so long, but I always hoped…." Realizing she was rambling, she stopped. "I need to call the Harbor Springs Police Department." She walked toward her desk.

Sergeant Wilson followed. "Are you sure you're OK, Detective?"

"Yes, I'm sure. Thanks, Sergeant." She dialed and waited.

"Harbor Springs Police Department, Sergeant Brechisen speaking."

"This is Detective Hannah Bell from the Chicago Police Department. I understand you recently found the remains of a young girl in your area."

"Yes, Detective. Just yesterday out on the scenic drive north of Harbor Springs at Five Mile Point. They were excavating for a new home when the dozer hit a metal box. When the operator looked in it, he freaked out."

"I'll bet. Do you know any more details than what came over the wire?"

"We know for sure it was a girl, and she'd been dead a long time, at least twenty-five years. The animal in the box with her was a dog. They're saying it was a dachshund. The remains are already in Lansing for testing. They took them down there for DNA work and other tests."

"Where in Lansing, Sergeant?" Hannah's heart beat quicker at the news of the dog, but she couldn't quite put a finger on what it meant.

"At the Michigan State Police Crime Lab."

"Can you give me their number?"

"Sure. Hang on a minute."

While she waited, Hannah's mind kept repeating, The animal was a dog, a dachshund.

The Wilkins family had a dachshund, and the dog had disappeared the same day Heather did.

"Bess," Hannah said.

"Excuse me?" the officer on the other end asked.

"Nothing. I was thinking out loud. Do you have that phone number?"

He gave her the number.

"Thanks, Sergeant. I'd like to leave my name and number and ask someone to call me if you hear anything more. I know a family to whom that child might belong, and I want to tell them how this is going. They've been looking for their daughter a long time. I'll stay in touch, too. Thanks again."

"You're welcome, Detective."

Hannah felt a little better. If she could continue viewing it as a missing-person case, helping a family—which was her job—maybe she could handle the emotional part better.

Now she had to face her parents. That would be the tough part.

"Hi, Mom! Hi, Dad! I'm here!" Hannah entered their home.

"At last." Her mother hurried toward her with outstretched arms. "Don't they ever let you rest, Hannah, even on Sunday?"

Hannah laughed and hugged her mother a little tighter than usual. "Where's Daddy?"

"Napping. It's Sunday, but then, every day is Sunday to him now. Since he retired, he sleeps most of the time." She sounded distressed. "I have to get him interested in something that will take his mind off his endless guilt and nightmares."

Hannah cringed. She was about to add to his nightmares, but if she were very lucky, she might help end them. Her father had nightmares every night since the day Heather disappeared. He constantly said, "If only she hadn't been sleeping in that room."

"But she wanted to, Dear," his wife always replied. "She slept there before and was OK."

"I should have insisted she sleep with Hannah and Laine."

"Now, Freeman. You know that would never have worked. It's a terrible thing that happened, but it's not your fault."

Nothing soothed him. Neither Hannah, her mother, nor any of their friends understood why Freeman kept blaming himself.

"If only…" he kept saying.

"So glad you could make it, Detective," Freeman teased as he gave his daughter her usual bear hug.

"Wouldn't miss it for the world, Dad."

"You must be starved." Her mother was always ready to feed someone at any time.

"Actually, I'm not. It's been quite a day so far, and eating has taken a back seat to everything else."

The seriousness of her tone made her parents look at each other quizzically.

"Mom, Dad, I need to talk with you. Can we sit in the living room?" Hannah felt her stomach move to her throat. Suddenly, her legs were weak.

"Sure, Hon," Freeman said.

They walked into the living room and sat down. Hannah sat between them on the couch, trying to figure out the best way to explain.

Tell them flat out, she decided.

She took hold of their hands and said, "We received a wire this afternoon from the Harbor Springs Police Department. The remains of a young girl were found yesterday while a contractor was excavating for a new home along the scenic drive north of Harbor Springs."

Their hands tightened on hers.

"They believe she was between ten and twelve years old and has been dead for at least twenty-five years."

"Our baby's been found at last," Lena said. "At last."

"It might not be her, Mom."

"It has to be. We looked everywhere else. It has to be. It's got to be over." She began to weep.

"They found her at Five Mile Point," Hannah said. "Ironic, isn't it? That's the ploy I used to call her from the basement. I said we were going to Five Mile Point and would leave her behind. Little did I know she was probably already there—dead."

There was a heavy, dreadful silence.

"They found an animal with her," Hannah added.

"What animal, for God's sake?" her father demanded.

"A dog, probably a dachshund."

Hannah was shocked when her father flew off the couch, flailed his arms as if fighting someone, and shouted in rage, "You son of a bitch! I knew you did it! I've always known! I'll kill you!"

He tore around the room, smashing vases, throwing candlesticks at the fireplace, kicking over a lamp and end table, while his wife and daughter held each other in terror. Freeman Bell was normally a calm man of great dignity and decorum, but he was out of control.

Hannah stared in stunned silence, wondering what to do. That was her beloved father, but what happened to him? Who was the stranger she saw?

She had to stop him before he hurt himself or one of them. She gathered her courage and strength, rose from the couch, watched his movements for a moment, then she stepped up behind him, grabbed his arms, and shouted, "Freeman Bell, stop right now!"

Her sudden action made him sink to the floor, taking her with him. He cried like a child and kept saying, "You son of a bitch. I knew you did it. I knew. I'll kill you."

When he settled down, Hannah finally asked, "Dad, what are you talking about?"

To Hannah and Lena's surprise, he said, "Gus Wilkins killed Heather. I knew it all along. He killed my little angel, that son of a bitch!"

"Dad, that's quite an accusation against a friend."

"He's not my friend. When was the last time he was in our home?"

Hannah thought for a moment. "Probably twenty years."

"Why do you suppose that is?"

"I have no idea. I never gave it much thought. I just thought you grew apart."

"We grew apart all right. He killed my little girl, and I knew it, but I could never get in touch with the reality of it. I buried it deep inside me, because I didn't want to believe it, but when you mentioned the dog, it blew up in my gut. Now it's crystal clear. Gus murdered our Heather. There's no doubt."

He looked hopefully at Hannah. "They'll do a DNA test, won't they?"

"Yes. The remains are already on their way to the lab."

"That'll lock it. The dog locks it, too. Gus killed the dog, because he used her to lure Heather away. He probably thought Bess could give him away somehow. He killed them both and then cried over his lost dog, that son of a bitch! He knew where they both were all along."

Freeman Bell stood six-feet-five-inches tall and weighed 220 pounds. He lifted himself to his feet and calmly walked to the phone.

After dialing a number, he smiled warmly at his puzzled wife and daughter. When someone answered, Freeman spoke so fast neither woman had time to react.

"You killed my daughter, you low-living, filthy son of a bitch! Now I'll kill you! They found her remains and Bess', too, and they're doing DNA tests on them right now, but I won't wait for a trial! I'm coming out there to kill you with my bare hands!"

He hung up before anyone could stop him.

It was over.

He slumped in his chair, lowered his head to his chest, and closed his eyes. Hannah and Lena looked at him, then at each other, wondering what to say. The pain and anger Freeman Bell held inside all those years had finally come out, exploding from the depths of his being. Now they knew why he blamed himself. His sense of guilt and shame resulted from his lack of action on his gut feeling that his friend killed his daughter. It was simply too painful to think about. The police could find no evidence of foul play and eventually ended their investigation. But, Freeman never forgave himself for his inaction. Even though he was unaware of all this, consciously, his physical and psychological well-being suffered greatly over the years.

"If only," he said softly. "If only he hadn't been my so-called friend, Heather would be here today."

That thought must have burned through his mind a hundred times a day for twenty-five years, Hannah thought, her heart aching for him until she thought it would beak.

"Daddy," she said, crying, "it wasn't your fault."

They sat for a long time without moving or speaking. Darkness eventually engulfed the room, and still they remained where they were. In time, Hannah slipped off the couch and reached for her mother, laying her down as Sergeant Wilson had done for her earlier in the day. She covered her bereft mother with one of the many afghans in the room, then covered her exhausted, distraught father as he lay on the floor before lying down on the plush carpet herself, and falling into a deep, desperate sleep.

CHAPTER FOURTEEN

When Hannah arrived at work the following morning, she went straight to Lieutenant Rob Keys' office.

As soon as she walked in, he said, "Hannah, I don't know whether to be relieved or not, to be happy for you, if that's the proper word, or sad."

"All of the above." She had no idea how she should feel, let alone anyone else.

The night on the floor hadn't bothered her. She was so exhausted that she didn't awaken until the first rays of sunlight came through the living room windows.

Now that she was at work, she felt more controlled. She told Rob what happened the previous evening.

"I'm worried about my father," she said. "He's a peaceful man, and I never saw him like that before last night. It scares the hell out of me. He's been holding in his hate for twenty-five years, and I'm afraid he just might do what he said, try to kill Gus Wilkins."

"Where does Wilkins live?"

"Somewhere in Texas, near Houston or Corpus Christi. That's the last I knew. I'll check with my mother. I didn't ask this morning, because it seemed wiser not to. I'm sure she can locate his address and phone number.

"I'd like to call him. Somehow, when Dad said Wilkins did it, I knew he was right, even though I never consciously thought about it. Somewhere deep in my mind, I've suspected him all these years, too, but I couldn't let myself believe it. I buried it as deeply as Dad did."

She sighed. "It makes sense, though. We often wondered if it was someone we knew. That night at the party at Burt Lake, we talked about where everyone would sleep when we got home, and Heather begged to sleep in the napping room, as she called it. There was absolutely no evidence of forced entry. In those days, we never locked our doors in Bay View. Anyone could have entered the house during the night.

"Nor were there any signs of a struggle. We never found any fingerprints except for those of us who belonged in the house. None from Gus. Heather must have left of her own free will, and she would only have done that for someone she trusted, or for a dog like Bess. She would have gone to the end of the world for that dog."

Hannah paused, then looked at Rob with damp eyes. "That's just what she did, too—she went to the end of her world, and her life.

"I can't help thinking that Gus somehow arranged that night at the party for Heather to sneak out to meet him and Bess. Maybe he promised a guitar lesson on the beach or something. It would be their little secret. I...I don't know how else it could have happened, but then, we'll never know, will we?

"I just hope she didn't suffer too much," she whispered, tears running down her cheeks and falling onto her clasped hands. She was working hard to keep herself together. She wanted to scream and tear at her hair, to curse at heaven, to rip the pain from her heart, but she didn't. She just sat and wept.

Across the desk, Lieutenant Keys looked at her with tears in his eyes. When someone opened the door, he motioned him away. Rob felt genuine compassion for his colleague's pain, enhanced by his fondness for Hannah. He wanted to take her in his arms and comfort her.

Hannah looked into Rob's sympathetic gaze. "Rob, my father told Wilkins about the remains and the DNA tests. Wilkins must know he'll be found out. What if he runs? Worse, what if he kills himself? I don't know what his mind is like. My God, Rob, we have to get to him fast."

Hannah's voice rose with the last sentence. She was on her feet, her hands on the lieutenant's desk, almost shouting.

Rob picked up the phone. "Get me the Texas State Police, pronto!" He hung up.

"What kind of cop am I?" Hannah groaned. "I should have acted the moment I heard Dad say those words to Wilkins last night. He could be gone, or dead, by now."

"Not likely," Rob said. "Unless he has a passport ready and can leave the country fast, the best he can do is get in his car and drive. If he does, we'll catch him."

The phone rang, and Rob answered. "Thanks, Sergeant. Hello, Lieutenant Dalton. We need to locate someone named Gus Wilkins. We believe he may have been involved in the twenty-five-year-old murder of a young girl in northern Michigan."

Rob told Dalton what they knew. Hannah half-listened, but her mind kept slipping back to memories of Heather and her father's rage. She'd never heard him use such language or such a venomous tone before. The tone struck her the hardest. She couldn't get the words out of her mind.

"He'll get back to us the moment he has something," Rob said, hanging up.

"What? I'm sorry, Rob. I didn't catch what you just said."

"Lieutenant Dalton will check on Gus Wilkins. He has to see if there's such a person in Texas, how many there are, and where they live. Then they'll go from there. He'll get back to us as soon as he has something.

"Hannah, it would be helpful if we had more information. Can you call your folks and ask them for Gus' address and phone number, or would you rather I did it?"

"I'll do it." She picked up the receiver and called home, but there was no answer. She left a message on the answering machine for her parents to call her at Rob's office as soon as they could.

She hung up, then the phone rang immediately.

Rob answered, listened for a few seconds, and said, "I'll be damned. Where'd you find him? We'll need DNA samples from the body ASAP. Call me at once if anything else turns up."

Hannah stared at him in shock. Body? she wondered. What body? Gus' body? Oh, my God. He killed himself, and Dad made him do it.

Hannah felt as if her world were falling apart around her. Rob saw the panic in her eyes. "Get back to me, Lieutenant," he said, hanging up.

He moved around the desk and took Hannah in his arms without a second thought. He held her close and didn't speak as she clung to him, her body wracked with sobs as she whispered, "What will happen to him?"

"Nothing," Rob said firmly. "The man knew he was guilty and was at the end of the line. He'd been living with the guilt himself, too, for the past twenty-five years. He took the easy way out—for all of us. Now we won't have to go through the pain of a trial. Your father didn't make him do anything."

Hannah looked at him and tried to smile, then she softly kissed his cheek. "Thanks, Rob. Maybe you're right. It will be easier for all of us except Micky. I feel sorry for her. Her pain is just beginning."

Rob held her until she was ready to step away, then he gently released her. A moment later, the phone rang.

"Hello?" Rob asked. "Hello, Mr. Bell. This is Lieutenant Keys. Yes, we know about last night. Hannah told us. We just need to confirm an address for Mr. Wilkins." He didn't want to add that Gus had hung himself in his basement the previous night. "Thank you, Mr. Bell. We'll let you know what we find out. Thank you for calling."

Hannah waved to indicate she didn't want to speak to her father.

"Hannah's not available at the moment. Would you like me to leave a message for her? Yes, I'll do that. Good-bye."

Rob hung up. When he spoke, his voice was thick with emotion. "He said...to tell you that he loves you, and he won't do anything foolish."

Hannah smiled. "If I'd heard his voice, I would have given it away. Dad doesn't need to know Gus is dead yet. I have to pull myself together. I have a job to do."

They briefly discussed Gus' suicide in Houston. When Lieutenant Dalton ran a check on the name, he immediately received the suicide report. He promised to follow up with more details and would send DNA samples to the Michigan State Police Lab immediately.

Sharon arrived early at work on Monday morning and was sipping coffee in the cafeteria when Sergeant Linda Wilson walked in.

"Hi, Linda."

"Hey, Sharon."

"Care to join me for a cup of coffee?"

"Sure."

Linda poured a cup and sat at Sharon's table. "Have you seen Detective Bell today?"

"Not since yesterday morning when she arrested Mandy O'Brien."

"You've got some catching up to do, Girl."

Sharon looked puzzled. "What do you mean?"

"They found the remains of a young girl in northern Michigan, and Hannah's a wreck."

"Oh, no! Poor Hannah. Where is she?"

"In Lieutenant Keys' office. They've been in there over an hour."

As they spoke, Rob and Hannah entered the cafeteria. Seeing Sharon and Linda at a table, Hannah motioned Rob to walk with her toward them.

"Good morning, Ladies," Hannah said.

"Good morning, Detective Bell, Lieutenant," Linda said.

"Hannah, are you OK?" Sharon asked as the two newcomers sat down.

"Yes. I'm OK now. Did Linda tell you?"

"Yes. I'm not sure how to feel about it. I'm glad the search appears to be over. I hope the rest will go quickly."

"Me, too." Hannah sighed.

Rob went to get coffee for himself and Hannah. As he walked away, Hannah's eyes followed him. He's a good man, she thought, strong and confident.

Sharon always seemed to be able to read Hannah's mind. "And he's good looking, too."

"You know, Walker, sometimes I'd like to strangle you." Hannah immediately blushed.

"I know. You tried that recently, but you couldn't do it, remember?" Sharon rubbed her neck.

"Why are you always trying to hook Hannah up with someone?" Linda asked. "Hasn't it occurred to you she might not be interested?"

"No, it hasn't. She's just fussy. That's all."

"Good for you," Linda told Hannah as Rob returned.

"Good for her what?" Rob asked.

"Just girl talk, Lieutenant," Hannah said, smiling and praying Sharon wouldn't say anything more.

As Rob sat down, he said, "I had a long talk with Mandy O'Brien this morning. How was she after Hannah left last night, Linda?"

Hannah was grateful for the change of subject.

"She seemed a little scared but was fine when I left," Linda said.

"She's willing to help us catch the Irish smugglers," Rob said. "I talked with her about being a decoy, and she's all for it."

"A decoy?" Hannah blurted, staring at Rob. "She's just a kid, Rob. They'll see through her in a second!"

"No, they won't. She's a very smart kid, very intuitive. We'll turn her into a boy, and she'll speak only Gaelic, with only the appearance that she understands minimal English."

"How will you make a boy out of her?" Hannah still felt incredulous that Rob planned to use Mandy as a decoy.

"The same way it's always been done. We'll cut her hair and dress her like a boy."

Hannah didn't like the sound of his plan. Her newfound feelings for Rob began slipping away. How could he use a child in this way? she wondered.

Rob looked at her. "I know you don't like this, Hannah, and I wish it could be different, too, but it's the best chance we've got, and Mandy's eager to help. She told me some things this morning, things you might want to hear directly from her."

Hannah looked at him intently.

"You'll have to ask her," he said.

They finished their coffee and departed for their offices. Sharon and Hannah walked together.

"How are your folks?" Sharon asked as they walked down the

corridor toward the elevator.

"They're OK. My father lost it last night for a while. I just hope he'll be able to handle what's happened." She explained about her father's threat and how Gus was found dead.

Sharon whistled softly.

"Rob's in touch with the Texas State Police, so the wheels of justice are turning," Hannah said with a sigh. "In the meantime, I have to get back to the Allen thing. My mind's been totally elsewhere since I left Mandy here yesterday afternoon. What's this business of using her as a decoy? I can't believe Rob's willing to do that."

"You've always trusted his judgment before. Why not now?"

"I don't like using a young woman to catch a bunch of crooks. We don't know what they'll do if they catch her. We have two dead women already, and we don't know who killed them. We put her in that position, and she might become number three. I can't go along with this."

"Why don't you talk to Mandy before you decide?" Sharon asked.

"I intend to do just that!"

Hannah found Mandy in her cell, reading a novel.

"What's that?" Hannah asked as the officer unlocked the cell to let her in.

"A romance novel," Mandy said sheepishly.

"Aren't you a little young for that stuff?"

"I've read lots of them already. Anna gives them to me and tells me to learn from them."

"Learn what, I wonder?"

"How to handle men."

"Oh. I see. Romance novels are supposed to show women how to handle men. Then I'd better get busy. I have a lot to learn."

"These aren't the juicy kind. They're pretty tame, according to Sergeant Wilson. She brought me these this morning, saying they'd keep me entertained. She wouldn't give a young lady naughty books." Mandy smiled slyly. "Would she?"

Mandy folded down the corner of the page she was reading, closed the book, and laid it beside her on the bunk.

"May I sit down?"

"Sure."

"Are you OK? Comfortable?"

"Yeah. I never spent the night in jail before. It's strange. I feel a little like a criminal, even though I'm not. It just feels that way. I've had plenty to eat and some company, too. Sergeant Wilson is real nice, and Detective Walker and Lieutenant Keys have been to see me this morning."

"What did you and the lieutenant talk about?"

"Plans he has for catching the Irish smugglers." She wasn't trying to hide anything or be coy.

"How do those plans concern you?"

"Well, he asked me a lot of questions about how I came to America, questions I was afraid to answer until he said he knew I was illegal and there wouldn't be any punishment for me. He said the police believe that the smugglers who brought me and lots of others here are getting rich off us, and they want to stop it. I do, too." She paused to take a breath.

"You once mentioned a letter. Who was it from? Who signed it?"

"I don't know. I didn't pay any attention to that part. I didn't even read it. My mother read it, because it was sent to her. I didn't see it anymore after that. I just did what she said I should do."

"Did you wonder why such an offer was being made?"

"No. My sister came here three years ago after my mother received a letter like that. She was going to San Francisco. Before she left, she said she'd get me into the States as soon as she could."

"You never mentioned having a sister before."

"You never asked."

"What's her name?"

"Lilly."

"Did you ever hear from her?"

"No."

"Have you heard from her since you arrived in America?"

"No," Mandy said sadly. "Not since I left Ireland. I thought she was too busy, but, when that letter came, I knew she must have been the one who sent it." She paused. "I told all this to the lieutenant."

"He asked me to talk with you and to ask you to tell me what you told him. I had the feeling it was pretty serious."

They sat silently for a few minutes while Hannah gave the young woman plenty of time to gather herself and tell whatever she knew. Mandy reminded her of Heather. Maybe it's her naïveté or her free spirit, or both, Hannah thought. That's it. It's the combination. That was Heather.

She was only eleven when she died, and there wasn't much time for Heather to learn about the world. Perhaps if she'd known more, she would have known better than to allow someone to lure her out of her safe, warm bed, even if it was a family friend, to go somewhere inappropriate at night.

"When I told the lieutenant about my sister," Mandy began, "he asked for her name, then went away for a while. He came back with bad news. It seems she was forced into prostitution when she arrived. There was a bed waiting, but it wasn't as a domestic.

"Blessed Mother of Jesus." Mandy crossed herself. "My mother would die if she knew Lilly was a prostitute. It makes me feel sick." She placed her hands over her stomach.

"The lieutenant said that when some immigrants learn they aren't really free, that they're more like slaves, and that they owe a lot of money, they run away. They have to eat and live, so they do things that get them in trouble. Boys become thieves, and girls, prostitutes.

"The rest of us are inden...inden...."

"Indentured servants," Hannah said.

"The lieutenant says that's illegal."

"Very illegal—and cruel."

"The lieutenant says the bill is never paid. He said we remain indentured servants for as long as we live. Worse, he said my mother probably paid a lot of money for my trip here, and for my sister, too. She probably didn't tell me about it. She doesn't have any money, and...." Mandy began crying. "I hate those people! I want to stop them!" She pounded the cot with her fists, then repeated, "I want to stop them."

Hannah put her arm around the overwhelmed young woman, and they sat quietly for a while.

"The San Francisco police picked up Lilly a couple of times and questioned her," Mandy said. "Because of her heavy Irish accent, they pressured her about how she came to America. Finally, she told them what happened, and they sent her back to the street! They let her go back, Detective!" Mandy was incredulous.

"How could they do that? This is the United States of America!"

"It happens, Mandy, somewhere over here almost every day. It's not pretty, and we aren't proud of it, but it happens."

"I want to catch those people. I want to stop them." Mandy leaned against Hannah and shook her fist. "Some of the boys end up in jail for stealing, and some even kill people for money. It's awful. We were good people in Ireland." Her voice rose.

She jumped off the cot. "I wish I'd never come here! I hate this place. The United States of America is supposed to be the

Promised Land. Ha!" She slumped onto the cot again.

"You, Detective Walker, Lieutenant Keys, and Sergeant Wilson are the only nice people I've met here, and you're police officers. Well, Anna's nice, too. I like her."

"Is being a police officer so bad?"

"In Ireland, mostly yes. That's sad, too. Since many policemen are Protestants, the Catholics hate them, and the Protestant citizens expect to get away with things. They want the police to turn their backs on the things they do in the name of God and independence. That's rubbish. I don't believe for one minute God wants us to kill each other and blame it on Him."

So young, so naïve, and yet so wise, Hannah thought.

"Most people in Ireland are good, law-abiding citizens," Mandy said as if reassuring herself. "There are enough really bad ones that it makes all of us look bad. I've seen the news reports about Ireland. They're awful. All they show is the bad stuff. You'd think all of us were killers."

"That's just like America," Hannah said. "Most people here are law-abiding, too. They raise their families; go to work, to church, a synagogue or a mosque; visit friends and family, and obey the rules. It's the bad ones that give us a bad name, just like everywhere."

Mandy didn't answer.

"Have you ever heard the saying, 'One bad apple spoils the whole bushel?'"

"No."

"What do you think it might mean?"

Mandy repeated the words softly, then said, "I know one bad potato can ruin a whole bushel. It's the same thing, isn't it?"

"Yes." Hannah smiled.

"I like you, Detective. I'll bet you came from a good family. Do you have children? You'd make a great mom."

"Thank you. I'll remember that vote of confidence when the time comes. Now let's get back to business. What plans did you make with Lieutenant Keys?"

"When I said I wanted to catch those guys, he said maybe I could help. Maybe I could help the police!" Her voice became more animated. "We talked about a few things. He was concerned I not put myself in danger, but I said I wasn't afraid. I could do whatever they wanted me to do. He was worried I might be recognized, so I suggested they make me into a boy. You know, cut off my hair and dress me like a boy."

She laughed. "I don't have any boobs to worry about. That's what you say, here, isn't it?" She pressed her hands against her small breasts and completely hid them. "See? It would be easy to make me look like a boy. We can even dye my hair. How about black!"

They laughed.

"Are Irish women as obsessed with boobs as American women?" Hannah couldn't believe she asked such a question, but it was too late to retract it.

"No. We know we'll get them when we have babies. My mother has them. Boy, does she ever. She said she looked like me before she was married and had children. I hope mine don't get that big. That's a lot to carry around."

"Did you also discuss this part of your disguise with the lieutenant?"

"Goodness, no!"

They shared a women's laugh, a laugh understood in all languages.

"Even as a boy, Mandy, they might discover you," Hannah said seriously.

"I'll take my chances. I want to help my sister and those who come after me. I have two younger brothers at home who want to come here. I want them to come legally and make a good life, then bring our mother here, if she'll come."

"I hope that happens, Mandy. This really is a wonderful country." She took the girl's hands in hers. "When this is over, I'll show you some of the real United States of America."

Mandy hugged her. "Oh, yes. I'd like that very much."

"OK." Hannah gently freed herself. "Now we have to work out the details."

"Details?"

"All the things we need to work out to catch the smugglers."

"I think the lieutenant has them worked out already. He plans to do the sting thing, as he called it, before next Wednesday night's party. We have to be ready to arrest them all by then when they're all in one place."

"He's not letting any grass grow under his feet, is he?" Hannah asked.

Mandy looked at her quizzically.

"That's an American expression that means he isn't wasting any time."

"Right." Mandy gave her a thumbs up.

Hannah shook her head and smiled. "You're learning."

CHAPTER FIFTEEN

Hannah left Mandy's cell and walked toward Rob's office. He was on the phone when she arrived, but he motioned her to a chair. As she sat and waited, her mind wandered to an earlier time.

The girls were eight years old that year, and Grandma Mullen was there for Christmas. The Bells always saw Grandma and Grandpa Mullen at Christmastime, but always at their home in Wisconsin. Grandpa died that year, so Grandma was glad to be in Waukegan with her son and his family.

Grandma Mullen made the best Christmas cookies ever, and she made many different kinds.

"That's how we always did it," she explained. "A group of ladies got together and had a cookie exchange. Then we'd all go home with a large assortment of cookies, and we each only made one kind. Each year I made a different cookie, so I learned how to make many kinds."

"Grandma, you're the best grandma in the whole world!" Heather exclaimed in delight as she ate her fourth frosted-sugar cookie—her favorite.

"Grandma, can you teach us to make a different Christmas cookie each year?" Hannah asked. "That way, when we're grown up, we'll be able to make lots of cookies just like you."

"Sure. What would you like to make this year?"

"Chocolate chip with M&Ms in them like ornaments!" Hannah said.

"Frosted-sugar cookies!" Heather shouted.

"I want chocolate chippers!" Hannah said.

"I want frosted sugar!"

"Hmmm," Grandma Mullen said. "What to do?"

She soon found a solution that worked well for everyone. As Hannah grew older, she often thought, Grandma should have been a diplomat.

"I know," Grandma said. "We'll make two kinds each year. Then you two will surely have the best cookie assortment of all."

"Wow!" the girls said. "That would be great!"

"If we do this until we graduate from high school," Hannah said, "we'll know how to make twenty kinds of cookies."

"Wow," Heather said.

That was how it went for three years. Grandma Mullen died in the spring of the following year. People said she was just too lonely without Grandpa. In the three years she had to make Christmas cookies with the girls, they learned how to make six different kinds of cookies.

In honor of Grandma's memory, the girls planned to continue the tradition at Christmas. When Heather disappeared the same year Grandma died, Hannah and her mother maintained the tradition in memory of both of them. Hannah soon became an expert cookie maker.

I haven't been keeping up with the tradition lately, Hannah realized. I'd better work on that.

"Hannah, where are you?" Rob asked.

Hannah blinked. "Just remembering…." Her voice trailed off.

"Did you speak with Mandy?" he asked.

"Well, yes."

"Did she explain about her sister?"

"Yes."

"Did she say what she wanted to do?"

"Yes, she did."

"What do you think now?"

"I still don't like it, but I can see she's all for it. Rob, she's just a kid. We shouldn't let her put herself in jeopardy like this."

"Aren't you letting your personal situation guide your thinking here?"

"I might be, but even if it weren't for that, I wouldn't like it."

"Well, we're doing it, and one of the things I want you to do is show up at the Allen estate during the time we estimate the two groups are in their respective libraries." He looked at her intently. "Who have you interviewed so far in this case?"

"Mariah, Gloria, Anna, and Mandy. Detective Walker spoke with the other household staff. I also spoke with Mrs. Quigley at her home and with Mrs. Costello and Mrs. Reilly on the telephone, and I met Darren Brannigan."

"Damn."

Hannah looked at him. "What's that for?"

"With Mariah dead, we are primarily concerned now with the men in the library group, and I thought we might send you as a plant to that gallery for a portrait sitting. Mr. Brannigan is a suspect in at least one of the Allen murders, as well as, for smuggling illegals. "

"Why Darren?" Hannah interrupted.

After a slight hesitation, he asked, "On a first-name basis, are you?" with a hint of acerbity in his voice.

"I said we've met," she said defensively, feeling the blush rising in her neck. She took a deep breath and hoped it would disappear.

An uncomfortable silence fell between them.

"I'm to see Mr. Brannigan's studio today," Hannah said finally.

"I want to look around, see if there are any clues."

"Not today," Rob said firmly.

It was Hannah's turn to feel annoyed. "Why not? I'm supposed to be conducting an investigation, right?"

"Yes, but we need to discuss how any future conversation with Mr. Brannigan will be conducted, and that won't happen today.

"Is Mr. Brannigan aware that he might be a suspect as well as a witness?"

"I'm sure he is," Hannah said coolly.

"But you haven't mentioned it to him and told him not to leave town."

"No."

"We believe Mr. Brannigan is in this business up to his eyeballs, which also makes him a suspect in both deaths. His artistic abilities make him the one most likely to have created the phony documents for the immigrants, complete with fake official seal. Someone had to counterfeit those papers, and he's the best candidate. He also had easy access to the Allen household and the Allen women."

With her eyes closed, Hannah shook her head.

"He's the one who found Mariah," Rob continued. "Maybe he also killed her."

"She choked to death, Rob. There's no evidence of foul play."

"I'm not convinced. It's just too convenient. Wasn't Brannigan in love with Angela? Maybe he killed Mariah to avenge her death, if he suspected her."

Is he trying to get a rise out of me? Hannah wondered. Is he concerned with what appears to be more interest in a suspect than is appropriate? "He wasn't in love with her," she said quickly and felt her voice becoming defensive again. "He cared about her due to her situation at home, but he wasn't in love with her."

"How do you happen to know that?"

Hannah squirmed in her seat. She didn't seem able to control her defensiveness. "He told Detective Walker he cared for Angela and even contemplated asking her to marry him to get her out of that house, as he put it, but he didn't love her in that way, as he also put it."

"I see." Rob wasn't impressed. "Pity's a poor reason to marry someone, but it's certainly noble."

Hannah looked quizzically at Rob, remembering her own similar words. Did he speak them exactly as I said them? she wondered. Still, it was close enough to make her pause. "Well, then, OK. He might have done in Mariah if he thought she killed Angela. It's possible."

"Do you really think so?" He gave her a penetrating look.

"Yes, I do."

There was another moment of silence, then Rob's demeanor changed. His eyes and voice softened, and he took a deep breath. "Hannah…."

"What?" Irritation laced her voice.

"Do you think you could identify a piece of cloth they found in the grave of that child in Michigan?"

It took her a few seconds to make the transition to the new subject. When she collected herself, she said, "Yes. We wore identical nightgowns that night. We'd just bought them a few days earlier on a shopping trip to Petoskey. I never wore mine again after that night."

"I want to take you to the Michigan lab today. I've already spoken with Lansing. They're expecting us this afternoon."

"But, I…I…. OK." She didn't want to add to the tension between them. "When do you want to leave?"

"Now."

"Now?" she gasped.

"Now."

"OK. I need to make a call first." She rose to leave and barely heard Rob's last words as she closed his door.

"Meet you at the front desk in ten minutes."

Hannah was surprised at her disappointment when she realized she wouldn't be meeting Darren that day. A wave of nausea passed through her at the thought of having to look at Heather's remains, if they were hers, and the nightgown.

God, give me the strength to do this, she prayed. I don't know if I can bear it if that piece of cloth turns out to be Heather's nightgown.

She reached her office and called Darren. It took several rings before he answered.

"Hello?"

Hannah's heart skipped a beat, then it beat faster until her face felt warm. "Hello, Dar…Mr. Brannigan. This is Detective Bell of the Chicago Police Department."

"Hi, Hannah. I look forward to seeing you today."

"I have to cancel our appointment," she said more abruptly than intended. "Something's come up at the office. I have to reschedule."

"Let's see. How about tomorrow afternoon? That will work for me."

"I'll have to get back to you when I return."

"You're going away?"

"I'll call tomorrow, Dar…Mr. Brannigan."

"What's with the Mr. Brannigan, Hannah? I thought we were beyond that."

"I need to remember my professional manners." She tried to chuckle, but it didn't sound quite right.

"Are you all right?"

"Please, Darren, don't ask right now."

"OK. At least you said my name. I want to hear from you tomorrow. If you don't call me, I'll call or come over there and find out what's going on. Remember, I know where you live."

She laughed. "You sound like my father."

"I don't want to sound like your father. I have a very different kind of relationship in mind."

"Good-bye, Mr. Brannigan." She emphasized his name very carefully.

"Good-bye, Hannah. See you tomorrow."

The ride to Michigan was uneventful and quiet. Hannah didn't feel like talking, so Rob respected that. I-94 was fast and easy between Chicago and Gary, Indiana, although not very picturesque.

Whenever Hannah passed that way, she closed her eyes and imagined how beautiful that stretch of land at the southernmost tip of Lake Michigan must have looked in the past, before the Industrial Revolution and its sprawl ruined the area's natural beauty and changed it into the ugliest of eyesores. Lake Michigan was still beautiful—if one could see it. With the expressway finally finished in northwestern Indiana, drivers no longer saw endless miles of smokestacks, railroad tracks, old railroad cars, and abandoned, broken-down buildings that were visible on the old roads.

As they approached the Michigan border, the area's natural beauty returned. They stopped at a McDonald's in Coloma, Michigan, for a quick lunch. They were making good time.

Lieutenant Keys suggested they stop at the St. Julian Wine Gallery for a pleasant break. The thought appealed to Hannah, and they each bought two bottles of wine to add to their home collections. Then they drove toward Lansing, taking I-69 west of Marshall and straight to the state capital.

They arrived at the Michigan State Police Lab in midafternoon, as expected. Sergeant Swingle greeted them, told them the specimens were ready for viewing, and took them into the laboratory.

As they entered the room, Rob put his arm around Hannah's shoulder and squeezed gently, then he lowered his arm and took her hand.

She let him. His hand was warm, strong, and gentle. They followed the sergeant to a cubicle where someone else waited.

As they approached the cubicle, they saw a large, rusty metal box that measured three feet by eighteen inches and looked twelve inches deep. A man stood nearby.

Hannah faltered in her step, and Rob's grip on her hand tightened. She leaned against him. He slipped his arm around her waist.

There were two empty chairs beside the table that held the metal box. Hannah walked to one and sat down, while Rob followed but remained standing.

"Lieutenant Keys? Detective Bell?" the man asked, stepping forward.

"Yes," Rob said.

"I'm Dr. Chen. This is the metal box we found in northern Michigan. It's been opened, and we've made a preliminary examination of the contents. After you examine them, Detective Bell, an in-depth investigation will be made." He spoke crisply and to the point. "You've been advised as to what it contains?" He looked at Hannah, who stared up at him from the chair.

"Yes," they replied.

"Are you ready?" He looked into Hannah's eyes.

"Yes," she said softly.

Then she stood, looked at Rob, and nodded at the doctor. The two police officers had been through the routine many times from the other side of the situation, watching grieving friends and relatives of victims. No amount of past experience could prepare

Hannah for what she saw.

She stared at the contents for a moment, then sat down, putting her hands over her eyes. After a moment, she raised her head and said softly, "The nightgown.... It's the one. It's Heather's. It's...it's just like mine."

The doctor immediately closed the box. The look he exchanged with Rob indicated no further observation was needed. Since a preliminary identification had been made, the DNA tests would immediately follow.

"I'd like to take another look," Hannah said.

"Are you sure, Hannah?" Rob asked.

"Yes. I'll be OK. I need to see her one more time."

The doctor opened the box, and Hannah stared into it for a few seconds before looking at Dr. Chen and asking, "May I?"

"Yes, but very carefully."

She reached in and gently touched a piece of the fabric with one fingertip. Then she carefully stroked a small section of her sister's crushed skull, a leg bone, and the dog's tiny skull.

With horror, she saw her sister's legs had been cut off, probably so her body would fit into the box. She almost threw up when she thought of someone cutting up her little sister.

It's bad enough he crushed her skull, she thought. Did he have to cut her up, too? I only hope she was dead when this occurred.

Hannah was quiet for a long time. When she finally regained the ability to speak, she said, "My family and I want the remains as soon as the testing is done. The dog, too. We'll bury them together. Please take good care of what's left of my little sister."

"We will," Dr. Chen said.

Hannah slowly closed the lid of the rusty metal box, turned to Rob, and said, "I'm ready to go now."

"Please let us know as soon as all the tests are finished and you have the results," Rob said. "If we don't hear from you soon, we'll call."

"We'll get right on it, Lieutenant."

Rob reached for Hannah's arm.

"Good-bye, Dr. Chen," Hannah said, shaking his hand. "Thank you."

"You're welcome, Detective Bell." He shook her hand firmly. "We'll be in touch soon. I'm very sorry."

"Thank you."

Hannah and Rob walked back to the car in silence. As they left the parking lot, Rob said, "I'll call Texas in the morning and let them know you ID'd the remains. The rest should fall into place quickly, I hope."

"Me, too." Her voice was barely above a whisper.

After a while, Rob said, "Hannah, I'm sure you don't feel like eating at the moment, but somewhere along the way home, would you let me treat you to a fine dining experience in a slow-food restaurant with some atmosphere? We can take our time and try to settle our nerves, too."

Hannah was touched and amused by his phrasing, not to mention his cautious manner. "You can be very charming when you want to, Lieutenant." A smile crept across her face.

"You ain't seen nothin' yet."

Hannah looked at him askance, further amused at seeing a new side to her boss. Is he courting me? she wondered.

She knew he liked her, and she was developing new feelings for him, too. She had always liked and respected him as an officer and even as her superior, even when they disagreed. She didn't believe in fraternizing with male colleagues, though. It was too risky for many reasons. Close associations with other women was one thing, but not with the men. She'd always been adamant about that.

Department policy outwardly discouraged the casual mixing

of the sexes. Men and women who became involved found themselves transferred to different precincts. Often one of them left the force, usually the woman. Hannah had no such plan.

In her preoccupation with her thoughts, she wasn't quite sure what Rob just said.

"I'm sorry, Rob. I didn't hear you."

"I just invited you out to dinner."

"Oh. OK. I accept."

They rode in silence awhile. Hannah felt comfortable enough to nod off to sleep. She thought about how it usually was when she rode with someone she didn't know that well, or with whom she'd spent very little time one-on-one. There usually was an awkward feeling, the need to fill silence with idle chitchat.

She didn't feel that way at the moment. Maybe it was emotional exhaustion, or maybe she felt a comfort level with Lieutenant Keys she hadn't fully realized.

When they reached the Lake Michigan shoreline, Rob left the expressway and drove toward Michigan City, Indiana.

They drove along the Indiana Dunes National Lakeshore, a beautiful area, where they rolled down the windows to enjoy the lake's cool breeze. It was a hot day, but it wasn't hot there. As it was so often on the eastern shore of Lake Michigan, it was windy. They stopped at a stretch of beach to take in the view.

After sitting in silence awhile, Hannah suddenly bolted from the car and ran toward the water, slipping off her shoes on the way. She could still run like the wind.

Rob watched in amusement for a moment, then a frightening thought went through his mind, and he was out of the car in a flash. At a trim six-feet-two-inches tall, he was a good runner, too.

Hannah hit the water at top speed, swinging her arms like a child, laughing and crying simultaneously. Her clothes slowed her down a little, but soon, she was in water to her hips and dived into a wave. The water was cool and refreshing as it rushed over her head. She rose to the surface and found herself suddenly in Rob's arms.

"Hannah, what are you doing?" he shouted, terror in his eyes.

She understood instantly. "Oh, no, Rob. I'm not trying to drown myself, just the pain that's burning me up. I love water. It always makes me feel better."

He kissed her as waves swirled around them, and she didn't try to stop him.

"I love you, Hannah." He held her close.

She pulled away. "No, Rob. Please don't tell me that. I can't handle it. I don't know what to do with it."

"Don't do anything with it. Just take it in. I've loved you for a long time, and it won't change. I can live with it."

He smiled, took her face in his large, strong hands, and kissed her again. She felt weak all over, as if she were melting into the water and becoming part of the sea far, far away.

A huge wave washed them both underwater for a moment. When they came to the surface, they still clung together.

She kissed him.

They played in the surf awhile, then lay on the beach together for a long time, unaware of the wind swirling around them or the sand covering them. They discussed many things.

"Tomorrow morning, this will all be forgotten," Hannah said sadly.

"What makes you say that?"

"Oh, I don't know. Isn't that the way it usually is?"

"I don't know. Is it?"

She thought about that. "Rob, I'm not ready for any kind of relationship," she blurted. "You know what would happen if we became involved?" She kept talking without waiting for his answer. "I'd be out of a job, that's what. I'm not ready to stay home and have kids and all that."

"Whoa! Wait a minute. Where are you going? You've got us married already."

Hannah turned bright red. "Oh, no, Rob. I'm sorry. I didn't mean that. I don't know why I said it." She laughed. "That's what girls do, isn't it?" She tried desperately to hide her embarrassment. "They start thinking about marriage whenever some guy kisses them. It's pretty silly when you think about it."

"I've thought about it with you many times."

She stared at him in shock.

"I have, but I know you're not ready, so I'll just wait. You may go through half a dozen guys before you realize I'm the right one. I'm a very patient man, up to a point."

He reached for her again, held her close, and kissed her hair, forehead, eyes, and nose. By the time he reached her lips, she was ready.

In time, he stood, offered his hand, and said it was time to go home.

"I don't want to get in trouble for bringing you home too late," he added.

"With whom?" she asked innocently.

"With you. I don't want you yelling at me tomorrow because I brought you home late tonight and took advantage of you, too."

"You didn't take advantage of me!"

"I know, but by tomorrow morning, who knows what you'll think I've done?"

They both laughed. As she stood, he put his arm around her, and she nestled her head against his big, strong shoulder, feeling very safe and warm as they walked back to the car with their arms around each other.

The final leg of their journey passed too quickly, even though they spent almost two hours having a late dinner at a cozy, lakeside restaurant. When they parted at the station, they shared a good-night kiss.

"Don't forget me overnight," he said.

"I won't." She took one of his hands in hers. "Rob, thank you for today. I'm glad we went, and I'm glad you were the one with me. I couldn't have done it alone."

"I wouldn't have let you go through it alone, Hannah. I want to be as close to you as you'll let me during this terrible time."

She smiled. He kissed her again, then they said a final, "Good night."

CHAPTER SIXTEEN

"Hannah, you won't believe what they found at the Allen estate during the search on Sunday," Sharon said as Hannah arrived at the precinct early Tuesday morning.

"While you and Lieutenant Keys went to Michigan yesterday, we went through all the confiscated items and recorded them. One of the officers, Hubbard, I think it was, said when they were searching Mariah's bedroom, they found a safe in the wall. They had to call in a professional to open it, because no one knew the combination. Not even Gloria knew it was there. Can you believe that?"

"Yes," Hannah said matter-of-factly. "What did they find?"

"Boxes full of locked diaries. Everything we need to know is probably in those boxes. The problem is, we haven't been able to open them."

"The boxes or the diaries?"

"The diaries."

"I'll bet we'll find out something about the smuggling ring in those books, and maybe a clue about what happened to Angela. We might even find another clue, like who might have killed Mariah. This might be the break we've been waiting for. We'll get them open even if we have to break the locks."

"Is there any particular organization to them?"

"Can't tell right now. There are no external markings to indicate order, but, as meticulous as Mariah was about everything else, I imagine the diaries are organized, too. We just have to learn her system.

"From what I've seen so far, they don't appear to be stored in chronological order. Juvenile book styles are mixed with more sophisticated, mature-looking ones. Some books are well worn, indicating she read and reread them often, but those are mixed with books that look brand new and unused."

"Hmmm. I wonder how she kept track of them all?" Hannah muttered.

"My guess is that somewhere in the house is a diagram showing the whole layout. Maybe it's on a computer disk somewhere. She had to have something written down, unless she kept it all in her mind, which I doubt. She might have been smart, but she wasn't that smart."

"I hope someone dusted the books for fingerprints before everyone started handling them," Hannah said.

"Yes. We'll have the results back in a few days."

"Good. Then we'll know who else knows about the diaries and isn't telling us. Is there any way to tell which one she was writing in when she died? I take it there wasn't one of these books sitting on her nightstand in plain sight."

"That's the one book we're actively searching for. It wasn't on the nightstand, in the drawer, under the mattress, or in any of the other handy places people usually use for a current diary. Since we can't tell one box from the other yet, we don't know which box she might have kept it in."

"It makes one think she had something to hide," Hannah said.

"She had plenty to hide."

"Sharon, I want to start reading those diaries ASAP, and I don't care where we start. Perhaps the well-worn ones would be best. We'll have to figure out the system as we go."

"That's what it'll take. However, Gloria has hired a lawyer to keep us from opening them. I don't know how that will turn out."

"We'll find out right now." Hannah took her partner's arm and walked toward Rob's office.

As Hannah stormed in, Rob looked at her and said, "I'm way ahead of you. I've already spoken to the DA. The books were taken during a legal search, and you can open them anytime you like. I've called in Lenny the Lock to help us open them, hopefully without breaking them."

"Lenny?" Hannah smiled. "I haven't seen him in years."

"He was just released from jail after a two-year burglary sentence. By the way, how are you this morning, Detective?"

"Fine." She smiled.

"Did you rest well?"

"Very well, thank you." Hannah blushed slightly.

Sharon watched their exchange with great interest.

"How are you this morning, Detective?" Rob asked Sharon, looking squarely into her eyes.

"Very fine, thank you, Boss. I, too, slept very well."

"Must be something in the air," Rob said.

"Must be. Perhaps you and Detective Bell should take more trips to Michigan."

"Perhaps."

"OK, you two," Hannah said. "Knock it off. Let's get down to business."

"Yes, Ma'am," Rob and Sharon replied in unison.

"The boxes of diaries are in the property room," Rob told the women. "You'd better get started reading. Lenny should be down there by the time you arrive. Let me know if you find anything significant."

"We're out of here," Sharon said.

They hurried to the property room and found Lenny with an open diary, studying it closely. Lenny the Lock had been around for as long as Hannah could remember. He was an informant for the lieutenant—when he wasn't locked up for burglary. Lenny couldn't resist the challenge of a locked item. He was less interested in the contents of a safe or house, but he never left the goods behind, either. That was what constantly got him into trouble. He was equally good at being caught with the goods as he was at opening locks or breaking an alarm system.

"Hey, Lenny," Sharon said. "How are things?"

"As good as can be expected," came his usual pessimistic reply.

"I should think you'd be in heaven with all these locked diaries to open," Hannah added.

"I would be if they had money in 'em."

"You have a point, Len."

"Is that the latest diary, by any chance?" Sharon asked, resisting the temptation to snatch it from the man's hand.

"The inside cover indicates it's from June, 1992, to December, 1992."

"Four years ago?" Hannah asked. "Let me see that." She took the book and apologized for her abruptness. After flipping through the pages, she asked, "Which box was this one in?"

"That one." Lenny pointed to an opened box near Sharon. "We have yet to figure out what box it is. We want to find the last one. Guess we gotta keep lookin'." He shrugged.

"Yeah," Sharon said with resignation. "I guess you're right. Let's get started."

Hannah turned to the sergeant in charge. "Bill, we'll need some extra tables here and a couple more chairs. Detective Walker and I will be keeping you company for the foreseeable future."

"Yes, Detective." Sergeant Bill Bieber, the property clerk, beamed. He liked having company. Most of the time, the property room was a lonely place.

After perusing the books for an hour, Hannah said, "There has to be a pattern to the way Mariah stored these! How difficult can it be to figure out?"

One book she leafed through was from 1982. The next was for 1988. Currently she read through a diary for a date in March through a date in August, 1974.

"Sharon, be sure you guys document each diary as you read it. Include code numbers, dates, and its placement in the box. Also write a synopsis of what's in the diary. What are the code number and dates of the one you've got right now?"

"Number C83, dates January 10, 1994, to May 27, 1994."

"About four-and-a-half months. That was the book just behind the last one in the box Lenny opened, right?"

"Right."

"OK. Mine's B74, dated March 13, 1974 to August 12, 1974. Have you written down the dates for that book?"

"Yes, Detective." Sharon was beginning to feel annoyed by all the interruptions. Besides, she was intrigued by what she read. A few minutes later, she was the one interrupting.

"Hannah, listen to this. It could be interesting." She read from the book. *"I met him today at the Pleasing Portraits Gallery, a newly opened portrait shop in Oak Park where in-house artists will paint your portrait for a sizable fee. He's beautiful, tall with blue eyes, blond curls, and a...."* The next few words were unintelligible. *"I'm eager to know...."*

Sharon suddenly stopped reading aloud but kept reading. After a few moments, she sat quietly and stared at the diary in her hand.

"What is it?" Hannah asked.

"Whoa!" she said softly. "It just goes to show you can't judge a book by its cover."

"Whatever are you talking about?" Hannah was now fully intrigued. Previously, she'd been half-listening.

"She always appeared to be so ladylike. A tough, cold lady, maybe, but still a lady. It seems she was anything but." Her voice trailed off.

"Give me the book, please," Hannah said hand outstretched.

Sharon handed her the book. "You read it. I won't read that trash out loud."

Hannah set down the diary she'd been reading and took Sharon's. As she read, the dreaded blush rose up her neck to her cheeks and forehead, then to the top of her head.

"Oh, my God," she said.

"Well?" Sharon asked.

"She sounds like one of those oversexed babes out of a Harold Robbins novel." Hannah handed the book back. "Keep reading. At least the subject matter will keep you awake. Just think of it as one of the more unpleasant aspects of your job. Maybe she'll say something about the Irish immigrants in it."

"If she can get her mind out of the gutter." Sharon retrieved the book.

Hannah smiled and went back to her diary.

It was late, and Laine's voice sounded concerned. "Hannah, I'm sorry to call so late, but where have you been? You haven't answered my calls for days. I've been worried about you. I couldn't go to bed tonight without trying to reach you again."

"No need to worry, Dear One. I've been pretty tied up with work. I've also been to Michigan."

"Oh."

"They found Heather's remains at Five Mile Point. Can you believe it? They're doing the DNA testing in Lansing." With each word, Hannah felt she couldn't continue, that she couldn't go over it all again. Neither could she stop.

Laine sensed Hannah's reluctance and wanted to say there was no need to discuss the subject right away, but before she could speak, Hannah added, "Gus did it."

"Gus? But how? Why? Oh, Hannah, how awful. How's your dad?"

"Out of his mind with grief and rage."

"And your mom?"

"Trying to make everything all right, as usual."

When Laine spoke again, she chose her words very slowly and deliberately. "The reason I called, Hannah, was to tell you I spoke with someone from Bay View this past weekend, and he told me about a beautiful new memorial garden beside Stafford's Bay View Inn. It's a cremains memorial garden started a few years ago.

"It made me think that when the time finally came, it might be a perfect resting place for Heather. Remember how she loved to play by the water there? It's beautifully landscaped with peaceful paths winding under the pines. There are benches along the path, among the flowers and trees, where people can sit and meditate, and view…view the bay…." Laine began crying.

"Oh, Hannah, I'm so very sorry. I loved her so. She was the only little sister I ever had. I don't know if my heart will ever mend."

"I know, Laine. I know how much you loved her, and she loved you. I like the idea of the garden in Bay View. It would be a perfect place for her. I'll talk to Mom and Dad about it. We should have the remains shortly."

"Hannah, I want to see you. Jimmy and the kids do, too. It's been too long. Please find a way to come for dinner tomorrow evening. It doesn't matter how late. We'll get the kids up to see you if we have to. We need to see you."

"Whatever did I do to deserve you?" Hannah's voice cracked.

"You were born."

They spoke briefly of other things, then they hung up.

Hannah's dreams that night were a bizarre mixture of the strange childhood of Mariah Allen, about which she'd been reading, about another little girl who never had the chance to grow up, and the convoluted lives of two young women who grew up amid pain and death within a wounded family.

CHAPTER SEVENTEEN

"Have you figured out the filing system for those diaries yet?" Rob asked Hannah as they sat in his office, going over the latest findings in the Allen investigation.

"No. It's still a mystery." Hannah thought for a moment before adding, "There's some sort of coded arrangement in the way they were stored, so there must be a document in that house that has the system on it, or else a computer disk, except there's no computer in the house. It might be she kept it in her head. Was she capable of that, or that paranoid?

"On the other hand, her compulsion to write down everything would favor a written document somewhere."

"I'll send a team out there to take another look around," Rob said. "I'll add two more to the reading detail, too."

"Great. Just make sure none are yappers. We don't want any leaks. The good judge might have some spies around."

Rob nodded.

"Someone really ought to take those diaries once we're finished with them and write a book. People love to read about the wealthy and their often miserable lives. Fiction can't touch the real lives of many of them. It would be a bestseller. For example, Mariah's parents were a major piece of work."

Rob listened, occasionally shaking his head or nodding.

"It also appears the Allen sisters weren't twins."

"What?" Rob asked.

"It seems Mariah had a baby girl when she was eighteen. That makes sense. Both girls are supposedly twenty-six—was twenty-six, in Angela's case—and, according to Mariah's birth certificate, she was forty-four when she died.

"It seems Bernard Allen's older brother, Jamie, was Angela's father. Mariah had an affair with him and ended up pregnant, but he would have none of her after that. So she seduced Bernard, who really loved her, married him, and went off to England before anyone knew she was pregnant. The baby was premature, very small and sickly. They named her Angela."

"What about Gloria, then?"

"I haven't gotten that far. Her birth would be recorded in a different diary, but she had to have been born less than one year later to pull off the twin act. If Mariah became pregnant right away, and Gloria was big and healthy...."

Rob raised his eyebrows. "Somebody doctored a birth certificate, probably Angela's, so the two girls' certificates would show the same date, time and place of birth. What about the doctor, the signatures, and whatever else would have to be changed to make it work?"

"If anyone could have pulled it off, it was Mariah," Hannah concluded.

"What about her husband? Wouldn't he have something to say about it?"

"From what I've read in the diaries and learned during our investigation, Bernard was a very good man but a weak one where Mariah was concerned. I doubt he had much to say about anything at home. I'd guess he gave in to Mariah no matter how selfish or inappropriate she was. He probably didn't dare rock the boat."

"The guy was a doctor?"

"Uh-huh. It's interesting that a man in a profession where he's revered as a god can have a home life where he's basically a peon."

"Sounds like a soap opera." Rob sat back and sighed.

"Sure does. If Mariah's life wasn't a soap, I don't know what else to call it. Reading those diaries is like building a jigsaw puzzle. I can't wait to see the complete picture."

"I see what you mean about the book. Once all the pieces are in place, it'll make a hell of a story. Hollywood would love it."

"Yeah. The diaries may also be the only way we'll ever be able to solve the how and why of Angela's death—and Mariah's, too. The answers have to be in them."

The phone rang, and Rob answered. He spoke briefly while looking at Hannah, then said, "OK, Sergeant. Thank you. I'll let her know." He hung up. "That was Sergeant Swingle from Lansing. He wanted us to know they've been in touch with the Texas State Police and are working on matching the DNA samples from Gus' body with material found in the box. They're putting a rush on it and hope to have the results in a few more days."

"I'm impressed." Hannah was pleased the agencies in both states were working so hard. She told Rob about the memorial garden in Bay View, Michigan, and he agreed that would make a perfect final resting place for Heather.

Gloria must be as torn up inside over the loss of her sister as I am over losing mine, Hannah mused. It's hard to believe otherwise, but it's hard to tell just by looking at her or talking with her.

She mentioned her thoughts to Rob.

"Or by spending time with her," Rob added.

"How many grieving siblings, especially twins, do you know who'd go on a major personal shopping spree two days after her sister dies?"

"I can't imagine it, but that could have been her way of dealing with her grief. She may bury her pain deep, pushing it so far down she no longer feels it. That certainly fits the family dynamic."

"This is the first time I've been so directly involved with the death of a twin," Hannah said slowly, "or supposedly a twin, in my work. It turns out to be the time my own lost twin is finally found long dead.

"Ever since the Allen case started, I've thought more about Heather than I have in some time. The pain is always there, of course. I mean conscious thought—remembering her and our lives together. Perhaps it was the universe's way of preparing me for what would be found in northern Michigan.

"I've thought about being twenty-six years old with her, then being thirty-something, about what her husband might be like, and about Heather as a mother. She'd have been a good one."

Hannah stopped and smiled ruefully at the man across the desk who smiled back with kindness and understanding.

"As much as she might try to deny or hide it, Gloria must be in some pain," Hannah said, "even if she's the killer."

"The pain, enhanced by guilt, may be greater in that case," Rob said. "Then she'd need to bury it deeper. Do you think if you had a heart-to-heart talk with Gloria about your common pain, you might gain some insight into what happened to Angela?"

"I don't know."

"She might disclose something without being aware of it."

"I'll try." Hannah felt a small surge of hope. Rob's suggestion had potential.

The room was silent for a moment.

"Don't tell her you're attending the next party," Rob said. "I've been thinking about that idea. It wasn't very good. All it would do is give the smugglers time to regroup."

"Agreed. Anyway, we need to work seriously on solving this case before next week. Besides the risk to Mandy, there might be others at the Allen estate who are in danger. I, too, find Mariah's death a little too convenient."

Rob nodded, pleased they agreed. "Immigration has been checking the files of all Irish immigrants over the past several years to see if there are any irregularities on file, including whether any of them are counterfeit. It helped a lot that you and Sharon found specific names to check. We'll see how their stories and dates stack up against the data on file.

"Even if we get lucky there, these crooks are smart. They plan for the long term and are meticulous in carrying out their plan, unlike their Chinese or Mexican counterparts—and other Irish smugglers. Most of the other groups don't even bother with any semblance of legality. All they want is fast money.

"These Irish rogues, on the other hand, run a high-class operation and have covered it well. Hopefully the diaries, and Mariah, will be their undoing."

"They're smart, all right. I worry they might become suspicious that we're on to them. I want these guys bad, Rob. I don't want them to get away."

"They won't. We're getting too close. We'll get them soon."

"I'd better get back to my reading. That's where the key lies. No pun intended. I'll read until more recruits show up. Then I'll talk to Gloria face-to-face."

"I'll get more people down to the property room."

"Thanks." As she turned to leave, Rob spoke again.

"Hannah?" His tone was softer and less professional. "May I take you out to dinner tonight?"

She hesitated. "I'd like that, Rob, but I don't know if it's a good idea." She saw disappointment in his face and added, "Let's wait for the weekend."

"OK." His mood improved again.

Hannah turned back toward the door just as Sharon burst into the office.

"She did it!" Sharon said breathlessly. "She killed her husband! It's in this diary. The whole thing, from the first drop of cyanide in his coffee to the last on the day he died! Read this!" She handed the diary to Rob.

Hannah closed the door and remained in the room.

"This is the account of the day he died in a car accident and her relief that he was finally, as she put it, out of the way. She wrote she wouldn't have to be bothered with him anymore. He had served his purpose."

As Rob read, Sharon added, "We're closer to how Mariah filed the diaries, too."

"Take a breath, Detective," Hannah said.

"Sorry." Sharon paused to calm herself. "Anyway, the boxes these diaries are kept in were made for the express purpose of storing them. The inside bottom of each box has a latticework of labels that match codes on the inside front cover of each book.

"I made a large chart to record the identifying information from each diary. As we read a book, we write the data on the chart. Eventually, a pattern will emerge. There still has to be a blueprint or disk somewhere. We need to search the Allen home again."

"Yes, we do, Detective," Rob said. "I was about to send a detail there before you entered my office so exuberantly." He set down the diary and reached for the telephone receiver.

Sharon turned to Hannah. "By looking at the designs on the diary covers, I can tell they were probably bought in groups. She was planning ahead. They also reflect the times in which they were purchased. Did you ever keep a diary as a kid?"

"Yeah, for about half a year once." Hannah chuckled. "I was given one for Christmas when I was thirteen. It was part of a desk set. I couldn't stick with it, though. The last thing I wanted to do at night was sit down and write about my day. Thinking over the day's events was one thing, writing them down was another. I could think lying down and drift off to sleep lost in thought."

"What did your diary look like?" Sharon asked.

"It was a pink, plastic-covered thing with a teenage girl on it. She had long, straight hair."

"That's what I mean. We can tell the ones she started with, at least the ones we've come across from the early days of her writing, because they all have teenybopper motifs. There are also some psychedelic ones that reflect the late sixties and early seventies. As she grows older, the books show more style."

"Interesting." Hannah rubbed her chin thoughtfully.

"They're all high-quality books, of course. I want to check some of the upscale stationers to see if we can find books that match something we have. That might help us identify the most current books. We'd probably find what we want then."

"Good idea."

"It's all set for the Allen estate," Rob announced, hanging up the receiver. "Hannah, do you want to go with them or by yourself?"

"I'll go alone. Since Detective Walker has things under control here, I can go right now."

"Keep up the good work, Sharon," Rob said.

Sharon beamed with pride. "Thank you, Sir."

"It's too late to do anything for Bernard Allen, but we might find out who killed Angela," Hannah said. "I'd at least like to do that. If Mariah killed Angela, I want the world to know. She can't keep secrets anymore."

Hannah and Sharon stepped outside the office and saw Sergeant Wilson approaching with a handful of phone messages.

"Mr. Darren Brannigan left several messages for you, Detective Bell. You might want to call him. He sounded very eager to speak with you. Said it was important."

"OK. Thanks, Linda. I'll take care of it right now."

Hannah walked slowly to her office, not wanting to deal with the call. She'd been thinking about Darren, and her thoughts weren't very comfortable. In the end, she felt she couldn't trust him. Rob's comments and attitude were part of her decision, too.

Hannah picked up the receiver and dialed. "Hello, Mr. Brannigan."

"Hannah! Where have you been? I've called over half a dozen times and haven't heard from you."

The comment sounded oddly possessive. *What business does he have assuming I'd call right back?* she wondered. "I've been very busy, Mr. Brannigan, and I've also been out of town. You're lucky I'm able to call back this soon."

"Well, I...I was worried something might have happened to you."

"You needn't worry about me. I'm a big girl, not to mention a cop, remember?"

Sensing her aloofness, Darren tried to regain control by inviting her out to dinner that evening.

Two dinner invitations in one day? Hannah thought. *My social life is getting better by the minute.* "Mr. Brannigan, are you asking me for a date?"

"Yes, and stop calling me Mr. Brannigan."

"I'm more comfortable with that, if you don't mind. I'm sorry, but I can't go out with you."

There was a pause. "Why not?" he asked, confused.

"I already have a date."

"Break it."

What an arrogant ass! she thought. "I beg your pardon?"

Obviously taken aback, he was clearly not accustomed to being turned down. "I'd really like to see you, Hannah. I need to talk with you about Angela and Mariah."

"Really?"

"Please?" He sounded wounded.

"It's against departmental regulations to go out with you, Mr. Brannigan. My lieutenant would have my badge."

"I don't believe this!" His usually pleasant, confident voice suddenly had an angry edge to it. Darren Brannigan was not going to take this rejection lying down. "Is your lieutenant a man?" He asked.

"Yes." Hannah realized immediately her answer was a mistake.

"He's probably got the hots for you himself."

"Be careful, Mr. Brannigan. Your true colors are showing."

There was an uncomfortable silence.

"I'm sorry, Hannah. That was uncalled for."

"I'm well aware of that, but at least it was honest. I'll give you that. You do plan to stay in town, don't you, Mr. Brannigan? We'll need to talk with you again during our investigation into the deaths of Angela and Mariah Allen."

"Mariah? She choked to death. What's to investigate?"

"That's an interesting question, and it portrays a very different point of view than your statements to Detective Walker."

"That's why I want to see you. That was just talk."

"Just talk? Really? OK. I'll make a note of it. You don't need to see me to tell me that. You just told me what I needed to know."

Darren became exasperated. "I told your detective friend a lot of things the other night, one being that I wouldn't leave town. Didn't she tell you?"

"It's all in the report of her interview with you, along with several strong statements you made regarding Gloria Allen as the primary suspect in the death of both her mother and sister."

He didn't answer.

"I have to go now, Mr. Brannigan. I have many things to attend to."

"The comments I made to Detective Walker were speculations," he said desperately.

"That's not what it sounded like in her report."

"Then she misunderstood. I don't understand what's come over you, Hannah. I thought we had the beginning of something special."

"Well, you were wrong. It's not that I don't appreciate your interest. It's just not appropriate."

He didn't answer.

"Someone will be in touch with you soon."

"But not you."

"Perhaps, but not one-on-one."

"I'm sorry to hear that."

"Good-bye, Mr. Brannigan."

"Good-bye, Detective Bell."

Detective Bell? she wondered. At least he's given up on that phony first-name business.

CHAPTER EIGHTEEN

Hannah pulled into her garage, parked, and walked into her duplex through the wet room door. She'd been to visit Laine and her family and had dinner with them. She was tired, but, even though it was late, she knew she wouldn't sleep for a while. The day had been too full—and emotional.

She made a cup of chamomile tea, sat at the kitchen table, and mentally reviewed the day's events. As was her custom, she kept a pad and pencil at the table in case she wanted to write down a thought or remind herself of something that needed to be done.

After she spoke with Darren earlier that day, Hannah prepared to leave for the Allen estate. There were several questions that came to mind over the past few days, and, most especially, after reading some of the diaries. It was only a matter of time before the books revealed all they needed to know concerning recent events at the Allen home.

Mariah was a compulsive writer concerning events in and about her life. Many things she wrote about were highly unpleasant. It would be difficult to determine from her stately manner that she was actually an extraordinarily unpleasant, selfish, and evil woman. Her primary concern was for herself, and she worked to ensure her wants and needs were the concern of those around her, too, no matter what it cost them.

Even as a child, she had a dark side that was frightening. In one diary, she wrote about an incident that occurred on her sixth birthday. According to the date in the diary, she wrote the account when she was fourteen.

Mariah's parents gave her a kitten.

I can't think about that now, Hannah thought. It's unbelievable and heartbreaking.

She forced her mind to another subject. They were close to figuring out the key to how the books were stored. Hannah hoped those who worked on them, reading through the night, would find something critical to the case.

The department had been informed that Mariah had also been cremated. Then the ashes of Angela and Mariah were mixed and strewn over the gardens at the Allen estate.

"I'm not sure whether to be touched or horrified," Sharon said when she heard the news. "It could be a lovely thing to do, to keep one's loved ones close, but since being loving wasn't that family's style, it makes me wonder what it really means."

"One barely has the chance to attend a funeral anymore," Hannah said distantly. "Maybe that's not so bad. I wonder if there'll be a memorial service for the women?"

"I'm sure we'll be the last to know."

"The physical evidence the bodies would have provided is gone, not that it matters anymore. The diaries are our only real hope."

"Hannah," Sharon interjected, "I've been meaning to tell you about the vial Anna and I found in the fridge at the Allen estate when we searched the place. It turned out to be poison gathered from venomous frogs. Isn't that strange? Why would Mariah keep a vial of frog poison in her refrigerator?"

"To apply it to a needle and stick it in her daughter's foot is my guess," Hannah said without pausing.

They looked at each other.

"Doc," Sharon said.

"Yep."

"Now we'll never know."

"I'll bet one year's salary that Mariah Allen wrote it all down for us, because she couldn't keep it to herself. Just like Bernard, she'll tell us. She'll even reveal where she found the poison. Since she's already paid for her deed, I suppose justice has been served. I just want to prove it, and I'd like to know who else might be involved—in both deaths."

"Like Darren Brannigan?"

"Yeah, particularly in Mariah's death. We know lots of people didn't like her, but who else had the reason and the opportunity other than Gloria and, maybe, Darren?"

"Anna." Sharon looked surprised at what she'd just said. She and Hannah exchanged a look, then both women said, "No."

"Still," Sharon said, "stranger things have happened."

"But how? I might be able to see a reason for it," Hannah said slowly, choosing her words with care. "She's seen a lot in her life with Mariah, much of it awful. She knows more about Mariah than anyone left alive. If we accept she might have done it, then the same question applies—how? If we can't figure out how Darren could have done it, how could sweet, gentle Anna carry it off?"

"Anna knew Mariah better than anyone else," Sharon said. "She knew what she was really like. Maybe Anna knows about the Irish thing, too. Maybe she knew the girls were snooping and were finding out what was really going on at the parties. If Anna knew Mariah was on to the girls, then maybe she knew Mariah killed Angela and might have been planning the same for Gloria. Anna might have extracted her own payment, as unlikely as it seems. Maybe that was the last straw in a lifetime of watching Mariah destroy everyone around her for her own gain."

"That's a lot of maybes."

"If it turns out to be true, we should give her a medal. I'd hate to see Anna go to prison for killing Mariah Allen. That wouldn't seem like justice."

"Agreed. I'd better talk to Rob before I see Gloria…and Anna. We've got a new wrinkle to consider. As hard as it is for me to believe Anna's capable of such a thing, I can see it. My gut tells me you're onto something, Sharon.

"As sweet and gentle as she is, Anna's a woman of strong convictions, and, I believe, has the courage to back them up. If it turns out she had a hand in Mariah's death, I want a plan in place on how to handle the situation before I go out there. The only way I can see Anna being involved is if she didn't help when Mariah started choking, assuming she was within earshot…."

Hannah paused with a look of consternation on her face. "Sharon, we should have asked Anna in the beginning if she heard Mariah choking, or, at least, if she heard a commotion coming from the garden room."

They exchanged a puzzled look.

"I never thought to ask." Sharon wondered how two experienced police officers could have overlooked such an obvious question. "Still, as far as I'm concerned, if Anna was responsible for Mariah's death by ignoring her, she paid the penalty before committing the act."

"What do you mean?"

"She spent her entire adult life putting up with that awful woman. That's punishment enough."

Hannah nodded. "Perhaps a jury would agree."

Hannah felt weak in the stomach thinking back on that conversation and what happened at the Allen estate that afternoon.

When she shared her conversation with Sharon with Rob, he decided to accompany her to the Allen home.

"Do you think you should?" Hannah asked. "You might intimidate Anna into not talking at all. She hasn't met you, but she knows me, and I believe she likes me. I can get her to talk."

"It's time for me to make an appearance. We'll say I came along to keep an eye on the search, to keep things moving so we'll be out of their way as quickly as possible."

"Then you'll leave me alone when the time comes?"

"Yes."

"OK."

When they arrived at the estate, the contingent the lieutenant sent out earlier was already at work. After being introduced to Anna, Lieutenant Keys made an excuse to go talk to the crew busily at work searching for anything that would enable them to figure out Mariah's storage arrangement for her diaries.

The place was crawling with cops. They were taking the estate apart, piece by piece. They wouldn't give up until they found what they believed had to be there.

"Where's Gloria?" Hannah asked Anna.

"She's out. I don't know where."

"Well, that's encouraging. Sounds like she's finally spreading her wings."

Anna smiled. "Yes, she is."

"Anna, I came here primarily to speak with you, because I believe you're honest. I hope to get some straight answers."

"What do you want to know, Detective?" Anna answered coolly.

"I've been reading some of Mariah's diaries. Did you know she kept diaries?"

"I knew she kept them as a teenager. I didn't keep up with her writing habits as an adult, Detective. Besides, she was very secretive about things like that."

Hannah sensed a little discomfort in Anna, who wouldn't look her in the eye as she answered. So much for honesty and straight answers, she thought.

"You're sure? We found a couple of gray hairs in one of the diaries, and we're having them tested right now. What if they're yours?"

Anna became quiet, and Hannah noticed that she was visibly shaken as she sat down, clasped her hands in her lap, and lowered her head.

"We've also dusted each diary for fingerprints. We expect those results very soon."

There was a long silence. Anna sat staring into the distance while Hannah waited.

After several minutes, she pulled a few hairs from her head and handed them to Hannah. "Take them, Detective. You can compare them to those you already have."

"Thank you." Hannah wondered what to make of the gesture. Her statement about finding the hairs had been a ruse. She wondered if Anna was calling her bluff.

Anna nodded without speaking as Hannah placed the hairs into a plastic bag and put them into her pocket.

"Anna, tell me about the kitten," Hannah said gently. ploy

"Kitten? What kitten?"

"The one Mariah received from her parents when she was six."

Anna stared at her with wide eyes, her skin suddenly ashen, but she didn't speak.

"Tell me," Hannah said firmly but gently.

"You have read the diaries." Anna's voice was weak.

"Some. We might need your help there, too."

Another long silence followed. It seemed Anna was preparing herself for the ordeal of dredging up the terrible memory she'd been asked to recall, one she had buried years earlier.

Finally, she began, her voice shaking. "Mariah received the

kitten for her sixth birthday." She shrank away inside herself, trying to hide from having to speak the horror out loud to a stranger.

"Go on," Hannah said. "Tell me what happened to Ivory."

"Do I have to?" Anna whispered.

"No harm will come to you from telling me, and there's no one to hear except me."

In a faltering voice, Anna told the story of a beautiful, fluffy, white kitten named Ivory, given to Mariah by her parents on her sixth birthday. Mariah seemed delighted with the gift and showed affection toward the kitten when she received it. She took it into her arms and hugged it, but then she began squeezing.

Before anyone understood what was happening, she squeezed the kitten so hard blood poured from its mouth, and its eyes bulged. As blood ran down Mariah's dress, she smiled. Those present watched in disbelief, but no one moved until it was too late. Anna was the one who finally retrieved the fatally wounded animal from the child's arms.

"It took only a few seconds," she said softly, "almost too fast to respond. It also seemed no one wanted to be messed up with the...the blood...and all."

Then she told how Mariah looked up at her parents and said, "See, Mommy and Daddy? I love the kitty—to death."

Then, with a six-year-old's giggle, she threw herself toward one of the remaining gift packages and tore off the wrapping.

Anna stopped speaking.

"What happened then?" Hannah asked.

Anna struggled to speak. "Mariah's mother told me to clean her up and bring her back to the party. I...I did, and the party continued as if nothing had happened. I called the gardener, who came and took the kitten away. He buried it somewhere in the gardens."

Hannah took Anna's hands in hers. "Mariah wrote about the incident almost exactly as you described it, as if it were of no consequence at all. Nothing was ever said or done about such a cruel act?"

"No. I told Mariah when I took her to clean her up that she'd done a terrible thing. I said she should never squeeze a living thing so hard again. A hug was supposed to be gentle and loving."

"How did she respond?"

"She didn't. It was as if she didn't hear me." Anna wept into the handkerchief she held clutched in her hand, and Hannah wiped tears from her own cheeks as they sat in silence.

"Anna, the next question I have to ask is very difficult, but I must. Please don't let it frighten you. It will work out all right."

Anna looked at her plaintively without speaking.

"Did you have anything to do with Mariah Allen's death?"

Anna's eyes widened, and she stammered, "How…how could I have? She choked to death."

"Yes, she did, but did she have help, or, rather, did she not have help?"

Anna sat motionless for several seconds, and then appeared to be about to faint. Hannah quickly reached out for the distraught woman and put her arms around her.

"It's all right, Anna," she said softly. "We'll help you if you were involved in any way. Just tell me the truth. Please?"

Finally, Anna said, "She was the devil's own, Detective. I had to stop her before she hurt anyone or anything else."

"But how? There's no physical evidence that anyone touched her."

"No one did."

"How could you have known Mariah would choke on her lunch? That's a hard thing to predict. Did you wave your magic wand or something?"

A slight smile came to Anna's face. "No."

"Anna, you're entitled to have an attorney present. Do you have one you can call, or do you want me to call one for you?"

"No."

"To what?"

"To either. I don't have an attorney, and I don't want you to call one for me."

"OK. We're the only two people in the room. It's not bugged, is it?" Hannah smiled as she glanced around.

"No."

"OK. No more jokes. It's your turn."

Anna sighed. "Sometime ago, Mariah was diagnosed with myasthenia gravis. Do you know what that is?"

"No. I've heard of it, but I don't know what it is."

"It's a disease that affects the nervous system. It can cause the eyelids to droop and the throat muscles to weaken so you can't swallow. It's my understanding that some people who die from choking actually have this disease and don't know it. They develop difficulty swallowing but don't know why, and they choke, because their throat muscles don't work right. Then one day, they choke to death while trying to swallow food or pills."

"Awful is right. Now I'll be paranoid forever that every time I choke on something, I have myas…myasthe…."

"Myasthenia gravis."

"Yeah. That."

"You'll get over it. Mariah seemed to be losing her appetite. She didn't have a big one to start with, but I noticed she wasn't eating much at all. She also didn't have her usual energy. Then she started having difficulty swallowing. When she noticed one of her eyelids drooping one morning, she called the doctor. He ran some tests and diagnosed myasthenia gravis. As far as I know, she never mentioned the disease to anyone but me.

"The only reason she told me was to make me more responsible for her. I gave her the proper dose of medicine, refilled the prescription, and made her doctor's appointments. Making appointments was part of my job, anyway. She didn't like bothering with things like that, saying it was a waste of her time. Besides, she always thought I needed more work to keep me busy.

"Since the disease is life-threatening, you don't want to miss a dose unless you're willing to risk death."

Anna stopped speaking for a moment.

"I think I get the picture," Hannah said thoughtfully. "When it began to appear to me that Angela's death...murder...wasn't going to be solved, I decided to do something before Gloria ended up dead, too. I know this family very well, Detective. I stood by for years while Mariah worked her evil on many decent people."

"I'm sorry for interrupting, but did Mariah kill her husband?"

"You know a lot, don't you?"

Hannah nodded.

"Yes, she did, although it was never proven in court. She poisoned him and got away with it. I couldn't let her get away with it again!" Anna's voice rose.

"I believe you. The proof's in the diaries. Did you know that?"

"I always thought so, but I couldn't find the right one."

"So, you have looked?"

Anna, suddenly realizing what she'd just confessed, looked worried.

"Don't worry, Anna. That's water over the dam. Bernie's dead, and so is Mariah. She paid for her deeds. Your having read the diaries...."

"Some of them. I only read a bit here and there."

"Quite probably, your having read some of the diaries will turn out to be in your favor."

"Maybe so, but I'll still have to pay for causing her death,"

Anna said in dismay.

"Not so fast, my dear. It's highly unlikely you'll spend any time in prison. Whatever you say right now is inadmissible in court, especially if I don't tell anyone."

"Can you do that?" Anna was incredulous that an officer of the law would choose not to tell her superiors what she knew about a murder. "Won't you get in trouble if someone finds out?"

"You let me worry about that. Do you trust me, Anna?"

Anna looked relieved. "I do."

"So. Go on with the MG thing."

"On the day Mariah died, I replaced her morning medication with an aspirin product that looked like the same pill. I'd done the same with the pill the previous evening. Since she paid little attention to her medication, I doubted she'd notice, and she didn't. All that mattered to her was taking the pill. She never paid attention to the pill itself. I was always there to give it to her. I was the only person she trusted. For that, I feel shame, but I couldn't let her continue."

"I understand."

"I thought she might die in her sleep. That would have been best for everyone, but she didn't." She stared into the distance for a moment. "I made her chicken salad sandwich drier than usual that day, then I served her and waited. If it didn't happen then, I would substitute her nighttime medication again. I felt that would do the trick for certain.

"I planned to keep substituting medicine until it worked, or she found out. I felt no remorse. I wanted her to pay. It was time. If she found out, I didn't care. It had to stop.

"I expected her to complain, to ask me to remake the sandwich, but she didn't. When I was in the kitchen, I heard her choking and did nothing. When there was silence for a few minutes, I went to look. She was dead, or so she seemed. I went back into the kitchen.

"I planned to find her after a while and call the police, but, before I could, the front bell rang. It was Mr. Brannigan, asking to speak with Mariah. I didn't know what to do, so I took him to see her. We found her dead, and he called the police."

Anna had regained control of herself. She sat up straight and looked Hannah in the eye. "I'm not sorry, Detective. I'm just glad it's over. Keeping it inside was worse than being caught. I'm willing to pay the price."

They talked a little longer. Anna explained what she knew about the diaries, but she had no idea if there was any master storage diagram or disk. With some reluctance, she also discussed the smuggling ring. She didn't know much about it except what she'd found in one of the diaries.

At first, she thought it was within the law and never realized they were actually smugglers. When the parties began, and she read a little more, and the men and Mariah became so secretive, Anna began to wonder. She snooped, unaware the girls were also snooping.

Anna's access to the diaries had been minimal—on the rare occasions when Mariah left one on her nightstand, and Anna managed to read a few pages.

"Weren't the books locked?" Hannah asked.

"Uh-huh." Anna replied.

"How…?"

"That's a trade secret, Detective."

"Anna?"

"Did you know that most diary keys are very similar?"

Hannah shook her head, then smacked her forehead with her hand. "You occasionally bought a diary like the one on her nightstand, didn't you? Sometimes, the key worked."

"I was lucky a few times. I even bought a diary and started

writing in it, but I didn't stick with it. As they say these days, it wasn't my thing."

"Mine, either. I couldn't stick with it." She now saw Anna in a different light. "You're one smart lady. We could use you on the police force."

"You'd want a murderer on the police force?"

"Don't bother sugar coating it."

"Maybe they'll sentence me to become a police officer." Anna gave her a wry smile.

"That would be true punishment." Hannah chuckled.

Lieutenant Keys walked into the room and asked Anna some questions about the diaries. The police detail hadn't found anything useful. He asked about the smuggling ring, but it became apparent that Anna knew very little. No mention was made of Anna's confession.

As the two officers prepared to leave, Hannah said, "Anna, you don't plan to go anywhere, do you?"

"No. I'll be here when you need me."

"You'll hear from us."

"I'll be expecting it."

Rob and Hannah walked to his car.

"What was that cat-and-mouse bit back there?" he asked.

"You're so perceptive, Lieutenant."

"I get paid to be, Detective."

"We'll discuss it on the way to the station," Hannah replied, reflecting in her own voice Anna's inner peace that the truth was finally out.

Hannah sat at her kitchen table, thinking of the kitten and the six-year-old who strangled it without a qualm. Then she thought about two other six-year-olds who stayed up all night to nurse a baby bunny back to health—and failed. The bunny died the following day from a respiratory condition common to rabbits.

Freeman Bell helped his daughters bury the bunny in the backyard. Heather and Hannah said a prayer and marked the spot with a small cross made of twigs.

Her reverie was interrupted by a loud knocking at her door. She almost jumped out of her chair, then looked at her watch, knowing it was too late for anyone to visit her.

An emergency! she thought. Daddy?

She bolted to the door. Without thinking, she flung it open.

Darren Brannigan stood before her.

In an almost hysterical voice, she shouted, "What the hell are you doing here?"

"I couldn't sleep, Hannah. I really need to talk with you. I heard about what happened today. I might be a jerk in many ways, but I can't let Anna take the blame for what I did."

"The blame for what?"

"Killing Mariah Allen."

"Where the hell did you get that idea?" She was aghast at the thought that Darren knew about her conversation with Anna that afternoon. How much does he know? Who told him? Was the room bugged?

"I just know."

"That's not good enough, Mister," she said harshly.

Realizing their conversation could be overheard by anyone who was near the house, she took Darren's arm and pulled him inside.

"I want to know what makes you think Anna killed Mariah?" she demanded.

"Anna told me."

"I don't believe you. Why would she say that?"

"She trusts me."

"Yeah, right, and I'm the pope's mistress."

"What is this sudden disdain you have for me?"

"Because…because…because you're conceited, arrogant, and, well, you just don't add up. Something's amiss with you."

He laughed. No one had ever described his shortcomings quite like that before, and he certainly had his detractors. "Something's amiss with me? That's unique, Hannah. I have to give you credit for that."

There was a long pause while Hannah paced in front of her guest, who stood in front of the closed door, waiting.

Finally, he asked, "May I sit down? If you let me sit, I'll tell you a tale that will answer many of your questions."

Hannah motioned toward the living room. They found comfortable places to sit, but she made certain she was a safe distance from him.

He told a story of a young girl in Ireland who had an illegitimate child. Leaving the child with her sister, she sailed to America to start over. Years later, she brought the child, now a grown woman who was married, to the States, along with her husband and two young sons.

The relationship between the older woman and the young family was never revealed, and the woman, now middle-aged, never married. She took a position in a wealthy household when she arrived in America and remained with that family for many years. When the youngest daughter in the family set up housekeeping in the States after spending time in Europe, she became the head housekeeper of that family.

"You mean Mariah and Bernard Allen," Hannah said flatly.

"Yes."

"So Anna had a child out of wedlock as a young woman. She came to the States, worked for Mariah's parents, then Mariah, and now here we are. What happened to her daughter and her family?"

"They settled in the area but didn't stay in close contact. The children never knew Anna was their grandmother as they grew up. The parents eventually divorced, and the mother and one of the sons died in a train crash several years ago. The father died of alcoholism a couple years ago."

"How do you know…?" Hannah suddenly realized what he was leading up to. "My God. You're Anna's grandson?"

"Yes. Now you're the only person, other than Anna and me, who knows."

Hannah stared at Darren in stunned silence.

"We share everything," Darren continued. "She's the real reason why I stop by the Allen estate. It wasn't for Angela or Mariah, just Anna. She's the only person I truly care about. I never forgave my parents for denying my brother and me our grandmother as children. Finn died at twenty-one and never knew her."

He paused to gather himself before continuing. "I'd do anything for her, Hannah. I'll swear on anything you can name that I was responsible for Mariah's death. I came to see her, she started choking as we visited, and I did nothing to help. No one will ever be able to prove differently."

She knew he was right. "Then we'll just have to settle for death by choking. Angela's death is another matter, Darren. We need to prove she was murdered. She deserves that."

"The diaries will tell the story," he said. "Mariah was compulsive about writing about herself. Her vanity was totally consuming. I tried to get my hands on those diaries once and gave up. It was too risky. I feared what might happen to my grandmother, not to mention Angela and Gloria, if I were caught."

Hannah knew she had the perfect segue into the smuggling business. It seemed natural to continue in that direction, but she didn't want to tip the police's hand. She decided to let Darren talk some more.

"Why were you looking for the diaries?" she asked instead.

"What could have been of interest in them for you?"

He thought before replying. "I made a decision about something I'd been involved in with Mariah…a business arrangement. I had second thoughts. I wondered what she might have written about it in her diaries. I knew she kept them, because Anna told me."

"What kind of business arrangement?"

"An illegal one."

"I see. What was illegal about it?"

"We'd been smuggling Irish immigrants into the country."

"That's pretty serious, Darren."

"I know. I also know that's an area you're interested in. My guess is you think Angela's death was connected to it somehow."

"Was it?"

"I believe so."

"Darren, we're getting into major illegalities. If you continue, there'll be serious consequences for you, like the possibility of prison. For my part, I don't want to botch an investigation. If we're going to continue, I want to read you your rights."

She waited tensely. Would he back down? Bolt? Try to harm her? She ruled out the last idea. Although he was in trouble, he wasn't a killer.

A moment later, she Mirandized him, set up a tape recorder, and listened to Darren's story about the smuggling ring and his part in it.

When he finished, Hannah called the precinct to have a nearby squad car pick him up. "Be sure it's officers I know well or I won't be turning him over," she told the dispatcher. Then she called her lieutenant.

After a brief conversation with him about what had just happened, she said, "OK, Rob, I'll tell him."

She hung up the phone and turned to Darren. "The lieutenant says that your cooperation with the district attorney will help reduce your sentence. I'm sorry you're involved in this mess, Darren."

"I believed in it at first," he said. "They said they just wanted to help bring people from Ireland to the States for a better life. I was in it a year before I learned about the money. Pretty stupid, eh?"

"You weren't being paid anything?"

"Not at first. When I learned about the money, they bought my silence. Suddenly, I had more money than I'd ever dreamed. I felt as if I'd signed a pact with the devil. I never told Anna, but I think she knew. I believe that knowing—or believing—that I was involved in the smuggling ring, combined with Angela's death, pushed her over the top. She couldn't let Mariah continue her evil deeds without being punished."

"That's essentially what she told me."

"I just hope I live to testify."

"We'll protect you."

"Yeah. I hear that all the time in the movies, but usually, the guy or gal ends up dead. The judge is powerful. He'll do anything to get what he wants. He also has a couple friends who are actually hired thugs who do his bidding. They're quite capable of murder, and I don't want one of them coming after me—or you."

"That's why we're acting so quickly."

"When are you going after them?"

"I can't tell you."

"Still don't trust me, do you?"

"Nope. Besides, it would be pretty stupid of me to lay out our plan to one of the suspects, wouldn't it?"

"Yes, I suppose it would."

There was a knock at the door. Hannah answered and let two officers into the room. She knew both of them well. They handcuffed Darren and led him away.

"Keep a close eye on him," she warned them. "We want him alive to testify. Lieutenant Rob Keys will meet you at the precinct and will take over from there."

As she closed the door, Hannah was impressed by how close they'd come to figuring out the case and how they'd been completely right concerning the smuggling operation.

Darren's confession and agreement to cooperate was more than she could have hoped for. All they had to do was keep him alive.

It's hard to know who might be a spy for the judge, she thought. Now we just need to tighten the case around Angela's murder. When we get our hands on the smugglers, we should get some more answers.

She fell asleep on the couch as she reflected on her conversation with Darren.

The phone rang, startling her awake. It was Rob.

"I have him here, Hannah. He's safe. I'm staying the night. We've got this place manned like a French fortress. We'll move tomorrow."

"I want the judge, Rob."

"You've got him, Hannah."

Detective Sharon Walker had become obsessed with the diaries. She was determined to figure out their order and to find the critical ones, if that was the last thing she ever did.

She was getting closer. The chart was filling in, and the pattern of the book designs was taking form. In addition, the readers found some interesting passages, some of which they shared aloud. All agreed the diaries should be written up into a movie or soap opera. Several suggestions for a name were proposed. Officer Shafer's suggestion, The Many Faces of Mariah Allen, was a popular one. All the producers needed to do was find the right actress to play the lead role.

"They could stretch a soap out for the next thirty years, telling the story of this woman's incredible, twisted life," another officer said.

As they read, they found information that would help the smuggling investigation. It appeared Mariah Allen had tried to write in code. Although clever, it looked amateurish, and Sharon was confident experts could reveal the true meaning of the words.

"Detective Walker," Officer Shafer said. "Take a look at this. I think we've got something."

Sharon set down the book she'd been reading and went to look. She read only a few words before realizing that diary held some of the evidence they needed. Even though it was in Mariah's code, references to sabotage and stranger in the tunnel told her what she needed to know, along with a date in April that coincided with the time Gloria said Angela had been in the passageway.

She continued reading. Mariah had veiled some of her diary entries in the form of little stories or vignettes that were intended to camouflage the truth involving certain events in her later years. Her earlier writings were forthright, and, Sharon believed, truthful. However, she noted in a couple of the diaries that were from more recent times that the use of the encrypted writing became more common.

As she read on, her heart beat faster, and she thought, This is it!

It was a medieval story Mariah had written about a pretty little blue frog, lovely to look at but deadly to touch. The frog belonged to a gentleman of the king's court. Its poison was deadly, and it caused the death of the gentleman's beautiful young daughter, Angel.

The girl accidentally stepped on a poisoned needle with her bare foot, a needle prepared by the family gardener to kill a rabid cat, but he dropped it in the grass. The girl stepped on it and was dead a short time later. Since the gardener never admitted dropping the needle, and it was never found, the family never knew what happened to their little girl, only that she died young and unexpectedly.

Mariah commented on how sad the story was and that sometimes things happened in life that just couldn't be explained.

"Interesting," Sharon muttered.

The next part she read made her jump out of her chair and shout, "Eureka! She couldn't leave it alone! She had to tell the real story and take the credit! Now we can prove how Angela died."

Mariah wrote, The story I just told you is a fairy tale. Let me tell you what really happened....

Mariah then described in detail how she planned and carried out the murder of her daughter, Angela, because Mariah suspected that Angela and Gloria—who would also have to die eventually— were onto the smugglers. She became obsessed with her plan and wrote about it every day.

Mariah suspected that her daughters were attempting to gather evidence to turn her and her friends in to the authorities. She was furious that her own family would spy on her. Ingrates! She wrote.

Darren Brannigan was the other one mentioned who might have to be taken care of. He seemed to have too much interest in the people in her household, especially Angela, Gloria, and Anna. He would have to go, too.

Then the diary ended.

"OK, Everyone," Sharon announced. "We're looking for this kind of cover." She held the diary up for them to see. "Find every diary that looks like this and check the dates on the inside front cover. Any book dated near this time is one we want to read now."

She entered the date on the chart on the wall and circled it in red.

CHAPTER NINETEEN

It was one week ago today that Doc died, Hannah thought, pulling into the precinct parking lot early Thursday morning. *It seems like yesterday. I miss you, Doc. This case has become one of the most interesting and challenging of my career. I wish you could share it with me*

Her thoughts turned to other things. It would be an eventful day. Important decisions had been made, and actions had been taken, with more to come. It would soon be over except for the trials. She knew some innocent, or, at least, unsuspecting, people would suffer. She thought of Kathleen Quigley.

The information gleaned from the diaries, along with Darren, Anna, and Gloria's testimony, would provide the evidence needed to charge the smugglers. The readers had broken Mariah's code the previous night and found the evidence they needed. Mariah had, indeed, written it all down in great detail.

What a fool, Hannah thought. *Her cronies will be shocked, not to mention pissed, when we arrive on their doorsteps in a few hours with arrest warrants. At least Mandy's off the hook.*

She thought of Mandy—dear, sweet, terrified Mandy. *Life will settle down for her now. Gloria will look after her, and Anna will teach her to be a good head housekeeper. She's got gumption and brains. She'll probably strike out on her own someday. Who knows? Maybe we'll take that trip around the States yet.*

Hannah smiled at that thought. *Guess there won't be any more* parties, unless Gloria wants to keep up the rendezvous with the wives in the music library. With their husbands in jail, they'll need things to do, no doubt.

It was 5:30a.m. In one hour, the arresting officers, including herself, would make the arrests.

Revenge is sooo sweet, she thought, imagining Judge Quigley's horror at what was about to happen. He wouldn't know how sweet was her own revenge, but that was fine. She knew.

They'd done their paperwork very carefully, calling the DA in the middle of the night to go over the details and making sure they followed all the proper procedures. They were ready.

It was over quickly. The officers arrived at their targets' homes simultaneously. Liam Reilly was arrested at home in bed. James Costello was also home, but he was arrested sitting on his patio enjoying an early morning cup of coffee with his wife. The only difficulty came with the judge.

As careful as the investigative team had been, word must have reached Judge Quigley's home moments before the officers arrived. As they broke down his locked study door, he shot himself in the head, the final craven act of his life.

"He didn't even have the balls to take his medicine," Hannah said later. "A coward to the end."

The judge's thugs were rounded up, one in bed with his wife, another in bed with his mistress, and another drunk at a bar. The one in the bar tried to run and was struck by a city bus.

"He'll be in the hospital for a while," Sharon reported. "He has two broken legs, some broken ribs, a broken arm, a fractured skull, and internal injuries. We'll arrest him when he's well enough to go to jail."

Hannah felt sorry for Kathleen Quigley, who'd been totally dumbfounded by the whole affair. Has she really been in the dark all these years about who her husband really was? Hannah wondered. Or did she know, and that's why she drank?

At any rate, Kathleen collapsed at the scene and was taken to a rest home. As far as Hannah knew, she was still there, babbling incoherently about a dead child named Merrilee.

"There's probably another horror story there," Hannah told the nurse when she visited one day.

"Best to leave well enough alone," the nurse replied. "The woman has enough to deal with. We'll leave her whatever sanity she has left."

A few other minor gang members were also rounded up.

"If only we could be this successful every time," Rob wished aloud.

"It's a good thing we moved when we did," Hannah said. "Someone—I'd love to know who—warned the judge. We were so careful. Why is there always a rotten apple in the barrel?"

"Because we're dealing with human beings," Rob replied.

"Yeah."

"We've already launched an investigation into the matter. We'll catch the bum."

"I just hope it wasn't someone in our department. That bastard would have been gone if we'd been half a day later getting to him. With his connections, he could have left the country by noon."

"Fate and luck were with us," Sharon said. "This time."

"You got that right," Hannah said.

In a search of the Costello home, the portrait of Angela Allen was found hidden in a storage closet. When the back was removed, two diskettes were found. One held the originals of all the counterfeit documents the smuggling ring used. The other had a database file of diaries, complete with their code numbers, dates, a description of each cover, and a synopsis of each diary's contents.

Forensics concluded two people had hidden the disks in the back of the canvas at different times. Darren told the authorities he hid his diskette of document file originals there when he painted the picture. He put a high price on it to keep anyone from buying it. He didn't know that James Costello had recently purchased it.

"Why would he do that?" Darren asked.

"We're still working on that one," the officer replied.

It was also later concluded that the portrait of Angela must have been at the Allen estate for some time, and that Mariah had hidden the diskette in the back of the painting during that time period, unaware of Darren's disk. Why she did that, and how she planned to update the information on the disk without a computer at home and with the painting in a gallery, was still being debated. The consensus was that there was another disk somewhere, and a computer.

Jim Costello said he received a call from Mariah in the early morning hours following Angela's death to go buy the portrait at whatever the price and stash it at his house. She promised to repay him. He didn't ask questions and did what she told him.

"Another example of Mariah's power," Sharon commented. "Some of what Mariah was planning we can only guess, but we've got hard evidence in her own handwriting that she murdered her own daughter."

"The ultimate evil act committed by a totally evil woman," Hannah said sadly.

With the diaries and Darren's willingness to cooperate, the authorities had all the evidence they needed to arrest the smugglers and make their case airtight.

"Rob, what do you think he'll get?" Hannah asked.

"Get?"

"I mean prison time."

Rob looked intently at her. "Do you care?"

"Oh, not really. I just don't think he's such a bad guy. He just got in over his head, became greedy, and started worrying about his grandmother."

Rob thought for a moment before replying, "I'm sure he'll get a good deal. It might cost him five to ten years, but that's not bad for swindling innocent people out of a lot of money, and being mixed up in a murder."

The room was quiet for a few minutes. Sharon, who'd been quiet for some time, asked, "What about Gloria and Anna?"

"Gloria's well into her new role as matron of the mansion," Hannah answered. "Time will tell how that works out."

"I still don't understand why Mariah accused Gloria of killing Angela that first day. It just doesn't make sense," Sharon stated, puzzled.

"Read the entry in her diary for that day," Rob offered. "You'll find out why she did it, though I doubt you'll understand it any better."

There was a long silence.

"And Anna?"

Hannah looked around the room and then squarely into the eyes of her two colleagues. "That one's on my conscience."

"How so?" Sharon asked.

Hannah shook her head.

"You spoke with her, right?"

"Yes."

"What did she say?"

"'Tis better left unsaid."

Sharon glanced at Rob, who shrugged. "Whatever was said in that house that day would be thrown out of court for many reasons," he said. "Detective Bell wasn't at the top of her form during that interview, so nothing will happen to Anna."

The lieutenant spoke without expression or inflection. Sharon couldn't tell if he gave a silent blessing to her partner's actions, or if he was totally opposed to them. He gave nothing away.

Although she knew she shouldn't, Sharon smiled. Anna had probably contributed to the death of another human being, but Sharon wasn't sure how. The cause of Mariah's death was officially listed as by choking.

Had fate taken a hand, and Anna just watched it happen? Sharon decided she didn't want, or need, to know.

"Guess we'll all have to live with that one," she said soberly.

CHAPTER TWENTY

As Hannah stood in the wings of the auditorium, she felt the same nerves she always felt before going on stage—butterflies in her stomach and the need to take long, deep breaths to calm the shakes. The nerves would always be there, but she'd finally learned how to handle them and make the energy from them work for her.

It was great to be there. She loved performing. As always, in those few moments, she promised she wouldn't let so much time pass before doing it again. When the lights came up, and the first strains of music came to her ears, she was ready.

She strutted onstage in her royal-blue Victorian gown, sweeping broad-brimmed hat with huge, purple, plumed feather, and carrying a matching royal-blue and purple parasol.

At just the right moment, she would turn the parasol inside out, and it would suddenly resemble a large pot. The lining was cleverly filled with glittering blue and silver confetti, so when she tipped the pot, water would appear to spill out. Simultaneously, a fabric figure of a man in a black and white bathing suit of the period would tumble from the pot and dangle as the water poured over him.

That had been the idea and product of a very resourceful prop man friend many years earlier, and the trick delighted every audience who saw it.

As she moved across the stage, she looked toward the back of the auditorium, as was her custom. Then her eyes moved forward and glimpsed her smiling parents. It was good to see the wide smile on her father's handsome face. In that brief instant, she thought of her sister, finally at rest, and a family finally at peace.

In the row ahead of the Bells sat Laine and her family—husband Jim, and their three boys, Ricky, Danny, and Tommy. Laine's cousin, Barb Herrick, was there, too. Barb came to Bay View with the Yahrs a couple of times when the girls were young. She and Heather became pals.

Closer to the stage was a group of colleagues from the precinct. Sharon and Linda were there, and Rob. He had dropped Hannah off at the theater earlier, given her a kiss, and told her to break a leg. She winked at him. He smiled back.

Then she glimpsed Benjamin Russell Stratton sitting in the middle of the front row. He smiled broadly, and on his lap was a bouquet of large pink roses wrapped in clear cellophane.

The vase! she thought.

The image of the exquisite, and very valuable, crystal vase filled with beautiful pink roses she'd received that summer from a secret admirer shot through her mind like a bullet, and she smiled.

"They call her Hard-Hearted Hannah, the vamp of Savannah, the meanest gal in town..." she sang.

Printed in the United States
1108200004B/76-105